THE PLAYER

21st Century Courtesan: Book One

P. S. DUMOND
PAMELA DUMOND

Pamela DuMond Media

PLAYER
ISBN-13: 978-1-941731-03-1
Print: ISBN: 9781941731062

Stock photo
Cover by Glammypammy
Published by Pamela DuMond Media

ALSO BY PAMELA DUMOND

THRILLERS

21st CENTURY COURTESAN series

THE PLAYER #1
THE MOVIE STAR #2
THE BELOVED #3
THE HUSBAND #4
THE DEVOTED FAN #5

MORTAL BELOVED TIME TRAVEL series

The Messenger #1
The Assassin #2
The Seeker #3
The Believer #4: Jack & Clara — STAND ALONE

COZY MYSTERIES

ANNIE GRACELAND COZY MYSTERIES Stand Alones

Cupcakes, Pies, & Hometown Guys
Cupcakes, Sales, & Cocktails
Cupcakes, Diaries, & Rotten Inquiries
Cupcakes, Paws, & Bad Santa Claus
Cupcakes, Bats, & Scaredy Cats
Cupcakes, Bars, & Rock Stars
Cupcakes, Spies, & Despicable Guys
Cupcakes, Lies, & Dead Guys

VON PUMPERNICKLE COZY MYSTERIES

Goldmitten

'SWEETER' ROMANCE

ROYALLY WED ROM-COM series

Part-time Princess #1
Royally Wed #2
Part-time Poser #3
Royally Knocked Up #4

PLAYING SWEETER ROM-COM Stand Alones

Ms. Match Meets a Millionaire
The Story of You and Me

'HOT' ROMANCE

THE CROWN AFFAIR series

The Prince's Playbook #1
His Majesty's Measure #2
The American Princess #3
The Duchess's Decision #4

PLAYING DIRTY ROM-COM Stand Alones

The Client
The Matchmaker
The Bodyguard

21st CENTURY COURTESAN: Book One

DESCRIPTION

Beautiful, broken billionaires pay Ma Maison Agency ungodly sums of money to be with me so I can help them heal.

The work is brutal enough but now someone's stalking me. I've made enough money to support my family and I'm getting the hell out. I'm down to my last four clients.

One wants to play me. One wants to buy me. **One wants to marry me. And one wants to murder me.** *Will I get out in time...*

PRAISE

"If **Sierra Simone** and **Skye Warren had a book baby** it would be **PLAYER.**" *USA TODAY* Bestselling author Samanthe Beck

"...**breath-taking, beautiful, and brilliant.** A must-read..." *USA Today* bestselling author Maggie Marr

"...**original, suspenseful, mysterious, sexy**, and dramatic... a captivating read." Angela Hayes

"An **addicting read**... I was hooked pretty much instantly." E. Walsh

"I am **ADDICTED!** If I could give this book more than five stars I would. **I devoured it in less than 4 hours...** I can't wait for the next installment." Liz Vrchota

"...was **completely enthralled and blown away** by this book!" Vegas Daisy

"...she was a **strong independent woman**... she was **covering up** for things that had happened in her past." Katie83

"...loved this novel and **could not put it down**... addictive." M. Ratclif

"... **These two were hot, hot, hot!** Like, keep a tall glass of water, and a fan nearby, hot." Liz Vrchota

"Player is the first book in the 21st Century Courtesan series and **what an amazing story it is.**" Erica Wojdyla

"This book **grabbed me from the first page** and didn't let go until the last..." Ashleigh

---

21st CENTURY COURTESAN is a **sexy, dark, addictive** series filled with love, lust, family loyalty, deceit, revenge, and *all the sweet little things in life worth killing for...*

For the Survivors

Because the wounds aren't always visible.

"Oh, what a tangled web we weave when first we practice to deceive."

Sir Walter Scott
"Marmion" 1808

BEFORE

BEFORE

IT IS A COLD WINTER DAY IN WISCONSIN. THE KIND OF mean-girl cold where my eyes water from the winds gusting off the lake, not from the fact that I'm terrified that Mom is once again, full blown manic.

I stamp my galoshes on the snow-embedded gravel trying to center myself as she pitches trash bags bloated with papers, clothes, and food, into the back of our salt-stained beater SUV. Mom's bad episodes happen twice a year. On occasion, a psychotic split lands her in a place with a 72-hour hold, and they keep her locked up for a few weeks or months.

When Mom's able to function, when she's able to swing through normal highs and lows and not crash like a meteor to earth, they release her, and she comes home to me and my sister. She comes home to people who love her. "Hey, Mom," I say. "Ms. Portman my ballet teacher decides who goes to recital today."

"Ballet's on hold," Mom says squeezing over-stuffed grocery bags into the car.

I peer down at my winter boots – mid-calf length galoshes, and focus on the dangling laces. If they can stay attached, I can too. I silently recite the words the social worker, Miss Williams told me over and over until they earwormed into my brain. 'You are strong, Evie. You are sturdy. Not a rickety shed shaking in a twister's path. You survive when the storm blows through.'

"In the car. Now." Mom says slamming the back door over and over until it latches.

I climb in the back next to Ruby who is already strapped into the seat next to me, absorbed in her tablet.

Mom slides in behind the wheel yanking the door shut. "Check your sister's safety belt."

I know it's fine yet I tug on it to make Mom happy. "Good."

"Again," Mom says, turning the key over and over, the engine grinding until it fires.

"Good," I say, passing a hand over it, unzipping my backpack, staring at the ballet slippers that I packed in the hopes that today might be uneventful: that our spur of the moment trip is simply a run to the store for milk, or eggs, or something special Mom's cooking for her boyfriend, Kyle, when he gets home from work at the hardware store.

Mom revs the engine. "I am done with Kyle and his shit for good."

My heart wobbles. "This time."

"Forever time," she says. "Buckle up. We're out of here."

I cinch the belt across my lap.

'When the storm blows through, Evie,' Miss Williams told me, hold onto something. A person. A feeling. A thought. Something solid with heft and grit that keeps you grounded no matter the twister spinning around you.'

I think. I reach. I find it. Ballet. I'm still hoping Ms. Portman picks me for the recital. "Mom, about ballet..."

"Ballet's not happening today." Mom throws the car in reverse, squints out the rear window and backs like a bullet out of the long, skinny driveway, snow piled high on either side.

"Uh-oh." Ruby clutches her stomach, a frown on her face.

This isn't the first time we've left home in a hurry. Most likely we will be gone for a few days, maybe a week. Nine out of ten times we return. Quietly. Shamefully. Apologetically. 'Please. I didn't know what I was thinking,' Mom would say to the live-in boyfriend. 'I'm sorry. It will never happen again. I don't know what got into me.'

She screeches out of the driveway onto the rural road, a skinny patch of gray asphalt, lonely against the white winter day, and I hope that I don't puke, 'cause I'm feeling sicker by the second. She throws the car in drive, and we pitch forward. Thick clouds bump across the open skies. It's as if the heavens unzipped them, and a big sloppy mess of snowflakes hit the windshield.

Ruby burps, her cheeks popping apple red.

"If I miss ballet today Miss Portman won't let me be in the recital," I say. The nerves in my stomach sizzle like drops of grease dancing in a frying pan.

"Miss Portman can be a bit of a bitch," Mom says. "There'll be other recitals." We shoot down the stark, narrow road, blow past telephone poles, skeletal trees, heaps of snow plowed in odd shapes like puzzle pieces that don't fit. Crows circle high in the cloudy gray skies over the fields.

A knot grows thick and hard, curling and tightening in my stomach. Queasy and Hope, my usual team of advisors, give me a heads up when something's not the norm. When something's playing out a little different.

3

'Pay attention, Evie, take a ticket, and hop aboard. Your ride's leaving the station.' Queasy says, always the worrier.

'Maybe everything will turn out just great!' Hope's the eternal optimist.

They've been dogging me since I was five years old. The first time was when I'd spiked a fever, Mom shoved the thermometer in my mouth, declared I had the flu, and tucked me into bed. She pressed a cool cloth to my warm forehead, rubbed my shoulders, soothed me with a story about bears and beds.

I finally slept, but Grandma Berlinger popped up in my dream, shaking a large baking spoon with an owl's head carved into it. 'Look out for your Mother, Evie Beanie. I am past tired, and taking a trip. Not coming back any time soon. Love you, munchkin.'

'Grandma?' I asked, blinking my eyes open, but she'd vanished.

Mom got the call the next morning that Grandma had passed.

We traveled to her house to pay our respects. To collect Grandma's jewelry that she promised to mom before Uncle Nate could steal it. After graveside prayers, I wandered into her kitchen, spotted that same wooden spoon with the owl head on the counter and jumped half a foot. I wandered right back out and kept on walking down the crunchy gravel driveway until Mom ran after me and asked me if I was okay.

I shook my head. "Grandma's spoon."

"The owl spoon?" Mom rubbed my arm in the way that quieted me.

I nodded.

"Damn bird always scared the crap out of me, too." She ruffled my hair and kissed my head. "We'll get through this together, Evie Beanie. Love you, baby."

And we always do get through whatever the problem is,

but there's a more determined set to Mom's jaw this time. I don't know why, but this time things feel different.

There are no other cars in our lane and we fly down the highway like a bullet, passing a few vehicles headed in the opposite direction, moving a lot slower than us. One car flashes its lights repeatedly and I wince, the beams boring holes in my brain.

"Fucking asshole." Mom keeps her foot on the gas. A T-shaped intersection looms. A traffic light swinging from overhead cables hooked up to poles turns from yellow to red.

"Red means you're supposed to stop," I say, squeezing my hands together, feeling heat blossoming on my face and chest.

Mom grumbles and taps the brakes.

I worry about Ruby. Does she know Mom's freaking out? Is she scared? But she's still playing a game on her tablet.

Mom hits the brakes harder and we grind to a halt. A hundred yards ahead the road ramps up to train tracks, its guard rails painted candy cane colors. She taps her fingers on the steering wheel.

Maybe I'm thinking too much. Maybe we're just picking Kyle up from work. Maybe my warning signals really are the flu? I place the back of my hand to my forehead. Hmm. Feels normal.

The warning lights adjacent to the train tracks flash, a *ding-ding-ding* of alarms as the striped protective guard rails lower, crossing in front of each other.

Mom taps faster.

Harder.

An incoming text *pings* on her phone. "Crap no." She digs her hand in her purse and drags it out, staring at it. "What does he want?"

Queasy wriggles its thin, hairy toes down deep into my stomach and digs in. My stomach lurches. I wince and clutch the front of my parka, my breath shallow, my heart lurching about in my chest.

I am not a rickety shed.

I survive when the storm blows through.

Mom tosses her phone onto the passenger seat. "I don't care what he wants. I am done. We are out of here." She glances up at the freight train chugging down the tracks toward us. Her hazel eyes narrow and I can almost see her brain calculating options like time lines drawn on a white board in History class. She takes a deep breath and white knuckles the wheel.

"Fuck it," she says and hits the gas.

The car pitches forward and I fly back in my seat. The gates close in front of us. *Ding-ding-ding* the approaching train shrieks.

"I can totally be late today," I say— *ding, ding, ding*—as we hurl toward them. "I've only been late once before. It's fine. *Really,* Mom." Panic rises inside me elbowing Queasy out of first position.

Ruby's face blotches red and she hiccups uncontrollably.

"Is your sister, okay?" Mom says, hunching forward.

"Mom!"

The conductor will see us and brake. He will see us and stop. But the train doesn't slow and no one brakes. I glance around, panicking, panicking, but all I see is white. Snow surrounds us. Snow hushes us. Snow will bury us. Who will hear one creaky car? Who will hear the whir of an old engine over the rumble of an approaching train? Who will hear the screams of a 13-year-old girl?

We rocket up the incline and slam under the gates. The little hairs on my arms stand straight up in my thick down winter coat and my lips burn like I've accidentally brush them against hot sauce, the kind Kyle likes with his taco chips when he watches football games.

6

I squeeze my eyes shut as bad feelings, horrible feelings, surge inside me. Feelings that this is it. I will never get to dance in Ms. Portman's ballet recital. I will never graduate middle school. I will never eat a sandwich in the high school lunchroom.

We fly across the tracks and are airborne for a forever second. The car dips, front wheels slam onto the road with a thud that rattles my bones and the candy cane barriers crash across the flat hood. My eyes pop open, my head swivels, and I stare wide-eyed out the back window as the train thunders down the tracks behind us, sparks flying off its wheels.

We bump, rattling fenders and thumpy old tires down the decline and rocket toward the line of cars queued on the highway's opposite lane. Maybe Grandma Berlinger in Heaven said a prayer for us, because we escape. I am flooded with happiness and silly words pop out my mouth. "We can still make ballet!" But then I spot the Wolfe boys crossing the two-lane highway and my breath catches.

Wyatt Wolfe and his older brother, Easton, wear headphones as they walk along the road a hundred or so yards in front of our speeding car. They are oblivious.

Wyatt has floppy black hair, a wiry build. We sit together during lunch, play mobile games, and study at the library. Wyatt is my escape from crazy mom and I am his from his angry dad. Wyatt was my first kiss at last year's mixer. It was a meeting of awkward mouths lasting fifteen or so seconds before we separated – me giggling and him smiling sheepishly, rolling his eyes. When I stare up at the glow stars on my ceiling at night before I fall asleep, I imagine that some day I will marry Wyatt Wolfe.

Snow falls harder.

Meaner.

Wyatt wears a backpack, a thick winter coat, and galoshes that look just like mine. "I got those stupid boots you like," he said in study hall last week, leaned back in his chair, and stuck his foot out in front of me.

"We're twinning!" I extended my leg, and indeed we were wearing the same fleece-lined galoshes. We laughed and shared a look as my heart bumped around in my chest in a weird way.

Now the Wolfe brothers step out from across the path next to the tracks crossing the line of cars waiting for the train to pass and my heart falls into my boots. "Mom!"

Easton is three years older than Wyatt, a high school junior, almost a man. He glances up, spots us barreling toward them, and panics, one arm flying in front of his face.

But Mom doesn't see because she's absorbed in her phone.

"Stop!" I reach between the seats and punch her arm but she doesn't slow down so I punch her again, harder. "Look!"

She finally glances up, her shoulders hitting her ears. "Fuck!" She hits the brakes.

We skid across the snow toward the Wolfe brothers and I scream. We plow into them with a series of sickening, heart-breaking thuds. The brothers bounce off our car, and fly through the air like broken birds.

"Damn." Mom grimaces, the car screeching until we stop a dozen or so yards away, spinning out on an angle on the side of the road.

Nausea consumes me.

Nausea *is* me.

I can't feel my hands.

I can't feel my feet.

I claw at my neck because my throat is trapped in there and I have to get it out or I will suffocate and die. I tear off my seat belt.

Ruby, her lower lip quivering, points a shaky finger to the tablet on the floor of the car that had just flown out of her hands and smacked me above the eye. She bursts out crying and pukes, yellow liquid burbling out of her lips, spilling down her chin.

I gag. I push the door open and crawl out, collapsing knees first onto the pavement, my heart bursting out of my thin chest.

I am not a rickety shed.

I will survive the storm that blows through.

Using the car door I pull myself to standing, my legs like noodles beneath me. I stumble forward, my forehead throbbing.

Easton is laying in a snow bank, cursing. His left leg and right arm splay out, his blood has sprayed random patterns, so red on the white snow. Sirens ring in the distance.

"Evie?" He grunts. "Evie?"

I'm clueless what to say, clueless what to do. I stagger past him – *so cold, so mean* – toward his brother, Wyatt, the floppy haired boy who I love. He lies half in and out of a ditch and I drop to my knees next to him. "Wyatt?"

Sprawled on his back, his headphones on the ground, a thin, twisted trail of blood trickles out of his nose. He doesn't answer. One leg lies twisted at an impossible angle, his twinning boot stuck in a snow bank a few yards away. I can't tell if he's breathing. I screw up my courage and place a gloved hand on his chest. "Wyatt?"

He blinks his eyes open and stares up at me, his pupils round, his beautiful pale lips breathing thin, smoky puffs, barely visible in the frigid air.

"Wyatt? Can you talk?"

He does not answer.

"It's Evie. Can you hear me?" *Drum. Drum. Drum.* My heart beats so loudly in my ears.

He blinks.

I lean and stare into his heartbreakingly beautiful face.

Black hair, white skin, full lips. My Wyatt has the face of an angel. "It's going to be okay," I lie.

He blinks.

Hot tears slide down my cheeks. I need to feel him—no —*I need to save him.*

I know then and there that God, and Grandma Berlinger, and anything good in the world that just saved me from that train has put me in charge of saving Wyatt Wolfe. And I wonder, *can* I save Wyatt Wolfe if I touch him?

Sirens shriek. People spill out of parked cars and race toward us. The crows circle the field, cawing.

Hands shaking, I rip off my gloves. I unzip Wyatt's jacket and place my bare, shaking hand on the soft v-shaped divet where his chest meets his neck. His breath ratchets up, his chest rising and falling unevenly under my palm. "Help's on its way," I say. "We can do this. Just like we twinned on the galoshes. Just like we aced history test."

His eyes meet mine. Our gazes lock. "You and me? We'll always be together, Wyatt. We've got this."

A quirk of a sad smile tugs at the corner of his pale lips. But then his eyes glaze, his lips grow bluer.

My stomach lurches. "No."

I cannot lose him now. We are laughter. We are hope. We are each other's way out of mean dads and crazy moms. I *will* life back into him. *My life.*

"Stay," I command, staring into his pretty blue eyes, eyes that are so hazy. My blood warms, my face flushes, tingles zip down my spine. I take his hand in mine and squeeze it. Hard. Just as hard as my need, my want, my intention to make him stay here on this earth. "Stay, Wyatt. Please. *Please.* Stay for me. For your friend, Evie."

But he ignores me. He's slipping away. He's leaving me.

"Stay," I command. Desperate. "You have to stay."

Beautiful, kind, lovely Wyatt Wolfe shouldn't lose his life

on this cold, snowy, mean winter day just by crossing a path. My hand grows cold, then colder, my warmth traveling from me into him.

His breath billows. "Evie?" he rasps.

It feels like Christmas and I smile. Healing is working. "Yes! We are doing this. Hold onto me."

He smiles. Just like he smiled after he kissed me. *We've got this.*

Grandma's owl spoon stomps into my brain.

Wyatt shudders, and his eyes roll back in his head. His limbs twitch, muffled against the snow. Only now do I see the blood pouring out of the back of his skull, pouring into the snow, the red warmth staining the white cold in angry blotches.

"No!"

Paramedics pull me aside. Mom envelopes me. It's too much. Too close. She pulls my face to her chest, suffocating me. "Don't look, baby. Please Jesus, don't look."

I struggle to break free, throwing elbows, blindly striking out with fists. "I'm not a baby! Wyatt needs me."

"Evie. You're thirteen. You can't heal everybody. You can't fix everything."

"You don't know that!" I burst into tears. "You don't know anything."

"Coding," one paramedic says.

They hustle my floppy dark-haired, broken boy to a gurney, then into an ambulance. A paramedic alternates between compressing his chest and breathing into his mouth. The van pulls off, the dull clump of tires on snow. The tail-lights flash red against the white.

First responders transfer Easton, a thick brace secured around his neck into an ambulance. He has to pull through. He has to help Wyatt survive this disaster. "Easton, I'm so sorry. We didn't—"

"Fuck you," Easton says as the paramedics slam the doors. The van spits chunks of snow from its back tires as it pulls away.

A police officer approaches us. "Ma'am."

"Yes, Officer," Mom says.

I stand in the cold and the snow, blood staining my hands, my coat, my twinning boots.

Ruby cries, still tucked securely in the car. I want to cry as well but I can't find the air. Where has all the air gone? I hear a few 'caws' and stare at the sky. The crows stop circling the field and fly off for parts unknown.

I am not a rickety shed.

Will I survive the storm that blows through?

HEALER

HEALER

Thirteen years later

I STAND IN FRONT OF THE FLOOR TO CEILING WINDOWS ON the 25th floor in the One Magnificent Mile office on Michigan Avenue, shiver from the chill of the air conditioning, and pull the thin cashmere sweater tighter across my chest. I stare out at the upscale bustling urban scene below me.

Madame Germaine Marchand sits behind the Louis XIV antique desk in the corner office of Ma Maison Agency. She slides an elegant manicured hand over her short silver bob. "Did you figure out who's been tampering with your mailbox?" she asks.

"Not really. Maintenance is putting in another security camera. In the meantime, I rented one at the post office. Anyway, that's the least of my worries right now. I talked to Mom's shrink a few days ago. He thinks she's stable enough to travel." I stare out the window. To the right traffic is thick on Michigan Avenue, even more congested on Lake Shore Drive, brake lights more solid than flashing. To the left choppy, white-capped waves on Lake Michigan crest far below on this steamy, summer day. I love Chicago. It's beautiful. It's my home. And yet I'm ready to shake all the 'city' off, and blow out of here.

"That's terrific, Evelyn," she says. "Check mom out of the clinic and take her someplace pretty for a weekend," Madame says. "A quaint B&B filled with antiques. A parlor where they serve tea with homemade scones and fresh jam."

"I rented a lake house in Wisconsin for a month," I say. "Her doctor said some down time in the country will help her brain reboot."

Madame Germaine frowns. "The timing's not going to work. I have a new client for you."

"Time in Wisconsin will do my family good." I say, hearing the irritation expertly contained in her voice; feel the manipulation in the thirsty vibes radiating off her. "Everyone needs to mix it up once in a while. Foliage. Farms. Even healers need healing. Vacation's not a dirty word."

"Time off *with* your family sounds like the opposite of healing. Do you ever just take a real vacation?" Madame assesses me behind her expensive, tortoiseshell cat- eye glasses. "Fly off to Rome or Paris or Aruba for 'me' time?"

"Wouldn't that be a luxury?"

I used to despise Madame but over the past two years I've learned to tolerate her. She's cold and manipulative, but she's pushier than usual today. I tune out the faint sound of traffic far below me, tune out Madame, and silently count backwards: *Three. Two. One.* I open to the intuitive layer that lies beneath the surface. The empathic layer. The layer where I access feelings that belong to other people and sense them in my own body.

The first emotion I tune into is obvious: disapproval. Clouds of disapproval billow inside me but I know they're not mine. Madame owns all of that. If I squint I can practically see disapproval roll off her shoulders like a miniature tank.

She's not thrilled I'm taking a break from work. And yet, master chess player that she is, she pinches out a smile. "Fall will be a terrific time to take a holiday. You'll catch the changing colors."

"I'm not going in the fall," I say. "I'm leaving next week. I don't want to miss out on all the excitement of mosquito season."

"They'll eat you up alive this time of year." She is brilliant at bargaining. Quiet. Relentless. She could turn her talents to high stakes poker or chess, but chooses to be a madame instead. She has no biological kids that I know of and I suspect this is her way of mothering.

"Re-think the timing on your vacation, Evie. The new client requesting your services has specific needs," she says, clicking off her tablet. "His people are not looking for an average escort. We ran his profile through the software and the results indicated that he'd best be matched with someone like you. Someone who heals."

I cleared seven figures last year. I'm one of the highest paid escorts in Chicago. I'm twenty-six years old and on a good day I feel like I'm going on forty-six. I need a break before I explode in a million bloody pieces splattering everyone within splattering range.

Madame Germaine purses her lips and lifts a white 8 X 10 envelope from her desk drawer. This is where she tries to talk me into doing something I don't want to do. Something that will earn us both more money in a month than most people make in a year. She clears her throat, a tell before she hard sells. But the last two years working as an astronomically-priced escort with a rare expertise has turned me into a decent negotiator.

"If they specifically requested a healer, Madam, a few other courtesans are excellent with that," I say. "Scarlett is great with emotionally damaged men. Lily knows how to help those who are physically broken."

"Yes, yes. The three of you are a small but potent division within Ma Maison," she says. "But this client specifically requested you. Sit." She points to the chair assuming she has schooled me like an expensive, well trained dog. Funny, I could say the same about her.

"Specialty. Ha," I say, making my way toward her desk. "Teaching five-year-olds was a specialty."

A few years back I was a kindergarten teacher with a Master's in Education. It didn't matter how much insight I had into what made people tick—my education left me with staggering student loans and creditors crawling out of the woodwork like determined termites chewing their way through a rotting fence.

I worked hard. I pulled a fifty-hour week, squeezed out the minimum loan payments every month, along with the last drops of soap from bottles, recycling them for cents on a dollar. I told myself that I was making a dent in my loans when the reality was 90 percent of that went to interest. I told myself I did it to save the environment, because plastic parts killed ocean animals. But the sad truth was I needed every nickel collected because the electric company had this sneaky habit of turning off the electricity on the exact date stamped on the pink notice.

One day over pudding cups in the teacher's lounge my new pal, Amelia, third grade teacher and best margarita maker ever, confided she'd started moonlighting as an escort. Not only was she paying her rent in a timely fashion, she was squaring off her credit card debt, and hacking away at student loans. "I'll set you up with my agency, Evie," she said. "It's just like dating. You don't even have to have sex with the guys."

"But they want to, right?"

She licked the remainder of the butterscotch from a spoon. "What guy doesn't want sex?"

Being an escort sounded creepy. Tawdry. Dangerous. "Thanks, but I'm going to pass."

"I hear the judgment," she said. "Come on. If you join, I'll get a commission."

"Do I have to buy a three month supply of laundry soap too? No thanks. Everyone does whatever to make ends meet. No judgment. It's just not for me."

But a month later Mom's insurance company doubled her premiums, stopped paying for half her treatments and a chunk of her pricey prescription drugs. As her proxy, I argued with them over the phone and fired off letters. When none of that made a dent, I scheduled an appointment at their local branch office.

I took half a day off work, and caught the bus downtown to plead Mom's case. I wore my most sensible suit, fashioned my long hair in a neat bun, and waited an hour past my appointment time for the adjustor. He drummed his fingers on the particleboard desk and talked nonsensical bullshit for five minutes. *He* was just an innocent pawn in this difficult situation. *He'd* do what he could do, but please don't be angry, *he* was only the messenger. We stood up and eyed each other.

"Thanks," I said. "Anything you can do, I appreciate it."

"You got it." He passed me his card, but it slipped from his hand and fluttered to the floor. I bent to pick it up and upon arising discovered his dick had magically busted out of his zipper. He clutched it in his hand and yanked it to and fro in my direction, a ridiculous look on his turtle face.

"Ugh." I gagged, raced out of his office, and tried to delete the 'squishing' sound from my brain. I made it home without puking only to find an eviction notice plastered on my door.

"Aw, fuck." I peeled it off the threshold, pulling the paint along with it. Not only was I soon to be homeless, but my douche landlord would deduct the 'property damage' from my security deposit.

I was twenty-four-years old. I could either crumple into a ball on my sorry mattress, or clear my head. It was spring and the Chicago weather was a psychotic ride between chilly, spring showers, and warm, sunny skies. Home sweet home. *Ha. Yeah, thanks a bunch, universe.*

I hopped on my bike, pedaled on the path adjacent to Lake Shore Drive, and rode for miles like a madwoman. I biked past sailboats dotting the harbor and sleek condos – the constellation of wealth gathered like members of a private club hovering around a mahogany bar at Lake Michigan's edge.

I braked at a stop light, watched the cars pass in a blur and wondered how, after four years studying to get a liberal arts degree, a year and a half to earn my teaching certificate, all the hours I'd spent learning alternative therapies and eighteen thousand different ways to meditate — how had I landed like last year's fashion in life's bargain basement bin once again? More importantly, how could I get out?

And then Amelia texted me:

Amelia: *In a bind. Pretty please double with me tonight. 8 pm. No funny biz. I'll pay you five hundred. Cash.*

Evie: *Yes.*

I shot back.

I biked home, showered, and flipped through clothes in

my closet at lightning speed wondering what kind of dicey situation I'd signed up for.

Now, two years later, in Ma Maison's posh corner office, I take a seat next to Madame Germaine's desk. The white envelope resting on her immaculate table contains details of a potential client – a high profile client. I can feel her desire for coin depositing into Ma Maison's bank account with a hefty clink.

"He probably doesn't even need me," I say. "Most of these guys just need a good therapist or someone who can mother them, not an astronomically-priced 'girlfriend' healing immersion."

"He wouldn't have requested you if he didn't need you. Money is nothing to these men," Madame says, templing her fingers. "They see their shrinks, go to church, synagogue, prayer services. They pay for pricey escorts for events, or kink, or whatever bug is up their ass. Yes, they come to Ma Maison for that, but they don't request someone like you unless they want a girl who can help them with their darkest, deepest concerns. A girl who can help them heal."

I wave a dismissive hand. "He'll do fine without me."

"Maybe yes. Maybe no."

The night I accepted Amelia's request to go on a 'date' for $500 cash, I was a big, fat bundle of nerves. I met Amelia and two well-dressed, thirty-something guys for drinks at a trendy River North restaurant. They were in from Kansas City for a trade show. We chatted and flirted. No one pulled down his pants in the middle of dinner. No one snuck their hand under the table in a shady attempt to slide it between my legs and cop a feel. I had the best meal I'd eaten in years. Two and a half hours and four courses later, Amelia and I hit the ladies room and she slipped me five bills.

"Was that so awful?" she asked.

"No," I said, my fingers trembling as I tucked the cash into my wallet and zipped my purse up tight.

"Told you." She leaned into the mirror, fluffed her hair, and applied a fresh coat of lipstick.

"It's not always this easy, is it?"

Amelia was always impossibly coiffed, had everything together, and I was the weirdo, sweating the details, not knowing how or if I'd pay the next phone bill.

"It is tonight. Say goodnight to your date on your way out. Take his card to be polite. No, you don't have to call him."

I thanked the guy for a lovely evening and accepted his card. No wizened penis wanking in my direction. Instead he shook my hand, a perfect gentleman. I stared at the ceiling that night on my lumpy mattress and imagined all the debt I could pay with those five bills. It was so easy. I was smart. I was better educated than the vast majority of people making a better living than me. Why *couldn't* I become an escort?

'Bah, who becomes an escort?' My old pal Queasy, opined. *'You want some ancient man peppered in liver spots feeling up your private bits?'*

Er, no. What was wrong with me? Was I losing it like Mom did? This idea was batshit crazy. I could get another job after my twelve-hour work day. Sell something weird on eBay and make a fortune. Become a Walmart greeter on the weekends.

The next day Mom's shrink phoned and told me she was a candidate for TMS.

"What's TMS?"

"Transcranial Magnetic Stimulation. It's similar to ECT. The next wave of technology for re-setting the brain," Dr. Winters said.

"But electro convulsive therapy never worked in the past."

"This is different," he said. "They use magnets. Early study results are amazing. If we get your mom into a study program it could turn her life around. She could live on her own again."

"You mean live with me again. She can't live with my sister Ruby − she's in college." As much as I loved my mom, we were like oil and water when it came to living under the same roof. It's a wonder we hadn't killed each other all the times we'd tried to make that work.

"No, Evie. If successful, she might be able to live on her own."

"What's the catch?"

"It's pricey."

"How pricey?"

"Six figures pricey."

"Got it," I said, my throat closing.

"I already spoke with the program's administrator. She's a friend. I'm almost certain I can get your mom in."

"Great," I said, my skin turning hot like someone had doused me in alcohol, lit a match, and tossed it on my head. "Then we have to do it."

"Excellent." He breathed a sigh of relief. "The down payment is due upon program acceptance."

"Right. I'll get to work on that." I hung up the phone and sobbed, kissing my life as I knew it goodbye. I called Amelia, catching her on a night between dates. We ordered pizza at her place, drank beer, and binge watched *Alfred Hitchcock* movies.

"Want another slice?" she asked.

"No. Thanks to you I can't get fat ever again," I said, smelling the fresh basil mixed with freshly grated cheese, my stomach growling. "I should still do this, right?"

"Yes. Do you really have other options?" she said. "Besides, some guys love curvy girls."

"Fuck you. Give me a slice of pepperoni."

She grinned and passed me a plate.

"Thanks. You've been doing this for a while. You know the ins and outs, no pun intended." I tore into a piece of pizza. "I'm the new girl, and I doubt they'll hire me for my ability to pull someone's thumb out of their mouth, or convince a five-year-old to lay down on his mat and take a nap."

"You'd be surprised how often the thumb in the mouth and the napping thing cross over." She sat back on her sleek, designer couch and pointed to the TV. "Resume streaming please. I love *Notorious* with Cary Grant and Ingrid Bergman."

I signed up for the Ma Maison agency the next day. I helped the tech girl fill in my fictitious bio, got my hair and makeup done and took the boudoir pictures. I reminded myself that sex with clients was not required because that would constitute prostitution. Ma Maison didn't want to get busted and neither did I. Besides, I'd been assured that sex with clients was *optional*.

I'd date. I'd pay my bills and pay for my mom's psych treatments. And everything went according to plan – for a while: Arm candy for middle-aged men in town for a convention, an engagement with a lonely guy returning for his high school reunion. Lots of prepping to look polished. Hair. Nails. Waxing.

I taught kindergarten in the morning and went on dates on nights and weekends when Ma Maison booked me. I earned decent money but didn't get big tips. I didn't make the big bucks because I wasn't banging clients. When I had sex with a client. *If* I had sex with a client, I wanted it to be with someone special. Someone I'd always remember. Maybe that was old-fashioned. I didn't care. I'd been accused of worse.

But everything changed when I met Dylan McAlister. Life shot a come to Jesus, Hallelujah sized hole through my chest when I met Dylan McAlister. Hard to believe that was nearly two years ago.

Now Madam Germaine pushes the envelope across the pretty antique desk toward me. "This man needs you."

"You say that about all the men."

"Open it. Take a look."

I reluctantly pick it up, fantasizing about casting a fishing line onto that Wisconsin lake. Feeling the tantalizing tug on the pole when I get a bite. The satisfaction of reeling dinner in. Pan frying it over the BBQ on the deck. Tossing back a few beers with some friends and my sister. After debilitating, exhausting years of bipolar depression, Mom's finally smiling again. I take mental snapshots, but when I hold one too close, one of her smiles threatens to melt my heart.

Now I hold the packet, solid in my hands, and suddenly my longing for fish fries, cold beer, and hanging with a relatively normal version of mom is replaced with a stirring of blood in my veins, goosebumps on the backs of my arms. And I know in my bones that this envelope holds the details of another broken man who – if the stars align – I'll uncover the bitter belief that shut him down. I'll help him heal.

I, Evie Berlinger, am no longer an average escort. I'm not paid to drop to my knees behind some shitty House of Pies and dispense blow jobs to sad men in town for a hardware show. My services are retained by powerful, privileged, wealthy men at the top of their professions who have lost their way; their self-confidence; the spark that made them great.

These titans could spend years in therapy paying brilliant shrinks to hack away at their issues. They could travel thousands of miles in their desperate search for answers. Vision quest to Peru, climb Macchu Picchu, drink the ayahuasca and trip the light fantastic.

Or, they could pay Ma Maison an ungodly amount of money to spend a few weeks with Scarlett, Lily, or me. We have the ability to help them uncover the screwed up core belief that shut them down and we do that quickly. If we take a liking to them they might have the best sex of their lives. Trip the light fantastic in a different kind of way.

"Do you mind if I look at this for a few minutes?" I ask and tap one finger on the white linen envelope. But I already suspect my vacation at the lake house is going to be put on hold. "Meditate on it for a few?"

"Take your time," Madam says.

I stand, hold the packet tight to my chest, already absorbing who this man is. I leave Madam Germaine's office and walk past her assistant. "Hey, Jay. Is there an open room?"

"Number four," he says. "Can I get you anything?"

"I'm good. Thanks." I enter room number four and close the door. I shut the blackout curtains, settle on a chaise lounge with the envelope resting on top of me, put on earphones and hit shuffle on my phone. Whatever music comes up is meant to be. And then the song starts to play. The one that reminds me of the man who changed my life.

I close my eyes, memories tripping through my brain. Memories of how I got here. Memories of Dylan McAlister. I let them dance around awkward and breathless and exhilarating like they are happening again for the first time. I slide into the deliciousness of Dylan McAlister: gorgeous, brilliant, tormented player.

TYCOON

TYCOON

Two years ago

WHEN A REQUEST FOR A 'DATE' COMES INTO MA MAISON from a new client, a non-refundable deposit is collected and the potential patron is vetted via the usual sources. Background checks are conducted for income, proper references, and a clean record for rape, murder, domestic abuse, and human trafficking.

Once cleared, a client (or if they choose to remain anonymous their representative), reviews and signs the standard contract. Then Madam Marchand and her assistant select the first batch of candidates. Most guys are looking for a few things when they hire from an exclusive escort agency: A beautiful girl on their arm to impress their friends, a girlfriend experience, or a young woman who can wrap her lips over their cocks and make them forget their sadness for a short, but glorious period of time.

In ninety-nine percent of the cases, the customer selects his date from the first batch of women presented to him in confidential files and documents. A pretty face, impressive breasts, shapely legs. Throw in decent conversation and it's not rocket science.

But Dylan McAlister is the odd man out.

I've only been with Ma Maison three months when he picks me. I normally wait ten minutes in the foyer for an appointment with Madam Marchand but this time her assistant ushers me into her office immediately. I don't think this guy is an average client.

"Why me?" I ask. I'm the new girl on the block. I'm not a client's exotic fantasy girl. 'No kink' is spelled out in my bio. I don't submit to dom fantasies. I don't crawl blindfolded across the floor holding a stick in my mouth. Nor do I flip roles, insist a client call me 'Miss Evelyn' while they kneel at my feet as I grind a heel into their ass cheek and beat them with a switch.

I am the girl next door they always wanted to ask out but never found the courage to. I am the fresh-faced high school cheerleader they always dreamed about screwing. I am the step sister fantasy. I am not the sought after Prom Queen because that role has already been locked down by Victoria, Amelia's frenemy. I don't really care because alpha girl status has never been my goal and I couldn't care less about becoming Ma Maison's head bitch.

This whole escort gig was going great until a week ago when I discovered during a random conversation that I was making a quarter of what the other girls made. I wasn't being considered for primo gigs because I wasn't actually fucking clients. I was pissed, half tempted to have more than a word with Madame Germaine, but she calls me into the office and beats me to the punch. I'm petrified she's going to fire me but instead she offers me a gig.

Madam slips off her cat-eye glasses, places them on her desk and rubs her temples. "I don't know for certain why Mr. McAlister picked you," she says. "He said he had a gut instinct. I pressed him a little. He said you had something special in your eyes."

"Probably eyeliner and mascara," I say, keeping a straight face while I mess with Madam Uptight. "Don't all the girls have that?"

"Remind me to highlight quirky sense of humor in your profile. Ask Mr. McAlister yourself when you meet him," she said, passing me the usual white linen envelope.

Ma Maison is old fashioned in that they don't transfer contracts via email. Apparently different laws could be broken via transferring information over the internet. "Mr. McAlister also requested that I give you a brief list of instructions of what he wants you to read before your first date. I took a peek. Nothing seems objectionable."

"Thanks," I say, sliding the envelope into my purse.

"Evelyn," she says, her frosty tone stopping me cold.

"Madam?"

She arches one thin eyebrow. "You're not technically a virgin, are you?"

I break out coughing. "No."

"Too bad. We could have gotten a lot more money for *that* kind of date."

"Sorry. My V card's already been punched." I practically bolt toward the door.

"Evelyn."

The room grows colder and goose bumps prickle on the backs of my arms. "What, Madam?"

"You're a pretty girl. A smart girl. You're the dream for the men who select you."

"Thank you."

"Don't thank me. Find a way to thank them. I'm certain you'll be richly rewarded."

I escape her pristine office, pound my fist *bam-bam-bam* on the elevator button and blow out of the pretty prison. I leave the frosty AC chilled building and step out into the swamp air of Chicago's humidity central summer. I catch the subway home to the Southside, keeping one possessive finger on the envelope tucked into my bag.

I slap the envelope on Mom's Formica table, pour a glass of lemonade, and fashion my long, thick hair into a loose bun, securing it with a stick. I turn on the rotating fan, positioning my face in front of it for a few seconds. Then I lean back and read Dylan's bio.

Dylan McAlister. Gambler. Player. Thirty-eight. Married once for five years, divorced for another five. He hails from a small town in Texas and his parents are church people.

Rich church people.

Tycoon rich church people.

About twenty-five years ago his dad moved up the ladder and became one of those superstar TV evangelist pastors at a mega-church that telecasts its services on cable. The McCalister's have money that can buy islands and mansions and private jets.

Dyla McAlister might be a player but at his roots he's a former church baby. What is a former church baby doing hiring an escort from a high-priced agency? Color me intrigued.

I hit up Google, search 'Images', and hunt down a few photos of Dylan hanging with his family on a pretty summer day on the steps of a gaudy cathedral. Father and son are cut from the same cloth: high cheekbones, full heads of hair, classically handsome. The house of worship, on the other hand, is an ostentatious palace of metal and glass with crosses beveled into the windows, with another gigantic cross erected on the front lawn.

The Lighthouse Cathedral is framed against a blinding beautiful Texas blue sky, the sun streaming down around it like even God himself is blown away. The brand screams money.

The same search reveals details about dollars enthusiastically deposited into the church's many collection plates, sizeable dollars inked onto checks, hundreds of thousands of green, green dollars reverently submitted via credit cards for church events and conventions. And then there are the millions dropped on the series of inspirational self-help books that his dad has probably dictated to a ghostwriter.

Money.

Beautiful money.

Come to Jesus money.

I find pictures online of Dylan's casually pricy Texas wedding to a petite, cute, coiffed blond girl, with dimples from here to eternity. His dad presided over the afternoon ceremony. A good-looking guy, who has to be his brother, served as his best man. His mom wore her Sunday best and beamed in the official wedding photographs, hanging onto Dylan with one hand, the other touching her husband's arm.

They look like a nice family. A handsome family. A happy family. What has pushed Dylan out of his marriage, out of Lighthouse Church? What has pushed him into a life of high stakes poker?

The vast majority of men that pay big money for a high-end escort are lonely. Something or someone is missing from their life, or they need their ego built back up. No judgment. I know lonely. I speak wounded ego. But staring at Dylan's photo I don't get it.

He's around 6 feet, with thick chestnut hair, blue eyes, and a smattering of freckles on his sun-kissed cheeks. His body lean, hard, and hell yes, darling, rocks a pair of blue jeans and a fitted T-shirt. He's smokin' hot in a three piece suit, his pants happy to be skimming his tight ass. What is Dylan McAlister doing hiring an escort, let alone a new one because he sees something in her eyes?

I skip to the 'About Event' page. He is traveling to Chicago for an underground poker game and wants a 'date' for the event. Someone trustworthy. Someone discreet. I open the envelope containing his instructions, half expecting to see something that might not have sounded suspicious to Madam Marchand but would raise my freak flag.

But the only weird thing is that his instructions are simple and handwritten:

"Dress elegantly. Look stunning. Wait, you already do. Hold intelligent, engaging conversation with attendees. Be witty and discreet. The job will last 16 to 24 hours. You will be compensated for the full 24 if the gig ends early. Bring a wrap. The room gets cold. And get plenty of sleep the night before, Evelyn. Can't wait to meet you, gorgeous."

My stomach flutters. I flip the switch on the fan up a notch and return to reading about him online. Dylan McAlister split from the church after his divorce and now he's one of the most successful players in recent years on the private poker circuit. He's legendary for spending small fortunes and winning even larger ones during games that last up to a few days. He tips generously. No known ties to Mafia, doesn't abuse drugs, alcohol, and is only called an asshole by people that squander their fortunes to him. The gorgeous, brilliant man with the thick chestnut hair and smattering of freckles has the Midas touch.

I stare at his picture, my heart *thump thumping* against my ribs. I could fall hard for those pretty blue eyes. Enjoy running a finger over the smattering of freckles on his sun-kissed cheeks, making my way down to his lips. I wonder what it will feel like the first time he kisses me. I suspect it will be magical – lips tingling, cheeks flushing, my body bathed in stardust after a meteor shower blows through.

Dylan McAlister is beautiful. If he wanted lips wrapped around his cock he could walk into any bar, or swipe right on a dating app. If he wanted to plunge his dick into someone warm and inviting, a dozen women would happily service him at a poker game or in a choir loft after 8:30 a.m. early church vespers and before the 10:30 a.m. late service. Who are you, Dylan McAlister? Who are you and what do you really want from a girl from an escort agency let alone a girl who has "a look in her eyes?"

I beautify for all my dates but I prep the holy hell for this one. I visit my fave budget salon. I'm still paying for Mom's medicals, so nothing fancy or overpriced for me. I pop for highlights, a cut, a blow dry, a mani pedi, and undergo the whole waxing ordeal.

Back at my dump, I turn on my bedroom window AC unit. It chugs along, coughing in fits and spurts as I rip through my closet searching for the perfect thing to wear. Clothes fly onto my bed, piling in miniature mountains. This outfit looks sleazy. That dress too old-fashioned. The purple skirt makes my ass look fat. The top I like on the hanger is too low cut making me look slightly slutty. I text Amelia.

Evie: *Panicking. A date. A new client. Absolutely nothing to wear.*

Amelia: *I doubt that.*

Evie: *Everything's too sexy or not sexy enough.*

Amelia: *Come to my place, Cinderella, and shop in fairy godmother Amelia's closet.*

Evie: *Yes, please and TY.*

I throw on jeans and a T-shirt and catch a ride to her new, two bedroom condo in Greektown. Escorting's been good to Amelia. She not only paid off all her debt, she's now a property owner. She lies back on her queen-sized bed swiping on her phone while I try on skirts, tops, and cocktail dresses. "Nothing works," I say. "I am tragically un-dressable."

"Stop, drama queen." Amelia tosses her phone, jumps up, and walks to the closet flipping through hangers. Half the stuff still has the tags on. Nordstroms. Saks. Bloomingdales. She pulls out a garment bag, unzips it, and pulls out a dress. "Here."

I take it from her and stare at it. This dress. Good God, this dress. It's red, fitted, mid-length, with thin straps and a deep V in the back. "Pretty," I say. Stunning is more like it. Out of my league is probably the best description. The only time I've laid hands on a dress like this is in the pages of a magazine.

"Try it on."

I pull it over my head, down my chest, and wriggle it over my hips. I turn and face the full-length mirror. "Wow. I look like a different Evie."

"You look like the same Evie to me," Amelia says, falling back onto her bed and returning to texting. "Albeit wearing a two thousand dollar dress. That's the one. It shows off your shoulders, and makes your waist look amazing. Your boobs are good, not too exposed. And it hugs your ass."

"How'd you score a two thousand dollar dress?"

"Ma Maison's giving me a clothing allowance for more exclusive dates."

"Nice." I stare in the full-length mirror and fuss with the skirt, smoothing it over my legs where it falls a few inches above the knee. "What about the length? Too old-fashioned?"

"It's elegant. What's up with you and the worrying? Want to tell me something?"

"Nothing to tell."

"Beg to differ," she says. "I've never seen you this wound up about a job. If Dylan McAlister was candy he'd be Red Hots. I think you're going to have sex with him."

"Oh, please. I haven't even met him."

"Someone's going to pop your escort cherry, Evie."

"Why?"

"Because it's expected."

"What if I don't want to do that?"

"Honestly?"

"Yes."

"Play the game or go back to being a full time kindergarten teacher."

"Stop being a bitch. Did you Google Dylan?"

"At least this bitch is your true, honest friend. Yes, I've seen his picture. I've seen his entire resume. Impressive."

My heart sinks. "What are you saying?"

"Madam Marchand offered the McAlister gig to someone else before you."

"You?" Disappointment mixed with a twinge of jealousy trickles like a pinch of poison through my veins. "She offered it to you? He picked you first?"

"Not me." She waves her hand dismissively. "Victoria."

"Victoria? Ew."

"You two share a similar fake bio. Written by the same copywriter, remember?"

"Except I don't do hard kink. And I don't spread my legs for just anyone let alone everyone."

"You don't spread your legs for *anyone*, Evie. I'm the last person to talk you into anything. I'm the last person on this planet to tell... you know what? Forget it. Do what you're comfortable with. Do what makes you happy."

"That's right," I say. "I'll do what I want to do. And, and... Victoria didn't want Dylan McAlister? What's wrong? Is he some kind of freak?"

"I don't know." She shrugs. "I don't think so. Victoria turned the engagement down because she's got a new boyfriend. He's taking her to Paris this weekend."

"Good for her,' I say, my excitement dashed. "If Dylan picked Victoria first, maybe I should turn down this gig too. There's a great concert in town this weekend. A guy from my gym asked me out, you know."

"Excellent." Amelia says, absorbed in her phone. "Do you like him?"

"No. But he could grow on me."

"Right. I think Dylan picked Victoria first because Madam pushed him in her direction. She manipulates, you know. Some girls pay her extra on the side. Who do you think she makes more money off of? You? Or Victoria?"

"That's not right." Indignation stomps around inside me like pissed off protestors in pussy hats at a protest. "That's not fair."

"That's the way the world works," Amelia says. "Fighting something that can't be changed isn't going to get you anywhere. Let it go. You remember what I told you how to protect your heart, right?"

I shiver. "My heart was broken forever, for good, a long time ago."

Even after all this time the wound lies just below my skin's surface, waiting for something to poke into it, rip the scab off.

Nothing good came out of that day we ran over the Wolfe brothers. I've been practicing the art of trying not to think about that day for years.

Every time images of Wyatt and Easton bloody and broken pop into my brain, I replaced them with balloons that float into the sky as light as feathers. Or birds winging away, just like those crows did for parts unknown. After I did that ten thousand or so times I got better at moving through the pain. The PTSD, on the other hand, was a bitch to lose.

At thirteen, the hard-working doctors employed through DCFS diagnosed me as having Generalized Anxiety Disorder because back then kids didn't usually get PTSD. Soldiers who went to war got PTSD. I wish they'd better explained that to my teenage nervous system.

The shakes started immediately following the accident, growing so fierce at times I could barely hold a pen. Students at my new school teased me, calling me 'Shake and Bake' Berlinger. The night terrors followed and I'd wake up time and again drenched in sweat. It wasn't that easy explaining damp sheets in foster care to the lady pulling them to her nose and sniffing with a fat frown on her face. "Are you sure, Evie?"

"I'm sure, Mrs. Smith. I didn't. I swear. I would know if I wet the bed."

And just when I thought things couldn't get any worse was when the empathic ability kicked into high gear. I started feeling other people's feelings in my own body, usually people in close proximity to me.

One day in 8th grade, I was late for gym class, hurriedly changing clothes in the locker room when the inside of my thigh began burning like I'd been stung by a bee. I put one foot up on a bench and peered down but didn't see any welts. Maybe I'd gotten my period.

I wasn't all that familiar with periods. I'd experienced

some cramps, but I didn't have a clue if they caused stinging. I wriggled my panties down and checked for blood. My cotton briefs were white as could be. But the stinging worsened. It burned, sliced, and then strangely there was relief, almost pleasure.

I suspected it was hormones. Just about everyone had warned me about hormones. A girl the next aisle over, sighed. I wandered a few yards over, popped my head around the corner of the row of lockers and spotted Lauren Caspberger. She was resting her foot on a bench and her legs were spread. She peered forward as she cut the inside of her thigh with a small knife.

I was embarrassed. It felt like I was interrupting a private moment. I didn't know if I should say anything but didn't know how I couldn't. "You okay?"

"I'm fine." She gave me the stink eye. "Go away, weirdo."

Twenty minutes later I was dribbling basketballs down the shiny gym floor – *thomp-thomp-thomp* – with twenty other girls aiming at hoops, when it dawned on me that the stinging wasn't mine. It was Lauren Caspberger's.

A week later I made my way down a hallway between classes when worry nipped at my heels so strongly I jumped. Would I have enough money? What would happen if I ran out of money? How would I take care of my family if I was no longer here? It was worse than worry, it was an almost quiet desperation. I stopped in my tracks and nearly got run over by a few guys.

"Out of the way, Berlinger," one said, pushing past me.

"Move it, Shake and Bake," his pal said, and they all laughed.

"Sorry." I was worried about a lot of things but walking the hallways of Beethoven Middle Grade School wasn't one of them. I leaned back against a locker and watched the kids pass. Some fast. Some slow. Some goofing around with their friends, others lost in thought. These feelings within me didn't belong to a student.

They belonged to the white-haired, stooped-back janitor wheeling a bucket with a mop impaled into it down the hall. He paused in an alcove waiting for the bell to ring, staring down at his bucket like his world was caving in. These weren't my concerns about money, they were his. I felt bad for him and said a silent prayer.

Eventually, I was diagnosed with PTSD, Generalized Anxiety Disorder, pre-disposed to panic attacks. They medicated me with a low dose of anti-depressants but they made me feel even worse than the anxiety. By the time I hit eighteen, I was determined to beat this crap and sought advice from alternative healers. I went to hypnotists, acupuncturists, body workers. One after the next told me I was 'empathic.' I picked up on the feelings of people around me, experienced *their* feelings in my body just like they were my own.

I could go crazy from this weirdness, split my brain into two or ten or five thousand pieces like Mom did, or I could compartmentalize and handle it with guided meditation, self-hypnosis, alternative medicine, and hard exercise.

I learned acupressure points to ground me. Meditation to calm me. Breathing exercises to bring me back to reality. And they helped. I never fully shut off the empathic spigot but turned it down to a low *drip-drip-drip*.

Now, seven years later, in Amelia's bedroom, my friend sighs. "I'm sorry, Evie. I'll cross my fingers that everything with Dylan McAlister goes well. I'm going to remind you what Victoria told me about boundaries in case you forgot."

"I don't need a reminder."

"Set boundaries within the confines of the date. Do not do anything you are uncomfortable doing. Ignore what I said before about popping your escort cherry. I shouldn't have said that. I say stupid things on occasion. Don't agree to anything that you know you'll have second thoughts about the next day. When the date is over, imagine yourself building a wall between you and the client."

"Can I make Mexico pay for it?" I snort.

"Build the wall. Keep your boundaries as intact as possible and keep yourself safe. If you get too close to these guys you can develop unhealthy attachments and confuse lust with love, a business relationship with a personal relationship and covet things you can't have."

"I've done pretty good so far."

"You have." She nods. "But you also haven't had sex with a client. Sex has a way of changing things. Enjoy the dress. It looks like it was made for you. Return it some day."

"I love you fairy godmother." I jump on the bed, throw my arms around her neck, and hug her. "You're my sister from a different mister." A pang of sadness pokes me because I wish I felt this way about my own sister.

"Yeah, yeah. Go before I turn you into a pumpkin."

"That's not how it works," I say, catching a glimpse of her texts − actually 'sexts.' "Fairy godmother sent the carriage. Technically it was a midnight thing."

"Go." She waves a dismissive hand. "I've got a date. Someone interesting for a change."

❧ 4 ❧

CINDERELLA

CINDERELLA

I DO MY HAIR, APPLY LIGHT MAKEUP, AND MEDITATE FOR half an hour to get centered. I slide into the money dress, zip it, and eye myself critically in the mirror. Cinderella indeed. Where are my glass slippers? Being that I was a lapsed Catholic and Dylan has the Christian background, before I step out the door, I bow my head in prayer.

Dear God. Please help me give my all for this job. Please help me do my best. And this I ask for in the name of the Father, and the Son, and the Holy Spirit. Amen.

Half an hour later I walk through the doors of a gorgeous five star hotel on Wacker Drive. I might look Zen but my nerves are sizzling, barely contained under my skin. Crystal chandeliers hang from the ceiling, casting rich light, flattering just about everyone in its glow. I ignore appreciative glances and questioning eyes from employees and customers, and navigate the marble floors, my high heels barely making a sound. I make my way toward the bar where I'm supposed to meet Dylan. I pause for a moment before entering.

Three, two, one, Evie. You've got this.

I smooth the skirt down my legs and remind myself that at the end of the day this is just a job. Dylan McAlister is just another client, just another guy in another elegant hotel with extra money to burn.

I slip the lipstick from the Chanel bag that I borrowed from Amelia, and swipe one last reinforcement coat on my lips. I'll do my best to be unemotional and remain professional. I'll give this job my all. I hold my head high, take a deep breath, and move into the bar's entrance. I've stared at Dylan McAlister's picture I don't know how many times now and yet I still worry that I won't find him.

I don't have to worry.

He finds me.

Immediately.

"Evelyn," he says, standing up from an intimate round table in the corner.

Wow. He's tall. Muscular. He's wearing crisp dress pants with an immaculate white shirt open a few buttons revealing groomed chest hair. Be still my heart. Dylan's hotter in person than he is in his pictures.

I make my way toward him feeling a little weak in the knees. I take in the smattering of light freckles on his high cheekbones, and the lock of chestnut hair that falls over his forehead. His blue eyes light up appreciatively. My pulse races, my cheeks feel hot.

Breathe, Evie, breathe.

He takes my hand, raises it to his lips, and kisses it. "Terrific meeting you. You're even prettier in person. How is that possible?"

My heart bumps about so hard I'm scared he'll hear it. "I don't know. I mean thank you, Mr. McAlister."

"Mr. McAlister's my father. Call me Dylan. Sit." He pulls out a chair.

I do as he asks and cross my legs.

A waiter arrives. "What can I get for you?"

"Mineral water, please," I say.

"Two Pellegrinos," he says.

The waiter nods and walks away.

Dylan pulls a small Tiffany blue box from his pocket and places it in front of me. "Considering I'm going to keep you working for the next 24 hours, I got you a little something."

I raise an eyebrow. "A super tiny espresso maker?"

"Ha." He claims the seat across from me. "Is this the first poker marathon you've attended?"

"Yes." I tear my eyes from his, and stare at the box, a petite pristine white bow on top. "You don't need to do this."

"I know," he says, smiling. "I want to. Open it."

I've never been one to rip open presents. I enjoy the unwrapping, the peeling away of the layers, the unveiling almost as much as I enjoy the actual gift. Besides, I've learned the hard way that too frequently men give you things to feel good about themselves. A way to feel like they are courting you instead of purchasing a fantasy. Or worse, buying a GWP.

I search Dylan's face for selfish motivations but all I see is kindness and anticipation.

"You're killing me," he says, looking like a kid waiting in front of a decorated tree piled high with presents on Christmas morning. "Open it already."

I bite back a smile. "Okay, boss man."

"Dylan," he says. "Boss man's my brother."

I pull the lid from the box, unfold the tissue paper. Inside is a delicate diamond necklace. "It's beautiful." I pull the pretty pendant in the shape of a horseshoe from the box, and dangle it in front of me. The dim lighting in the bar catches the sparkle of the diamonds like they're on fire.

"I think so too." Dylan beams and springs from his chair. "I read your bio, saw your pic and this feeling hit me." He thumps one hand on his chest. "Right here. You, Evelyn Berlinger, you are my lucky charm. It seems only fitting my lucky charm has one of her own." He takes the necklace from me and pauses, his hands just inches from my neck. "May I?"

Tingles zip down my spine and I nod.

He gathers my long hair with care, lifts it off my back, and places it over my shoulder. Its length trails down onto my breast. His breath is warm on my skin and it's all I can do not to fan myself.

He loops the necklace in front of my throat, the diamond charm landing possessively on my breastbone. The chain is delicate and cool in contrast to his elegant warm hands. He secures the clasp, brushing the little hairs on the back of my neck. The skin pebbles on the backs of my arms and my nipples grow hard in my lace bra.

The waiter drops off our drinks. Thank God, because I am in desperate need of something to cool me down right now. Unlike most of my clients, Dylan McAlister is hotter than sin. Also unlike most of my clients, Dylan isn't thinking about himself.

"Thank you," I say, completely rattled. I can't recall a time when a guy went was so generous to me. "This is so kind."

"It looks great on you," he says. "I wanted my lucky charm to be taken care of tonight."

"Lucky charm wants to help you tonight as much as possible. Make that easier for me," I say, reluctantly retreating from the dopamine hit and returning to the business arena. "Tell me more about you. Things that aren't on your profile."

"What do you want to know?" he asks.

I size him up. Those cheekbones. Those eyes. Those lips that beg to be bitten. "You look like the kind of guy who would rush into a burning building to save people. You've got the classic 'hero' look."

"Are you flirting with me, Ms. Berlinger?" He smiles, a smattering of crinkle wrinkles etched around his blue eyes, making him even sexier, if that's possible.

I shrug. "Just calling it how I see it."

"Aha. A straight shooter. I'm in trouble now." He shakes his head and sits down. "I've never run into a burning building. But you've obviously heard about the frog."

"The frog?"

"It was just that one time and yet, like a fairytale curse, the legend follows me wherever I go." He sighs theatrically and drums his fingers on the table.

"Wow. Sorry to hear that. Did you... kiss a frog?" I shove back a giggle.

"Gross," he says, and shakes his head.

"Did you think the amphibian incident would escape my scrutiny?"

"Nope. It didn't escape my biology teacher's either."

"Did you... I'm going out on a limb here, rescue a frog?"

"Yes. Biology class, freshman year in high school, but it feels like yesterday. Would *you* want to get pithed by a panicky, pimply high school kid?"

"Your lab partner?"

"Nope. Suzie Ashurst was cool as ice tea on a Sunday afternoon. Sadly, I was the panicky kid. I was the pimply pither who, at the last minute, couldn't go through with it."

I inhale bubbly water, and burst out coughing and laughing at the same time. One hand flies to my face trying to contain the seltzer that sprays out of my nose.

"Uh-oh." Dylan bites back a smile. "The curse of the frog rescue story strikes again. Are you okay? Or do I need to give you mouth to mouth?" He waggles his eyebrows.

I stop snorting, my cheeks turning warm, and I stifle giggles. "I'm fine. I'm fine."

"Albeit a little wet." He grabs a napkin and pats my wet face. My wet lips. My wet chest right above the dress where it takes a V turn down my cleavage.

"Sorry." My face might be flushed from laughing but that doesn't explain why the V between my legs is also warm, throbbing, and wet. "You crack me up."

"We're going to do just fine together, you and I," he says, removing his hand – dare I hope reluctantly – and regards me with something more than affection, his blue eyes twinkling.

We sip on our bubby water that I miraculously manage to keep inside this time, and chat like we've known each other forever.

"Cubs or White Sox?" he asks.

"Don't care as long as Chicago makes it to the playoffs," I say. "Dallas Cowboys or the Dallas Cowboy Cheerleaders?"

"That depends on what activity you have in mind."

"Point taken."

"Why is Chicago called the Windy City?" he asks.

"You did not include 'pop quiz' in your instructions."

"You read that?"

"Of course I read that."

"Geez, no one reads anything I write."

My nose scrunches. "I call bullshit."

He laughs.

"And Chicago's called the Windy City because the politicians talk B.S. all the time," I say.

"Get out. I thought it was the winds gusting off the lake."

It's a dance without a dance floor. And so it goes for another twenty minutes. Dylan's funny. Self-deprecating. Kind-hearted. Gorgeous. The more time I spend with him the more I like him. The more time I spend with him the more I want to spend.

"You're smart, Evelyn," he says inside the elevator as we ascend to the Penthouse. His gaze slides from my face down to my breasts, then back up.

His lips are so full, his cheekbones high and strong, and the glimpse of groomed chest hair revealed by the two undone buttons might be my undoing. Good God, this man is hot. "Call me Evie." I avert my eyes and fiddle with my hair, pushing strands behind my ear so I don't spontaneously combust right here, right now in the elevator.

"Evie, it is. Ready to meet an intimate crowd of my worthy adversaries, dearest enemies, and ruthless hosts? I've got to warn you. They're not the nicest people in the world. I should have put that in the instructions, but God forbid that goes public, these assholes will never let me hear the end of it."

"I'm not sharing anything you tell me with anyone."

"Good," he says. "I'm not kidding. Gamblers are a weird lot. Case in point. The Fast Food King plays tonight. I grew up down the road from him in Dallas. He's got this disturbing habit of licking his lips when he sees a pretty girl. If he stares at you and licks his lips, run for the hills, darling. His next move will be trying to get in your pants."

"The Fast Food King will fail because I'm wearing a dress."

"The heiress will take one look at you all gorgeous in that dress and get jealous," He eyes me appreciatively. "She'll toss pointed shade in your direction and speed text her plastic surgeon for an emergency appointment."

"The heiress can stand in line behind the rest of the chicks who throw shade at me."

"You're not going to sleep, the room's cold, you'll be breathing recycled air," he says leaning closer to me. "The internet connection is blocked, the food is impossibly healthy, and you might die of boredom."

"Perfect." I look up into his gorgeous face and shiver. "Sounds like my average Friday night."

"God, I like you." He takes my hand, squeezes it, and intertwines his fingers with mine. My stomach flip-flops and I can't help but wonder what it would be like if he kisses me. What if the elevator grinds to a halt, we are stuck between floors, he just leans in, puts a hand behind my head, pulls me to him and kisses me. Lips soft on mine at first, until he becomes more insistent, tangling fingers in my hair, his tongue exploring my mouth.

But the door slides open, rudely interrupting my fantasy, and he gestures. "Shall we?" We walk down the hallway, our shoulders grazing and I'm a little high from his touch. It feels like I've known him forever. It feels like I want to know him longer than that.

He raises his hand to knock on the last door at the end of the hallway and pauses. "Last chance to fold, Lucky Charm. Call it a night before you even start. I won't even ask for my money back. I haven't had a chance to tell the frog story in a few years. That was cathartic. Kind of like therapy."

"Hell, no, I'm not leaving." I'm standing on a tall cliff ready to dive off into choppy, white-capped waters far below. "I'm all in."

"That's what I was hoping you'd say." He leans in, and kisses me on the lips. *Finally. Yes.*

He is kissing me and his lips are soft, but firm. There's a hint of tongue and all the breath leaves my body in one spectacular whoosh.

And I'm diving...

❦ 5 ❦

BABY TEETH

BABY TEETH

DYLAN MCALISTER, TYCOON, FORMER CHURCH BABY, gorgeous player, kisses me in the hallway of the penthouse floor in this five-star hotel. It's a soft kiss, a sweet kiss, but the heat's been building between us since the moment I met him in the hotel bar.

A pretty woman opens the door, interrupting our moment. "Oops, sorry," she says and starts to close it.

"That"s okay." Dylan reluctantly pulls away from me. "No worries."

"Great to see you, Mr. McAlister." She flashes us a toothy, million-dollar smile.

Breathe, Evie, breathe, I remind myself, and we walk inside. Technically, Dylan and I met on an arranged engagement about forty minutes ago. This is a work gig. I'm not here on a real date. I've known him for under an hour.

And yet I feel like I've known him forever. We enter the

47

sleek penthouse suite – a confident, comfortable couple – that move in vaunted circles such as these with ease.

A pristine poker table is set up at the far end of the living room. Mostly men gather around it, chatting in that passive aggressive way white collar rivals do when they're revved up and ready to rumble, albeit in a civilized way. Right before they draw blood.

I recognize a few of the players from newspapers and magazines. The middle-aged man with the lean face and hawk nose owns Chicago's professional soccer team. His fortune was built from great granddaddy's newspaper empire. He parlayed those millions into an even larger domain. The beefy, red-faced short guy stars in TV commercials for his string of popular fast food restaurants across the Tri-State area. He has to be the Fast Food King with the lizard tongue Dylan warned me about. The sole, elegant, thirty-something woman standing next to the table has a few million followers on Instagram. Dylan wasn't kidding. She's the heiress to an elegant department store chain.

Yikes. This is a far cry from a 25th high school reunion at a VFW in the suburbs. This crowd is big money, big attitude, and I'm just a rental date wearing a borrowed dress.

"I need to be polite, civilized," Dylan says. "Go say hi to the crew before things get ugly. Before I figure out who are the Christians and who are the lions. It changes with every game. You need anything?"

"I'm fine," I say. "I'm great."

He leans in, kisses me on the cheek, and whispers, "Cast your lucky charm spell for me, Evie. I need this to be a good game." He pulls away and looks at me as if for a blessing. "A very good game."

I rub my hands together theatrically and blow on them.

He winks at me, turns, and heads to the table.

"McAlister," the beefy guy says. "Wasn't sure you'd make it. Thought you were still at church. Praying."

"I've been praying for you non-stop, Glenn," he says, taking off his jacket and draping it on the back of the chair. "Please stop all your sinning. It's exhausting."

"Prayer can be a dirty job," the heiress says. She shoots me a jealous look and regards Dylan with more than business in her eyes. "But someone has to do it."

No, no, department store heiress. You can just shut that shit down right now because I'll be covering all Dylan's dirty business needs tonight.

A bartender mixes cocktails at a bar set up in the corner of the suite overlooking downtown Chicago. A handful of waitresses circulate, taking orders and refilling glasses. I need to kill some adrenaline and movement always does that for me. Sadly, I don't think jogging around the room in heels will help me blend in. I make my way to the bar and order a drink.

"Evelyn," a woman says, touching my shoulder lightly.

I swivel and lay eyes on a pretty redhead in her thirties. Her dress fits her like a glove and looks like it cost more than the one I borrowed from Amelia.

"My name's Annie," she says, smiling warmly, holding out her hand with its neatly polished nails. "Dylan asked that I introduce myself. If you need anything while you're here, all you have to do is ask." She shakes my hand, her palm cool.

"Thank you," I say.

"Is this your first time attending a game?"

I nod and sip on a bubby water with a lime.

"You're in for a nail biter," she says. "An excruciatingly slow, exhausting nail biter. We brewed the extra strong coffee. You can always take a nap in the adjoining room if you need to lay your head down for a few minutes."

"People do that?"

"People do whatever they have to gain an advantage or to win at a high stakes underground poker tournament. Make yourself at home."

———

I HAVE PLENTY OF TIME OVER THE COURSE OF THE NEXT twenty-four hours to learn about the game. Players draw at the beginning to pick seats. It's a cash contest. The buy-in is fifty thousand, the lowest chip five thousand. Pretty masseuses massage players' tight shoulders and necks. Coffee is practically main-lined.

The room's kept chilly. Annie tells me it's done to help the players stay awake. I don't see any non-legal drugs but there are three bedrooms and multiple bathrooms in the back of the suite. Drugs aren't my thing, but I'm also not a cop and I'm not keeping track of anyone other than Dylan tonight.

About that. The look on his face is neutral but I find myself tuning into this man and I'm not all that happy about what he's feeling. When the sun cracks on the horizon, he's holding tight to five stacks of chips. By late afternoon his vibe is shaky and he's down to three. When the sun sets almost twenty-four hours after we walked into this penthouse, the confidence he exuded earlier bleeds through the cracks in his façade onto the sole stack standing.

At the end of the marathon game, Dylan wins more than he loses. According to my calculations, he leaves the tournament thirty thousand ahead, including the money he spent on me. He's not broke but he's not balls-out champion either.

That honor goes to Glenn. He's sweaty and beaming, brimming with bravado as he tips the dealer and staff generously. I don't look at him because I don't want to see him look at me while he licks his lips.

The bartender and waitresses close up shop. Servers

collect the remaining glasses, transfer food from silver plat-
ters to plastic containers. Players wander out of the suite –
some content, some pissy. All wiped.

Dylan smiles at the dealer, makes small talk, and tips her.
He walks over to me, face strained, like an overworked coffee
pot on its last legs at a Sunday church breakfast. "Ready,
Evie?" he asks, his voice cracking.

"Yes." I was not his lucky charm tonight, and for that I
feel like a jerk. Technically, I have no control over this and yet
for some reason it feels like I let him down. I want to make it
up to him, collect him in my arms, kiss all his worry away.
Promise things will go better the next game.

"Evie, what do you think?" Annie asks. She's still immaculate, and looks like she just slept an uninterrupted eight
hours. Not like she'd been up for twenty-four.

"Pretty much what you said. A nail biter, slow speed
chase," I say. "And somehow — still exhilarating."

"Exactly," she says, squeezing my arm. "I'm so glad I got a
chance to meet you."

"You too."

"See you soon, Dylan?" Annie asks.

"You got it," he says.

We exit the suite and hang with the small crowd of
players and their support crew loosely clustered in the
hallway waiting for the elevator. "How are you?" I ask,
rubbing Dylan's arm.

"Crap," he says under his breath. "But I have to look like
sunshine just spanked my ass and I liked it so much I invited
it back for more."

"That good," I say.

But Dylan suddenly hangs back when the elevator arrives.
"Go ahead," he says to the others. "I need a private moment
with my girl." He turns to me, his eyelids heavy. He manages a
quirk of a smile and nuzzles my neck. He brushes his lips

against me as if he's talking dirty. "Buy me time," he whispers and nips at my ear.

The scruff of his beard scrapes against my sensitive skin and the pulsing between my legs returns. Adrenaline. Hormones. This man. God knows what perks me up. Who needs caffeine? Who needs sleep? I suspect I'd wake up happy every morning if I took a daily dose of Dylan McAlister.

I pull it together, sigh, and giggle as if on cue. "Dylan. You're naughty. Stop," I say loud enough for the people crowding on the elevator to overhear.

"Perfect," he whispers, and kisses the length of my neck. My skin pebbles, my nipples grow hard.

"Get a room, McAlister," a guy says.

"Happy to loan you the spare key to my place," the heiress says. I clench my fist around my purse and I'm half tempted to punch her.

"Yeah, yeah." Dylan waves them off. The moment after the elevator door closes, he slumps against the wall and runs a hand through his thick hair. "Maybe we should take the stairs. I'm not sure I'm able to keep a straight face with these people."

"The game's over. You don't need to worry about them anymore tonight. Besides the lobby's twenty-five floors down and I'm the walking dead." I punch the button for the elevator. "Do you want to talk about it? Tell me what's going on?"

"What's not going on," he says, and checks his phone. "I'm off grid for twenty-four and all hell breaks loose."

"Like?"

But Dylan's eyes rip from his phone and train on the Fast Food King who won tonight's pot. "You were on fire, Glenn."

"I know," Glenn says, his chin thrusting proudly forward, his tongue snaking between his lips. He devours me with the look of someone who is flush with victory and desires his spoils.

Ew. I edge closer to Dylan.

The elevator arrives and we step inside. "You coming?" Dylan asks, holding the door.

"Nah," Glenn says and waves dismissively. "Grabbed a room down the hall. See you soon, McAlister. Be sure and bring the new girl with you." His eyes linger pointedly on my breasts, and slide like oil down my waist to my ass. He adjusts himself with one hand and my skin crawls as the gate slides shut.

In the elevator, Dylan leans back against a wall and berates himself. "I should have folded that hand earlier. I know this shit."

"I think you did great." I lean in to him, brushing a thick lock of hair off his forehead.

"I'm used to doing better," he says. "I'm used to doing a lot better. Truth is, Evie, I'm losing my game."

"You're being too hard on yourself."

"If I'm not hard on myself, I won't be around this business for much longer," he says, weariness rolling off him in waves that could drown a girl.

He's wiped. Beaten. It makes my heart hurt. I take his hand in mine and squeeze it but I'm not sure he even feels me. He stares off into space inside that pristine cage, replaying the game in his head, worry slicing lines across his handsome face.

"There was a moment when Glenn hesitated," he says. "I should have known he was bluffing. But he'd been playing fast and I didn't follow my instincts."

"We all make mistakes."

"Not these kinds. These were stupid." The elevator opens and we exit. I link my arm around Dylan's as we walk through the lobby. My feet hurt. I'm hungry. I'm craving a hard mattress and cool sheets. I haven't stayed up for twenty-four hours since I crammed for a final my junior year of college.

But then I remind myself that I prayed to God to help me do a good job tonight. I'm not about to let that go because all the adrenaline's worn off and I didn't get the outcome I prayed for. Sometimes unanswered prayers can be blessings in disguise.

We make our way through the lobby. There's a fresh crew of guests and workers and the attention directed at me isn't so appreciative this time. Curious looks circle thick around us like garbage running down the disposal. Judgment slops over me like a pail of dirty mop water. A well-dressed older woman hits me with one of those glares that lasts only a few seconds but carries a thousand words, none of them good. I avert my gaze just in time to catch the eye fuck from her husband. *Ugh.*

Sadly, no, I didn't spend the last twenty-four hours in bed with Dylan. I just look as though I did. But even if I had, who died and made these people Law & Order: Special Morals Unit? Their attitude irritates me, lights a fire under my ass, and I up my game. I raise my eyes, meet theirs defiantly, and throw some sass in my step.

Outwardly, Dylan's calm. Inwardly, he's a walking disaster, still lost in thought. We exit through the hotel's revolving doors. I can practically hear the clock tick-tocking down on our date but I desperately don't want our time to end. "Buy you a drink?" I ask. We pause curbside, a dozen or so yards away from the front door waiting on a ride.

Circles under his eyes, he's still so handsome, a few strands of silver in his temples, his white shirt rumpled with sweat and nearly twenty-four hours of playing a game of mental 'Chicken.'

"You're a sweetheart, Evelyn."

"Evie. Remember?"

He looks me in the eyes – really looks at me – and the fog evaporates like vaped weed in a college dorm. And boom, Dylan transforms back into the ballsy player who spotted me the moment I walked in the bar. The guy who gifted me a diamond horseshoe necklace. The man who made me go weak in the knees when he fastened that necklace around my neck and marked me his 'Lucky Charm.'

He wraps one strong arm around my waist, and draws me flush against him. "Where are my manners? I didn't thank you yet for tonight."

My throat turns tight, scratchy, and I smile up at him. "Hey stranger. I didn't do that much. But, it's nice to see you again." My body's flush against his, the heat building fast between us in the sultry Chicago summer night air.

Dylan's muscular, all hard planes and angles, the day-old scruff on his jaw making him even hotter if that's possible. He's the poster child for the boy next door who grew up to be the sexy as fuck man.

I want to strip off his shirt, rip off my dress, and get naked with him. I don't have to make a decision, it's already been made. Dylan McAlister's the first man I've wanted to be with in years. He's the client I'm going to sleep with.

"I checked out, didn't I?" His cock stirs against me, growing harder by the second.

"Yes."

Kiss me, Dylan. Take me somewhere private. Unzip this dress. Pull it off me.

"I'm back," he says. His erection presses insistently against my pelvis.

"I can tell." The V between my legs is *throb throbbing*, my skin's on fire, my panties pooling between my thighs. He's going to kiss me for real this time but is he ever going to ask to sleep with me? Oh, Jesus, why am I even wondering? The sizeable hard-on digging into my pelvis is a giant clue.

Kiss me, Dylan. Strip for me – first that shirt, please. Let me draw my fingers down your chest with one hand while I unzip your pants with the other.

My V card was punched a few years ago, claimed by one guy who I genuinely liked before I discovered his 'roommate' was actually his live-in girlfriend. But my real dirty secret is that I haven't had sex since then. I haven't been with anyone in two years. It used to embarrass me and I didn't talk about it because I thought I was some kind of freak who attracted unavailable men.

But right now? Right now, I am thanking God I waited. I am thanking God I said no to the extra money, no to the perks, the decent apartment that I could have afforded if I had slept with the last twenty clients I went on dates with. Instead, I paid for mom's psych treatment. I helped out Ruby with college. I lived in the same crappy apartment because part of me still wanted to believe that a happily ever after could happen for me too. I held out for a hero. I held out for Dylan McAlister. Finally, the waiting is over because the hero is here.

Kiss me, Dylan. I want to watch your hard cock release from those dress pants. I want to take it in my hand and stroke it from base to head.

He pulls me closer as if he heard my thoughts, his erection growing more impressive, more insistent by the second. "Evie."

He might be tired, but honey, under those rumpled clothes, he's tight and lean, all corded muscles. The scruff of his unshaven beard alternately tickles and scrapes against my neck as he leans in and whispers, "I might have lost tonight at poker tonight, but darling, you're my winning hand."

A small moan escapes my lips. "Good."

Will Dylan take me back to his hotel suite? Will he kiss me before or after we enter? Will he run his hands through my hair? Unzip my dress slowly, just as slowly as I unwrapped his present? Will he press kisses down my neck, his lips grazing mine, the scruff of his beard scraping against my skin?

Will he pull down the thin sleeve of my dress, push it further with impatient hands? Will he cup my breast, his thumb tracing circles on top of my lace bra as my nipple grows taut under his touch? Will he unhook my bra, lower his mouth to my breast, draw my taut nipple into his mouth, suck on it, scrape his teeth against it? Will I try not cry out as he unzips my dress with one hand, the other traveling down my stomach, landing on the edge of my panties where he plays with the edges of my lace thong?

'Delicious, Evie,' he'll say, cupping the V between my legs, as I grow wetter and wetter, arching into his fingers with need. Want. By the time he slips his fingers inside the lace, tracing my skin with skilled fingers, insistent fingers, making his way to my center, my pelvis throbbing, the ache building inside me, pulse, pulsing, his fingers reaching for me, brushing against my clit, detouring to caress the inside of my thighs, will I bite my lip in an effort to not cry out? Will I …

But my fantasy *pop-pop-explodes* like a kid on a sugar high tearing through a birthday party, poking a pin in balloons, because Dylan does *not* kiss me. Instead, he pulls away, sighs, and gives his head a shake. "I'm sorry," he says. "I'm so sorry."

"What?"

"I almost forgot." He lifts a fat envelope from his coat pocket and slips it into my purse. He sighs, reaches for me, but stops himself. He rumples my hair like I'm his kid sister and busses me on the cheek.

"Are you okay?" I ask, my stomach dropping hard.

"Sure," he says, and walks a few feet away from me.

"Right." I sway, a little unsteady on my aching feet. The need and urging and wetness of my desire is deflated by his return to professionalism. I'm completely thrown by the 180-degree spin and try not to stare at him in disbelief. "Is something wrong?"

Did I do something stupid? Did I ruin this thing we had

going on between us? Because I'll guarantee you I was not making up the chemistry. It was sizzling between us, alive, and ready to do the cha-cha.

"Nothing's wrong," he says. "Unfortunately, I've got to catch some Zzzs, catch a plane, and blow out of Chicago. Big game tomorrow night in Tulsa."

"Got it," I say, the pit in my stomach growing more vicious, like it's birthed baby teeth in the last fifteen seconds and is chewing on my insides. But now's not the time or place to push it with Dylan.

He's the client.

I'm the escort.

He's the boss.

I'm the employee.

But, boy oh boy did I read this one wrong. I feel like an idiot, a naïve, foolish girl. I might be wearing a two thousand dollar dress but honey it's not all that easy taking the insecure out of the girl who's been insecure most of her life. Dylan lifts an arm and signals a driver. Regret drills thin, mean holes in my bones.

I replay the last twenty-four hours in my head, desperately searching for the stupid thing I said, the stupid thing I did or didn't do that would explain his 180, when a truckload of fear and panic broadside me as if being hit by a runaway car.

Blood drains down my arms, a chill descends my spine like I've been shot up with Novocain. My fingers turn numb and I wriggle them just to make sure I still can. Crap. What did I screw up? What did I do to cockblock this man?

And suddenly I get it: the gut-chewing feelings bookend the heady ones I experienced twenty-four hours earlier when Dylan secured the lucky charm necklace and his fingers brushed the little hairs on the back of my neck, his touch making my nipples hard. His pride, generosity, and determination soared within me like a shot of courage mixed with premium single malt scotch.

But now all the bad feelings, the horrible ones — the funhouse mirror versions stomp about inside me like mean minions eating me alive.

And then I realize these aren't *my* feelings after all.

They're Dylan McAlister's.

And I'm having an empathic reaction.

❦ 6 ❦

A CLUSTERF**K

CLUSTERF**K

MY CHILDHOOD WAS A CLUSTERFUCK. I GREW UP WITH A bipolar mom who suffered psychotic splits. When you're around bipolar people, when you're around manic-depressive, hypo-manic, whatever the derivative is that is *not* treated, *not* controlled with a combination of therapy, treatment, and/or meds, you get schooled in moods that flip on a dime.

I grew up with highs so high my ears popped and lows so low I couldn't keep track of the times I was buried lower than six feet. Do you know how many days Mom couldn't get out of bed and it fell on me to get things done? Yeah. Me neither. I lost count. It fell on me to feed my sister. It fell on me to walk Chris the dog for the month we had him until Mom made us return him to the shelter. I made coffee at noon and waved it around next to Mom's face. "Come on. I know you want this. I made it super strong, just the way you like it. Sit up and it's all yours."

"No," she'd say, not even lifting her head off the pillow. "Go away. Just let me sleep, 'K?" A week later she'd be buying us burgers, shakes, and cotton candy, all of us squealing in delight, stumbling around a Halloween-themed maze in a cornfield.

Emotional rollercoaster.

Emotional funhouse.

Emotional whiplash.

Karma delivered me into this family, bought my ticket, and signed me up for this ride. I prayed I'd get through it, and I did. But survival didn't come free. I paid with anxiety, over-sensitivity, and empathic reactions. I'll never forget the feeling of being ripped apart, tossed to the winds, spun here and there like a twig in a tornado. I survived but I was never the same.

Trust me. You're never the same.

After years of sublimating, kicking away, flat out denying that I could sense others' feelings within my own body, my empathic ability has returned unbidden and unwanted with a special fury in the form of gorgeous Dylan McAlister. I shiver and I remind myself –

I am not a rickety shed.

I survive when the storm blows through.

But I know, the same way I knew in the car that day when we ran into the Wolfe brothers, that something is crashing, but this time it's not something – it's someone.

Dylan McAlister.

His heart is breaking. Whatever horrible, crappy thing is playing out inside him, he's dealing with it by shutting down. He's not sharing it with me. Why would he? We only met twenty-four hours ago.

My ride pulls up to the curb of the five-star hotel and Dylan opens the door. "Thank you, Evie. See you again? Soon, I hope."

"Absolutely," I say, getting in, knowing in my bones that I'm missing the puzzle piece that desperately needs to be snapped into place. "Sounds good." I so dearly want to be the person who figures it out but I'm not, and my failure makes me so mad I could stab myself. What is wrong with me?

I pray on this kind of shit. I meditate on it. I get it done. After all, I was in the car that ran over the boy I loved. I could blame my mom. I could blame her disease. But at the end of the day part of me believes I broke Wyatt Wolfe.

I made myself stumble past his old brother Easton – *so mean, so cold* – when he lay bloody, broken, and twisted like a liar's lies on the white, hard ground. I broke Easton Wolfe.

Oh sure, I sought redemption, sought healing. I shook like jelly but still managed to unzip Wyatt's coat, place a hand on his bare patch of chest, and did my best to save him. Paramedics hauled him away in that ambulance.

I might have been a kid but I knew that half of his bones and organs were shattered, and that he'd be messed up forever and ever amen. Yet I got down on my knees and prayed every day and night: 'Please, God, please save Wyatt Wolfe.' I would have given anything, done anything. I would have sacrificed myself on God's jagged, bloody, tear-stained altar if He would have just saved Wyatt Wolfe.

Eleven years later I am still seeking redemption. I long to help another person I care about, but I'm still tragically clueless. And I'm so angry about it that I swallow fat, five-thousand-dollar-poker-chip-sized tears whole before they rip a hole in my chest and bust out like a geyser.

"You were wonderful, Evie," Dylan says, standing next to me at the curb. "Thank you. I hope to see you again. Soon." He shuts the door with a harsh *thud*.

My driver pulls into traffic. I roll the window down, and wave. "Yes," I say, and immediately feel like an asshole, a disheveled homecoming queen visiting last night's float before the janitor tosses the dime store decorations into the trash. The driver turns a corner and I can't hold the tears in any longer. I wipe them away as fast as they trickle out.

I bite my lip to center myself. It's done. Dylan's gone. The arranged date's over. He hired me through Ma Maison Escort Agency. It's not like he swiped right, or his grandmother introduced him to me, or he really cares. *Get a grip, Evie. Get on with it. This thing happened so fast you'll never really know what you missed. Build the wall. Survive. At least you can do that.*

I roll up the window and focus on erecting an emotional barrier between myself and Dylan. I will not be a weakling. I will not be an idiot. Boundaries are the best way to keep one's sanity in an insane business.

I arrive at my crappy apartment, climb the rotting wooden steps two at a time, and slam the door so hard the walls rattle. I lock the cash tip in my safe, and ditch the dress, tossing it onto my bed in a heap. Funny, it doesn't look like a two thousand dollar dress anymore. I turn on my shower as hard as the piece of crap plumbing can handle and lean under the shower head. The water pours over me, washing away the stress, the dirt, the regret. I just wish it could wash away all the pain.

I prided myself on burying my empathic ability years ago. Why is my freak flag rearing its ugly head now? Probably escort attachment syndrome. *Ugh.* Terrific. Predictably, laughably, I'm falling for the hot, charismatic client with the full lips and muscular shoulders. I need to shut this down. Get my mind and my heart off tonight, off Dylan McAlister, and get back to uneventful, bland, and boring.

I text back and forth with Ruby. She's visiting Mom at the Institute tomorrow at noon, wants to know if I want to meet up. I pass. It's all just a little too much right now. Besides, I'm paying the bills. I'll see Mom in a bit.

And, it's back to the grind. A spur of the moment date

with a dentist on Monday. Cocktails with a foreign dignitary at the Brazilian consulate on Tuesday. I get a text from Madam Marchand.

Dylan contacted Ma Maison and asked if I was available this Thursday and I practically fall of my chair. He apologizes for the last minute request, didn't realize he'd be back in Chicagoland so soon. He understands if I'm busy and no, he doesn't want anyone other than me.

I text back faster than a game show contestant in a lightning round. "Yes."

❧ 7 ❧

MIDAS TOUCH

MIDAS TOUCH

I PICK UP DYLAN'S HANDWRITTEN INSTRUCTIONS THE NEXT
day at Ma Maison.

Madame hands me the white linen envelope. "The engagement is in St. Charles on Thursday."

"The suburb?"

"Yes."

"That's an hour west of the city. I can train it out there."

"I'll forward him that information." Madame says. "He
likes you. Two dates in one week? Impressive."

"Thanks," I say, slipping the envelope in my purse and
practically bolting for the door.

"Evelyn," Madame says.

"Yes?"

"He comes from big money, you know."

"No, I didn't," I lie.

"Big money clients can open doors and provide opportunities that average clients do not."

"Got it," I say, turning the doorknob because I'm itching to get out of here and read his letter.

"Evelyn?"

"Yes, Madame?" I pause, grit my teeth and toss my ponytail over my shoulder so hard it *thwacks* against my back.

"If opportunities arise for advancement, please seize them."

"Will do." I escape the pretty prison and wait until the elevator door closes between me and Ma Maison before I rip open the envelope.

"Dress summer country club casual, Lucky Charm. Be your beautiful, funny self. The job will last sixteen to twenty-four hours. You will be compensated for the full twenty-four if the game ends early. Can't wait to see you again, gorgeous."

I don't know what country club casual is, but I'm not going to make myself nuts picking the perfect dress. The dress isn't the problem. *I'm* the problem.

I want to help Dylan and my brain spins, thinking about how best to do that. Knowing a little more about poker can't hurt. I watch a few tournaments on YouTube and study up on terms and vocabulary. It's like learning French or Italian with Berlitz. "How much does that cost?" but in poker language.

I need to master the emotions spinning around Dylan, especially those catching me in a tangled, sticky web. Are they his? Mine? Hopefully, I'm not picking up on someone else in the room, like the Fast Food King. Unlike french fries, I'm not on his menu. Ever.

"How'd the date with Dylan McAlister, go?" Amelia asks that night. We're sitting around a polished high top table at a sports bar, TVs lining the walls, tipping back a few beers.

"Good. I'm seeing him again this week."

"Get your cash tip up front. Word is Mr. Midas is losing his touch." She dips into the plate of wings sitting on the table. "Chasing a nasty losing streak. Doesn't seem to be able to pull out of it. Was he a weirdo when you went out with him? Did he make you nervous? I know how sensitive you are."

I shake my head. "He was lovely. Kind. Funny."

"Even funny guys can be weirdos."

I nab a wing. "He's not a weirdo."

"Even funny guys can be losers."

"He's not a lose..." But my words take an unexpected hike because Victoria walks through the crowd toward our table. Yes – *that* Victoria – the escort that Madame Germaine pushed in Dylan's direction. A scab tears off a wound that I didn't even know was butterflied on top of my heart.

Amelia waves. "Victoria!"

"Hey!" She waves back and makes her way through the crowd toward us. She's drop dead gorgeous with mocha skin and hazel eyes. Guys stop watching the game, gawking at her like she's Moses parting the Red Sea.

"Did you invite her?"

"Yes," Amelia says. "You need to get to know her better."

"What if I don't want to?" I wipe my mouth with a napkin, crumple it, and toss it on the table.

"What if I don't care that you get everything that you want?" Amelia says. "You've gotta find more powerful friends than me. I'm not going to be around Ma Maison forever. I'm going to meet a good guy. Someone kind with money who worships me. In the meantime, Victoria's head bitch. It won't hurt to have her on your side."

I grumble. Victoria makes her way toward us – all groomed, with perfect tits, posture, and body by Pilates.

"Be nice," Amelia says, pinching my arm.

"I'm always nice."

"Girlfriend." Amelia smiles at Victoria and pulls out a stool. "Glad you could join us. You remember Evie?"

"Evelyn," I say, and muster a smile.

Victoria takes a seat and scooches in closer to the table. "Yes! You're the kindergarten teacher, right? I'm still amazed you can wrangle all those five-year-olds."

"It's not rocket science. I just tell them when to lie down and take a nap."

"No wonder all the clients like you," she says.

Amelia laughs. "I told her the same thing."

I'm nice to Victoria and in exchange she's nice to me. The three of us talk about fall fashion, wonder why Madame Germaine is so uptight, and offer increasingly silly explanations until we're all giggling so hard Victoria pretends to face plant into the platter of wings.

She rises back up theatrically, rolling her eyes, dark red sauce on her chin. "Maybe Madame Marchand is a vampire, grooming us as bait for undead blood suckers. Maybe Ma Maison is actually a high-end sex club for vampires."

"That kind of makes sense," Amelia says. "Madame's pretty cold. But except for the old guy who lost his dentures last week when he tried to kiss me, no one's bitten me yet."

"Ew," Victoria says. "Hey, I'm having a party next week. Both of you should come."

I'd planned on hating Victoria but she's totally charmed me.

"Tell her the story," Amelia insists.

"Which one?" Victoria hands off her credit card to the waiter before he even drops the tab on our table.

"You know. About how you started working for Ma Maison," Amelia says. "The one about the creepy stalker."

"Yeesh! I'm still getting over that," Victoria says. "Don't want to have nightmares. I'll save that one for another night."

"I had a great time." I extend my hand to her and we shake affectionately. "You're hilarious. I'm glad we finally spent time together."

"Hello?" Amelia says and rolls her eyes.

"Ditto, Kindergarten," Victoria says. "If you ever have any questions, feel free to ask."

"Actually, I do," I say. "What's country club summer casual?"

"One of your client wants you to dress country club casual?"

I nod.

"Page through *Town and Country*."

Amelia chimes in. "Check Ralph Lauren. Lily Pulitzer."

"I can't afford Ralph Lauren."

"You don't have to buy it," Victoria says. "Just nail the look."

I get home around eleven. I lie in bed Googling Ralph Lauren when suddenly I don't care about fashion. I switch subjects and do a deep Google dive on what's going on with Dylan. The gossip is he's lost his ability to read a table. He dropped a couple hundred thousand last month and has plummeted from being a player to chum. The sharks smell blood and circle.

Glenn's probably sharpening his knives getting ready to mince him into bits, stuff him into hot dog casings, and sell him to unsuspecting customers. I doubt the department store heiress gives a rat's ass how much money Dylan has. She'll seduce him if he's loaded or down to his last chip and totally give me a run for my money. Oh wait – after I pay for mom's medicals, Ruby's college, and my own bills – I won't have any.

I stare up at the ceiling and wonder what Dylan's doing right now. Is he still in Tulsa? Back in Chicago? Hitting a club or a bar? I hope he's not out with another girl, but hey, I've got no control over that and it would be silly for me to obsess about it.

Instead I obsess about our second date. Will our time together in St. Charles be any different? Will he kiss me? Will he touch me?

I slide one hand inside my cotton top and skim it across my breast. My nipple pebbles under my touch. I slip my other hand inside my briefs, glide it down to the soft skin of my abdomen, and trail my fingers through my groomed curls until I touch my sex.

I close my eyes and think of the look on Dylan's face when he gave me the diamond necklace and I circle my fingers across my folds. His lips were so full. His eyes, excited like a kid on Christmas morning. Chills zipped down my spine when he secured the necklace around me, his hands brushing the wisps of hair on the back of my neck.

Now, I clasp the diamond pendant with one hand, part my legs a little and let my fingers toy with my clit. I'm already wet, the hard nub sensitive to my touch, waves of pleasure building.

Like any teenage girl, I learned how to take care of my own needs but always hoped for fireworks with the right guy. I never orgasmed with Drew, the loser who punched my V card. His idea of sex was cock-centered. The 'non-vagina' part of the V between my legs was dutifully serviced for forty seconds immediately before he was ready to come. Now the combination of my fingers moving faster, memories of Dylan McAlister flooding my brain, the anticipation of seeing him in a few days, tips me over the edge and I climax in hard, abrupt spasms. Shivers travel down my spine and the backs of my arms.

I lie in the dark room, tired, content, almost happy. I'm going to see Dylan in less than forty-eight hours. I have a good feeling that this time things will be different.

———

THE NEXT MORNING, I SHOVEL DOWN EGGS, DRINK COFFEE, and Google *Town and Country* and Ralph Lauren. Country club casual is classic fashion. I can totally do this look, just not on my paycheck.

I hit the ground running and visit my favorite thrift stores. Goodwill has a hundred gray dresses lined up on one rack that look like they belong in *The Handmaid's Tale*. Salvation Army is having a run on shoulder pads and all things eighties.

I finally score at the Orphans of Foreign Wars when I stumble upon a vintage cotton dress for twenty bucks. It's tea length, has a modest neckline, and a skirt that flares below the knee. I take it home, hand wash it, tumble it on low, and iron it. I zip it up, put on the diamond necklace Dylan gave me, check out my reflection in the mirror, and smile. "Hello, Mrs. Ralph Lauren."

It takes me two hours to beautify and dress for our second date. I go back and forth on the earrings, finally settling on simple, petite white gold hoops. How should I do my nearly waist length hair? I curl it, fashion it into a loose updo with simple, pretty, rhinestone clips. Mom gave me one of Grandma's vintage cardigans in a light blue that pairs perfectly with this outfit. I check the clock. Just enough time to meditate for ten minutes and follow that up with a quick prayer chaser before I blow out of my hovel in time to make the 4 pm train departing Union Station.

Dear God. Dylan McAlister's a good man. A kind man. Please help me give my all for this job. Thanks for guidance. And this I ask for in the name of the Father, and the Son, and the Holy Spirit. Amen.

I cross myself.

I make my way down the sagging stairs and notice my mailbox is stuffed with grocery store fliers poking out the slats. I barely bother checking the box anymore. Almost everything is done online. But I don't want thieves thinking I'm gone for any length of time. I unlock the box, grab the stash, and walk toward the recycling bin, when I see an envelope addressed to me in a typed font with no return address. I slide it in my purse and make tracks for the station.

———

THE HOUR-LONG TRAIN RIDE SLIDES BY. ONLY TEN MINUTES remain before we pull into St. Charles. Best not to get too excited. I'm here on business. Traveling for him, not me or my fantasies. I pull a compact from my purse, check my reflection, and swipe on a layer of lipstick. When I return it to my purse I see the letter and open it.

———

Dear Ms. Berlinger,

May I call you Evelyn, or do you prefer Evie?

It's up to you. I'm good with either. You can let me know which you prefer if our paths ever cross in real life.

First, let me apologize for this message that most likely feels like it finds its way to you out of the blue. You're probably wondering, 'Who is this strange person contacting me via old fashioned paper correspondence?'

As much as I'd love to tell you my full name. As

much as I imagine it rolling around in your brain, tripping off your full lips, I've been advised to sit on that for a while. I can always share it with you later.

I just wanted to let you know that catching a glimpse of you on social media always brings a smile to my face.

Thanks for being a spot of sunshine!

That's all, really.

Best,

A Fan

ST. CHARLES

ST. CHARLES

THE TRAIN SCREECHES AS IT BLASTS TOWARD ST. CHARLES. My stomach churns like I just ate something dicey from one of those sidewalk food carts. I text Amelia.

Evie: Have you ever gotten a weird letter from "a fan?"

Amelia: Yes. Dick pics. Did someone send you dick pics?

Evie: No.

Amelia: What?

Evie: Just a letter.

Amelia: What did it say?

I skim it. Reading it the second time I'm not sure it says all that much.

Evie: *Not that much. Maybe I'm over-reacting.*

Evie: *I'll show it to you when I get back.*

 Amelia: *Forward it to me.*

Evie: *Not now. My train's getting in. Besides, it's snail mail.*

 Amelia: *That's even weirder.*

Evie: *I know. Talk later.*

"St. Charles. The next stop will be St. Charles," the conductor announces.

The train's slowing down and I make my way to the front of the car. I step off into a late afternoon summer, the sinking sun practically blinding me. I shade my eyes and glance around at the stretch of parking lot chock full of sedans and SUVs.

A wolf whistle pierces the air and I swivel. Dylan's leaning back against a Jeep convertible. "Lucky Charm," he calls out, moving two fingers away from his mouth.

"Hey." I go hot, then cold, then hot again, my knees practically knocking about under the twenty dollar country club casual dress, because I want his mouth on me and for that matter, his fingers too.

"Looking awfully pretty on this summer day. Need a ride?"

He's wearing black khakis and a fitted V-neck T-shirt showing a dusk of groomed chest hair and, oh holy hell, how did I miss the definition in those arms the last time I was with him?

"Yes, please."

"What? No overnight bag?"

"I assumed we'd be working," I say, my throat going dry. "Besides you didn't include that in your instructions."

"You actually read my instructions?" He leans in, kisses me on the cheek, and I could swear he lingers a second. His scent is subtle. Cologne? Soap? Does he smell this great naturally?

My cleavage flushes. It's hotter out here in the suburbs. Maybe the heat's rising off the asphalt or the train grinding away from the station. Maybe it's just shooting off Dylan McAlister like firecrackers leaving puffs of smoke trailing across a hazy summer sky.

"Of course, I read your instructions." I take a step back and execute a slow twirl. "Country club casual."

"Holy hotness, Doris Day."

"Thank you."

"Thank *you*." He opens the Jeep's passenger door and I climb in. Our arms brush and my pulse quickens, my mouth going dry. Like somehow this is fate. I'm supposed to be his lucky charm. Why do I get this weird premonition he's going to be mine?

"How was your week?" he asks. He drives down Route 34 and we motor past shopping plazas filled with parking lots bigger than the actual grocery and sporting goods stores.

"Same old, same old. Yours?"

"Nothing to write home about."

We cruise past VFWs, White Hen Pantries, Thai food take out joints, and gas stations on every other corner. The air is warm. It smells different than big city air. Fresher, greener, if that's possible.

"How'd the game go in Tulsa?" I ask.

"'How was the play, Mrs. Lincoln?'" His handsome facade cracks. Weariness seeps out.

"That good," I say, my updo breaking apart. My hair blows in the wind. I push back strands of hair.

"I missed you, Evie."

He might be tired but those reflective Aviators make him even sexier.

"I missed you back."

His thigh muscles contract and release under the black khaki pants when he shifts gears. I wonder what they'd feel like under my hand? I vote for hard and ripped.

He turns down a smaller four-lane highway. In a few miles it narrows to two lanes. We zip past subdivisions filled with upscale tract houses on large grassy lots surrounded by marshland. Ducks and geese make their homes here. Another ten minutes and we've left the suburbs behind for the country, passing farmland and hacked off corn fields.

It's yellow and green and lush and relaxed out here. So different from the grit, grime, and hustle of the city. Wouldn't it be nice to be doing this for real? Motoring down a rural road in a convertible, sunshine bathing my shoulders, hair flying about in the breeze, a handsome guy who seems to like me seated next to me in the driver's seat? I could get used to this. "Where's the game?"

"The Schillinger Batavia Estate and Inn. Historical landmark. Pretty place. Built by a robber baron as a summer home for his beloved mistress."

"His mistress?"

"Yes." He turns into a driveway and cruises up a black top road toward a three story Victorian mansion. "Schillinger kept the wife and kids tucked away on a lake front estate north of the Chicago," he says. "There's sixty miles between the two properties – a proper distance between his two lives."

A former 1800s mansion lies tucked back from the road on twenty-five acres of thick, lush Midwestern woods and farmland that now looks like an arboreteum. I didn't grow up with money, but I've seen plenty of it in pictures. This place could pass for one of those magazine spreads – it's big money – no wonder Dylan's request was for country club casual. I twist my hair back up into a loose updo and secure it with a few clips.

"Nervous?" he asks.

"Not really. Why?"

"Lots of hair fiddling going on."

"Good thing you're the one playing poker and not me."

He smiles. "That remains to be seen."

WE SIP ON BUBBLY WATER IN A COZY DARK BAR INSIDE THE 1800s mansion, sink back into old, comfortable leather chairs and fall into easy banter, just like the first time we met.

"Do anything interesting and different since last time I saw you?" he asks.

"Kind of."

"Cheer me up. Share."

Probably best not to confide I rocked out an orgasm fantasizing about his mouth on my sex. "Drinks at a sports bar with some friends."

"Sounds like fun," he says.

"It was. You?"

"Nothing all that interesting. I've been having difficulty concentrating lately."

"Tell me more."

He checks his watch and rises from the table. "I will. After the game."

We make our way down a cedar-chipped path through manicured lawns with a smattering of flowers, to a refurbished barn on the back of the property.

"Sorry," he says. "No gift for you this time."

My hand flies to the diamond pendant resting on my breastbone. "I'm already wearing the pretty one you gave me."

"And yet you're missing something." He reaches down into a bed of flowers, and plucks a daisy. He catches strands of hair between his fingers and smoothes them behind my ear. "Thanks for coming out to see me again. I think I gave you mixed signals the last time we were together and for that I apologize. The game's getting to me."

"We're cool." Wow – he realized it. This is good. Better than good – excellent. "Can I help?"

"You're already doing that. You make me calmer." He tucks the flower into my hair on top of my ear. It feels like an apology of sorts. "My beautiful, Evie. Ready?"

"Yes." We reach the door that mysteriously opens before he even knocks.

A pretty young woman smiles at us. "Mr. McAlister?"

"Dylan McAlister. And Ms. Berlinger."

"Great," she says. "We've been expecting you."

Sixteen hours pass. Monetarily Dylan's up and down – winning some, losing more. The stacks of chips in front of him dwindle. I'm chatting with one of the hostesses in a far corner of the room, not even watching the table when an empathic reaction rolls in, striking with a cold fury like I've been stabbed in the chest with a fat icicle. My gut twists. My heart hurts. And I know the game is over for him. I break out in a sweat and sink in a pit of crappy sensations.

"You okay?" the hostess asks. "You look a little green."

"I'm good. Just tired." I squeeze my eyes shut for a few seconds and pinch the thick acupuncture point on the fleshy web between my thumb and forefinger, the stabby sensation rooting me to reality.

'This isn't your quicksand,' Queasy says. *'Don't drown in it.'*

I'm not sure I want to shut this empathic hit down. It connects me to Dylan and if I hold on tight I might find a pony under this pile. It would be nice to do that before the skin crawls off my bones.

'Everything's a teachable moment,' Hope says.

'How so?' I ask.

'Identify the feelings. Name them,' she says. *'That way you own the pain, it doesn't own you.'*

If I get a grip on these emotions maybe I can mitigate the damage they're wreaking inside me, and help Dylan as well.

Three. Two. One.

I sink into the empathic layer and the world spinning out of control around me slows down. The twists in my gut soften, untangle and in the murkiness I identify the sensation: desperation.

Dylan's desperation.

Weird. As soon as I name it the feeling within me dissipates only to be replaced by the next wave. A bitter taste of bile blossoms in my mouth. I pull back, grow space, and identify it. The sensation is shame.

Dylan's shame.

Wow. I might be able to do something with this.

This time the poker marathon lasts twenty hours instead of twenty-three. Dylan folds at the end, hustled by a guy my age who made a fortune in a social media company. I catch myself the second before I cringe in regret and keep a poker face.

The players tip the help and the event organizer. Folks use the bathrooms, gather their stuff, and wander out of the bungalow. Dylan and I walk back down the cedar-chip pathway toward the main building and the parking lot. It's late afternoon, not as hot as the day before, and a gentle breeze rustles the greenery. I'm wiped – for both of us. I'd lay money that sex is off the table but my heart still sinks when he confirms it.

"I'll order you a car, or you can train it back to the city," Dylan says, slipping an envelope inside my purse. "I can drop you at the station."

Anxiety bubbles and I finger my necklace. Here we are again. What if this is the last time I see him? "Are you blowing out of town?"

He shakes his head. "I couldn't get a direct flight. I'm staying a day to recoup."

Hope pinches me. *'Opportunity knocks…'*

I square my shoulders. "What are you doing between now and then?"

"Sleeping. Talking to my mom. Doing something that involves nature. I miss nature. These games just keep going and going and eventually you forget to get outside and move. The great outdoors is literally a stone's throw away from where I've been holed up in a room breathing crappy recycled air but I forget about that because I'm going over the game in my head, or thinking about the next one."

"Do you over-think everything?" I bend down and pluck a daisy from a fat, happy cluster.

"Yes. For the most part, I do."

"Ever consider mixing that up a bit? You know, playing it a bit different?" I bring the flower to my lips, kiss it, and tuck it behind his ear.

He coughs and blood floods his cheeks. He looks healthier already.

"Yes," he says.

"Good." I give voice to the words that have been bumping around my brain since the last time we parted. "Want company?"

❧ 9 ❧

SUGAR GROVE

SUGAR GROVE

"OF COURSE, I WANT YOUR COMPANY." HE TRAILS A FINGER across my face, my lips. "I'd be a fool not to want your company. But I can't pay Ma Maison any more than I already have."

"Happy to say I don't care. Besides, it's not like Ma Maison owns me."

"You sure you want to do this?" His eyes sweep over me.

My heart bangs on my chest with a resounding *thump-thump* and the V between my legs throbs. "I'm very sure."

"What if I told you I wasn't staying at this gorgeous hotel?"

I glance up at Schillinger Batavia Estate's main lodge. Posh. Beautiful. The epitome of country club casual. Yet I get a feeling what Dylan's offering might be even more refreshing. "I'm not interested in the gorgeous hotel. I'm interested in the gorgeous man standing next to me."

HE'S BOOKED A ROOM AT AN IMPOSSIBLY KITSCHY LODGE twenty minutes away on the outskirts of a small town. "It's not a roach motel but it's not my usual 5 star gig," Dylan says, pushing open the door to the tiny wood-paneled lobby that looks like we time traveled to the seventies. Travel posters of Greece beaches, Italian food, and Roman ruins line the walls.

"It's adorable," I say and walk inside as he follows.

"Visiting on business or pleasure?" the middle-aged female motel manager asks, running his credit card, curiosity hanging thick and heavy on her plump cheeks just like her rouge.

"Business," Dylan says staring at the credit card machine, blinking when it flashes 'Approved.'

"Pleasure," I say, taking his hand, squeezing it. "Right honey? You always have business but you promised me some fun this trip. It can't always be about work, you know."

"Yes... *honey*." He plays along, leans in, plants a soft kiss on my lips, and I startle. "What is this foreign word 'fun'?"

"Um..." A rainbow of tourist brochures in a metal stand against the wall spark an idea. I focus my attention on the manager. "My first time to Sugar Grove. I hear there's a lot of fun things to do around here. Outdoor things. What do you recommend, Ma'am?"

Her eyes light up. "Oh, there's so much. Kane County Flea Market. Check out the Fox River bike path. We've got gambling at the casino. That's not outside but it's legal."

"Gambling!" I tug on Dylan's arm. "You've always wanted to try gambling."

"Nope. I'm a church goer. Whatever gave you that idea?" He kisses me again, teeth grazing my lower lip for a longer second.

I blush and smooth a hand over my hair. "I could swear

you mentioned it recently. What else do people do around here for fun?"

"The game. You don't want to miss the game. The Kane County Cougars are playing the Wisconsin Timber Raccoons tomorrow night at Northwestern Medicine Field. It's the best of minor league baseball."

"Thanks." I squeeze Dylan's muscular shoulder and his eyes light up. "Do you want to go to the casino? We could play the slots. Try our hand at blackjack. Poker --"

"There are sharks at those places. Besides, who can trust a gambler?" He brushes strands of hair off my face, his breath warm on my face. "Shady characters. Total players."

"I met a gambler recently." I shake my head. "He was sexy. Seemed nice, too."

"Really?" He asks quirking a chestnut eyebrow.

"Yup. Something intriguing about his intensity. His focus. All his smarts. You know -- I'd never go behind your back or anything – but he was hot."

"Newlyweds?" the manager asks seated behind the counter, her chin resting in her hands, snapping her gum, watching us like we're a tennis match.

"Not yet," Dylan says.

I blush.

"First date?" the manager asks.

"Nope," I say.

"I totally agree with your girlfriend," the manager says, "You know Kenny Roger's song, "The Gambler?" Who doesn't hear that song and not long to be a gambler? Or at the very least -- be with one?"

"Me," Dylan says.

"Not all gamblers are creeps," I say. "Come on, honey. Let's hit the casino."

"Not up for that," he says finishing the registration,

signing his name with a flourish. "Besides, I'm more a minor league ball kind of guy."

"If I had to pick one," the manager says, "I'd vote ball game."

"Ball game it is. 'Buy me some peanuts and Cracker Jack?'" I ask waggling my eyebrows.

He bites back a smile, opens the lobby door, and gestures. "Yeah, yeah, I have a feeling you'll talk me into it."

DYLAN CLOSES THE DOOR TO OUR SMALL MOTEL ROOM. THE window AC unit makes grindy noises, chugging along more enthusiastically than the half-assed one at my place. I take this as a good sign. "Have you thought about what you're doing?" He asks. "Staying overnight isn't in your contract."

"I know."

He approaches me, releasing the decorative clips and my hair falls down my shoulders, my back, hitting my waist. He loops a thick lock around his hand, pulling me closer to him with each turn. We stand just inches away from each other, heat sparking between us. I'd have to be blind not to notice the sizeable bulge in his pants. I wet my lips.

"Full disclosure?" he asks.

"Yes." My pulse races.

"I don't get involved with women I hire to accompany me to games. Say the word and we'll keep it PG-13."

"Got it," I say, staring at his full lips. Dying for them to be on my body. "Full disclosure?"

"Yes." He twirls my hair around his hand, reeling me toward him until my breasts flatten against his chest, his thick erection presses into my pelvis. He places one hand behind my head, leans in, and his mouth is on mine. The stubble from his unshaven beard scrapes my face. His tongue explores my mouth, and I moan softly, twisting my fingers in his thick chestnut hair pulling him closer to me if that's even possible.

His kiss isn't playful like in the motel lobby, not light like the first time he brushed them against mine at the fancy five star Chicago hotel. He's claiming me. Kissing him for real is exactly what I suspected: magical – lips tingling, cheeks flushing, my body bathed in stardust after a meteor shower blows through.

This man. This sexy man. "Full disclosure," I say, my breath ragged. "I've never slept with any of my clients."

"Really?" He stops and regards me quizzically. "But you're so smart. Pretty. I don't get it." He slides the strap of my dress off my shoulder with one finger, his touch raising goosebumps on the backs of my arms.

"Sleeping with someone isn't a given." My fingers fumble as I unbutton his shirt, each button popping open gives me pleasure, my breath coming faster. "FYI, not once in the history of the world has any guy said, 'Good God, I must fuck that woman. She's got tits to die for, but the best part is she's so smart.'"

"Hah!" He feathers kisses and bites down my neck onto my bare shoulder. My breath quickens. His hand finds the back of my dress and unzips it. My country club casual dress slides awkwardly down my body and he tugs on it with one impatient hand until it lands pooled on my calves. "Lose the dress, Lucky Charm."

I place one hand on his shoulder, balance on a summer sandal, and step out of it. I stand next to him wearing only my shoes, lace bra, and matching panties. Feeling nearly naked. Vulnerable.

Dylan inhales. "Wow." He takes me in from head to toe, one hand grazing my cheek, my neck, skimming my breast, my nipple already pebbling before he even touches it. "Good God, Evie, you're beautiful."

"Thanks." I shiver.

"Bed." He tugs me toward the queen-sized bed at the far end of the small room.

"Lose the shirt," I say. I've been dreaming about running my hands across his bare chest for over a week now.

He unfastens the remaining buttons, shrugs it off and thank you Jesus, this man's just as gorgeous as I imagined two nights ago when I strummed my fingers across my sex and rocked out an orgasm. I run an appreciative hand over his chest, his muscles sculpted and hard just like I imagined. The V between my legs grows wetter, warmth flooding my pelvis, my clit tingling.

He seizes my hand, walking backward, leading me.

"Are we're putting all our cards on the table?" I ask, following him willingly.

"Sure."

"I haven't slept with anyone in a while."

"What's a while?"

"Two years," I say. "Not because of anything horrible. Simply my choice."

"Oh, darling," he says, sitting on the bed, pulling me onto his lap on top of him. "You're so sexy, Evie. What's wrong with these Chicago guys?"

"Not their fault," I say, "It's just, well, before I started at Ma Maison, I was finishing up school. Dating was pretty random. But that doesn't matter because I can take care of my own needs, if you know what I mean."

"Tell me."

"I can come on my own. Girl's got different ways to get that done, thank you very much."

"Wait up, hold on." He and eyes me. "You've never come with a guy?"

"No. I mean -- I don't think so. It's probably my fault. I'm doing something wrong or --"

"A girl's first orgasm with a partner isn't the girl's responsibility, Evie. Making a girl come is her partner's responsibility. Oh, baby. I'd push all my chips into the middle of the table to be the first man to give you this."

HE BRUSHES KISSES DOWN MY ABDOMEN, ONE HAND grazing my inner thigh, traveling to the V between my legs, close to my clit, but not touching it. My breath ratchets up a notch as he continues stroking the inside of my thigh, licking and nibbling at the soft skin just inches from my pussy. My hips lift almost of their own accord because Dylan McAlister is a fucking tease.

"Touch me," I say.

"I am touching you." He looks up at me.

"You know what I mean."

"Where should I touch you, Evie?"

"My clit."

He sucks on his fingertips, then brushes a thumb over my bundle of nerves and I clench my thighs against him.

"You've got some place to get to?" he asks. "Someplace you'd rather be?"

"No." My heart *thump-thumps* in my chest.

"Then slow down and enjoy the ride, Lucky Charm." He flicks his thumb back and forth over my center, and I sigh. He reaches his other hand up and plays with my tits, grasping them, pinching my nipples, and they harden under his touch.

Desire moves through me and I bite my lip. I'm growing wetter and I want him inside me. "Dylan," I say. "Fuck me."

"Let's do this first," he says, pressing his hand against the wetness of my seam, sliding two fingers inside my pussy.

I moan.

"Good God, Evie, you're tight."

I clench my center around his fingers as he pushes deeper, before slowly drawing his fingers out and sliding them back in. "Good?" he asks.

"Good," I say, and lick my lips. "More."

"How do you want more? Tell me."

"Harder, Dylan. Deeper."

He thrusts fingers into me harder, moving in and out. Faster. Deeper. He finger fucks me, rocking out a rhythm, and I close my eyes and ride his hand. I'm on fire for this man. The sensation between my legs builds, my breath ratcheting up, and I pant. Pleasure ripples through me. It moves from my pussy, and travels down my thighs. It moves from my nipples down my arms. Bliss builds. "Oh, Dylan. Oh."

"Come for me, baby," he says, flicking his thumb over my clit, sucking the soft skin of my upper thigh as I ride his hand. "Come for me, Lucky Charm."

And I do, my orgasm exploding in spasms. "I'm coming, Dylan. I'm coming!" I squeeze my legs against his hand. Fireworks shoot off in my body and my brain. The sensation lasts a minute, an hour, I don't know, but when I finally catch my breath, I feel content. I feel different somehow.

I open my eyes and see him smiling like the proverbial cat who ate the canary. "So?" he asks.

"Let's do the recap later," I say, admiring his thick erection that he's already sheathed. "Inside me."

"So bossy, Lucky Charm." He leans down and kisses me, lining his dick up with my pussy, and pushes slowly inside me. I close my eyes, feeling him fill me. I am tight around this man and he takes his time with me. He thrusts slowly at first, easing in, easing out. "Oh," I say.

"Okay?"

I nod because with each move we get used to each other.

It's almost too much at first, but then it becomes just enough and I arch into him. He kisses me, claiming my mouth, taking my hand in his, interlacing his fingers around mine and holding it down on the bed. "Hot, Evie." His breath comes faster, sweat shining on his brow, his chest. He pumps harder, and releases my hand. "Legs up," he says.

I do as he asks.

He places a hand under each knee and angles my legs up, allowing him to penetrate me more fully. I glance up at him as he pounds me. Those muscles in his shoulders and arms flex and cord as he fucks me. He stares down at himself inside my pussy and rocks into me harder, and I hear my ass slapping against his stomach. "Oh, Evie." He sinks into me, releases my legs, and my feet hit the mattress. "Side."

We angle onto our sides with him behind me. He pulls my hair back through his fingers, and nuzzles my neck. Biting. Sucking. He circles one hand around my breasts and fondles them, playing with my nipples while he continues to fuck me brilliantly, fuck me beautifully. "Evie. Evie. I'm coming, baby." He's so deep within me and I feel him shake and shudder, thrusting a few more times as he empties himself.

He cradles me in his arms afterward, our breath returning to normal.

"I had no idea sex could be like this," I say.

"This is the only way sex should be," he says.

❧ 10 ❧

BET ON IT

BET ON IT

I wake up the next day cradled in Dylan's arms. "Good morning," he says, and presses his lips against my shoulder giving me goosebumps. His morning erection bumps the small of my back.

"Good morning." I stretch my arms overhead feeling better rested than I've felt in years. "What's on the agenda today?"

"Oh, I don't know." He cups my breast, rolling the nipple between his thumb and forefinger. "What are you up for?"

"You're a smart man." I push his hand down my stomach. "I'll let you figure it out."

"Ha." He kisses his way down my neck, and slides his fingers across my sex until I arch against him and moan. He straddles me, then leans down and kisses me, the scruff of his beard rough and sexy against my face. He palms my breast, tugging on the nipple and it pebbles. Pleasure courses through me, my breath coming faster. "Mmm."

He spreads my legs with his hands, kissing his way down my stomach, making his way to my sex, circling it with his tongue. He plants his hands on my abdomen as he buries his face between my legs, his tongue flicking across my sex.

He holds tight to me and I ride his face. I moan. The stimulation of his tongue and his mouth is almost too much, but he doesn't let go. I tangle my fingers through his thick hair until bliss explodes and I come in shudders and shocks, waves of pleasure coursing through my entire body.

He reaches for a small foil square on the bedside table, ripping it open with his teeth. He rolls the protection on his thick, hard, jutting out cock. "Legs on my shoulders, Evie."

"Yes, sir, Mr. McAlister, sir."

"Smartass."

I lie on my back, lift my legs, and wrap them on top of his shoulders. He lines his dick up with my sex and pushes inside, filling me. I stare up at him as he fucks me. He's all muscle: rippled chest, cut abdomen, square jaw, those blue eyes of his shrouded with desire. "You feel so good," I say.

He smiles, leans down, and kisses me. "You feel better."

I don't know how many minutes later he makes me come with his fingers on my clit and he pumps out an orgasm as he watches me. We collapse against the bed and catch our breath. I could do this with him forever but my traitorous stomach growls, interrupting the moment.

"Uh-oh," he says. "The beast has woken. I need to feed you."

Ten minutes later he's dressed in athletic shorts, a T-shirt, and a ball cap, and I'm zipping up my Mrs. Ralph Lauren dress.

"I'm starving," he says. "You're wearing out an old man. I need sustenance."

"You're not old."

"I'm thirty-eight. You'd better be legal or I'm suing Ma Maison." He pinches my ass.

"I'm twenty-four." I push back a smile. "Shut up, old man."

We hit a little grill where the plastic encased menu hawks twenty different kinds of omelets. It's bacon and eggs and endless fresh-brewed dark coffee. Perhaps I've landed in heaven and nothing else will ever taste or feel this good again.

"I didn't even ask if you wanted to hang out today," he says, eyeing me over his coffee cup. "It's Sunday. You probably already have plans."

"Nope, I normally chill on Sunday. I'd love to hang out with you." It dawns on me – it's Sunday. *God's day.* "Why are you asking? Do you want to go to church?"

"No." He frowns. "Do you?"

"I'm good." I signal the waitress for a coffee refill. She stops by with the pot and gladly accommodates along with dropping off the check. "I've got a deal with God. I pray to Him every now and again, confess my sins, do penance, and He lets me skip the weekly services."

"You have a nice God," Dylan says wiping his mouth with a napkin.

"A super nice God," I say. "We've had a rocky relationship for a while. Lots of fights and time outs. It took us years to get to a good place."

"Good for you," he says. "God and I are still in a fight. Let's hit the trail." he says, and throws down a few bills. "Ready?"

"Sure." I stand and follow him, wondering how I'm going to ride a bike in a country club dress.

TEN MINUTES LATER DYLAN WALKS OUT OF THE convenience store where we just grabbed bottled water and trail mix, stops in his tracks and stares at me, a funny look on his face. "Did I tell you the first thing I thought when I saw you step off the train yesterday?"

"No."

"That I was a lucky man. You looked so pretty I was half tempted to tackle you right there on the train platform."

"Thank you I think."

"Welcome. I wanted to skip the game. Drive back to my sordid little hotel and have my wicked way with you."

"Funny how life works," I say, heat building inside me. "Wish for something long enough and it happens. Maybe not in the way you expect."

"From your lips to God's ears, Lucky Charm," Dylan says. "Right now, I'm picturing you bike riding in that dress. A beautiful summer day on the trail. The wind blows your skirt up and I catch a glimpse of those lace panties." He drops a hand down my waist, grazes my ass. "You are wearing your panties -- right?"

I blush. "You're bad."

"You guessed my middle name -- Dylan Bad McAlister. Follow me," he says and holds out his hand. "I've got an idea."

We visit a nearby sporting goods store and suddenly I'm the proud new owner of jeans, a pair of shorts, a few T-shirts, and runners. "You dress down nice," he says, peering out at me from under that ball cap and his Aviators as the cashier rings up the purchases.

"No ball cap, honey?" I ask.

He snags a Kane County Cougars cap from a rack, sets it on my head. Leans back, pulls off his Aviators and checks me out. "Cute." He drapes one arm over my shoulders and throws down another bill on the checkout counter.

The checkout girl hands him change and gives me a

thumbs up. "Wear the hat if you go to the game tonight. They'll give you a discount."

"Awesome." I smile at Dylan. "Remind me to thank you, later."

"Bet on it," he says.

WE RENT BIKES WITH LOCKS AND HELMETS FROM A LITTLE sports shop in a mini-mall a hundred or so yards off the Fox River trail. We ride down a dirt path on a glorious summer Saturday. The weather's warm and humid with a scattering of cumulous clouds threatening rain at some point.

The sun pokes between the clouds as we bike along the Fox River taking in miles of curves and bends. We pedal pass people fishing, folks on the trail with their kids, others jogging with their dogs. A few aggressive bicyclists tear past us at breakneck speed needing to blow off excess energy. Not us – we already spent time in the fast lane – we're taking it slow, chilled, relaxed. We're here for some fun.

"Woot!" Dylan wheels off the path, skids down a leaf scattered muddy embankment dozens of yards to the river's edge. His shoulders have dropped off his ears. His complexion's warmer. The care and worry evaporated off his face, off his entire body. He seems bigger, freer, wilder. He's transformed into different person. This man needed to get outside, get back in nature. This man is where he belongs.

"Having fun?" I ask a few dozen yards away from him, still on the path.

"What do you think?" He regards me with a delicious grin and it's all I can do not to tear down the hill, tackle him, and kiss him.

But today isn't about me. "Race you," I say.

"Where to?" he asks, looking up, shading his eyes from the sun.

"From here," I point a ways off, "to the far end of the river. Where it turns around the bend."

"Sure, Lucky Charm," he says. "What's the bet?"

"Bet?"

"You throw out a challenge to a player, you need to sweeten the pot. What's the bet?"

"Hmm." I drink him in – ruffled hair, sun-kissed face, a sheen of sweat from physical exertion, not stress. He's delicious. I wish we could stay here on this path, stay here on this green leafed, sunshine filled day. That the Universe would draw a protective bubble around us and we could live in it forever.

"Cat got your tongue, youngster?" he asks. "No worries. I'll go first."

"Spit it out, old man," I say, "Before you forget."

"Hah! If I win?" He takes a swig from his water bottle, then squirts a generous helping of water over his face, slicks back his wet hair.

"Yes?" *Bumpity-bump-bump* goes my heart.

"If I win, we ride back to the motel, I peel off your bike shorts, and make you come a few times. Maybe watch you do that on your own. That would make me a happy man. Then we tackle more good stuff."

"Shh." I press fingers to my lips, the V between my legs already throbbing.

"No one's within hearing distance. After a few rounds of hot sex, we order pizza, cold beers, sit out on the porch on that rickety old swing set. You rest your head on my shoulder, I hold your hand, and we kick back and watch the sun set like an old couple," he says. "I'd really like that."

"That sounds nice." His words tug at my heart. "If *I* win?"

"Yes?"

"I play on a softball team and I've always wanted to see a minor league game. If I win you take me to the ballgame, buy me a hot dog, some chips, and a beer. Afterwards we go back to the motel room and play my favorite song. You strip for me – slowly might I add – while I cheer you on. You give me a lap dance. *Then* we have hot sex."

"I've never given anyone a lap dance before," he says, a quirk of a smile pulling up the corners of his lips.

"And I've never gotten one," I say. "It'll be a first for the both of us. A total win-win."

"Maybe old dogs can learn new tricks," he says and waggles his eyebrows.

"Good," I say. "Bet?"

"Bet," he says.

"Awesome." I push down hard like dynamite on the pedal and peel off as fast as I can. "See you!"

"Not fair!" He hollers, thundering up the embankment after me.

I laugh and pedal faster.

WE SIT IN THE BLEACHERS AT NORTHWESTERN MEDICINE Field on the third base line watching the Kane County Cougars play the Wisconsin Timber Raccoons. I'm wearing my new jeans and a T-shirt. The ballcap Dylan bought me entitled us to a free bag of chips and two bucks off a ticket. We nosh on hot dogs and drink cold beers. The sun sets late, the stadium lights popping on, the air damp and hanging heavy around us. "When's the last time you went to a ball game?" I ask.

"Long time," he says, his long legs stretched out on the empty bench in front of him one hand resting on my knee. "Maybe six years?"

Thunder rumbles low in the skies above us, lightning strikes a few miles away.

"Who'd you go with?"

"Family. My ex-wife, Dixie."

"What happened?" I ask. "Wait. Don't tell me if you don't want to talk about it."

"Family or Dixie?" He asks.

"Both," I say.

"The pretty version or the shitty version?" He asks.

"Whatever one you want to share."

He sighs. "I looked great on paper to Dixie. A pastor's son. A wealthy congregation. A built-in life of security and hero worship. There was one tiny problem."

"What?" I ask taking a sip of my ballpark beer. A crack of a bat as a batter hits a double, the crowd's up on its feet cheering.

"Marriage is more than paper."

"And?"

There's a swing and a ball flies out to deep left field.

"She thought she married the preacher's son." He shrugs. "Not the preacher's *prodigal* son. It wasn't what she signed up for. In her eyes, she got a raw deal. I was sadly regrettable."

The runner on third takes off and slides into home and the fans shout in excitement, throwing fist punches in the air. We jump to our feet and cheer with them. "Dylan," I say, rubbing his shoulder. "Never in a thousand years could you be regrettable."

Fat raindrops plop down from the skies above. Umps and coaches glance up, questioning looks on their faces.

"I was to Dixie. She re-married a Baptist minister and is now queen bee in a smaller congregation. She's got a new kid, a husband who comes home at decent hours and she leases a new SUV every two years. It's the life she signed up for."

"Do you have regrets?" I ask.

"No."

"What about your family?"

"That's a whole 'nother conversation," he says. "Tell me about you. Besides the bad sex former boyfriend. In a strange way, I feel like I owe him."

The heavens open up and a soft warm rain pelts us.

"How so?" I ask.

"Not every day a guy gets to give one of the sweetest girls he's ever met her first orgasm."

"Her first four orgasms."

"Only four?" he asks, a smile growing on his face.

I count on my fingertips as the skies open and pour, drenching us as if on cue. "Five."

"A sign from the heavens that I need to up my game." He takes my hand. "Besides, I've been figuring out my stripper moves all day. Come on."

WE CHECK OUT OF THE LODGE AT CRACK OF DAWN THE next morning. He drops off the keycards in the lobby while I sit on the porch swing, drinking a cup of thin motel coffee. The countryside has that fresh feel after a rain: a medley of green grass, cut fields, and a new start. My life has changed, even though besides the orgasms, I can't figure out how or why.

Dylan walks out the lobby door, wearing a T-shirt and jeans. A soothing warmth envelopes my chest like I downed a whiskey infused with honey – only to be pierced by pangs of sadness. I've already grown comfortable being around him but the weekend blew by so quickly. Now I'm going to miss him and I'm not sure what to do with this mish mash of feelings. Amelia was right – sex with a client changes everything. "When's your next game?"

"Tonight. Come with me," he says impulsively. "Come with me to Nashville."

"Nashville? Really?"

"Yes. No. Crap," he says and smacks his forehead with the heel of his hand. "I can't ask you to do this. I'm a complete, utter asshole. I'm sorry, Evie. I have to cut back on expenses. I love being with you, but, let's face it. Engaging you through Ma Maison is pricey. God, I hate that I'm in this position."

"I'm overdue for a few days off. I can take vacation days."

"You can't," he says.

"Why not? I haven't taken a day off since I started working for Ma Maison a few months back." Truth -- even though there's not one scintilla of fine print that guarantees me vacation days or anything else for that matter.

"You don't have to do this. I'd never want you to do something you're not comfortable doing. Never want you to get in trouble."

"I know." I pull out my phone to text Madame and immediately think better. Plenty of time to tell her about it after she tracks me down. I shove it back in my purse. "Nashville here we come."

NASHVILLE

WE TRAIN IT BACK TO THE CITY, STOPPING BY MY PLACE SO I can pack a bag. I sort through my closet while Dylan sprawls on my bed scrolling on his phone. He chews his lower lip and I wonder if he's having second thoughts. "I don't have to go, you know."

"My mind hasn't changed." He looks up. "Has yours?"

"No," I say. "Am I interrupting plans?"

"Nope. I just bought you a plane ticket." He drops the phone, his gaze taking in my bedroom. "You live simply."

"Yup," I say tossing clothing onto my bed.

"I wasn't sure what to expect," he says.

"PSF. Poor, simple and frugal," I open my bureau and take out underwear, bras, camis, a bathing suit just in case. "That's me."

"PSF. Pretty, smart, and funny," he says. "That's you. I'm assuming you know my background."

"Which part?"

"Church."

"You told me about church." I grab the cross Grandma Berlinger gave me from my jewelry box on top of the bureau and tuck that in my purse.

"Yeah, well there's more than church," he says.

"Tell me," I say.

"We're got time to talk about my life as well as yours on the flight there," he says.

"My life's boring," I say.

"Hah hah. Right. You need to tell me why you got into this nutty gig."

Yes, *dying* to tell him about my crazy mom and the sister who's dating the meth head. My phone pings and I check it.

> **Amelia:** *Haven't talked. Are you still creeped by the letter?*

Evie: *No.*

> **Amelia:** *Good. This stuff is usually nothing.*

Amelia: *A fourteen-year-old saw a pic of you online and he's jerking off in the bathroom.*

> **Amelia:** *How'd your date go?*

I glance at Dylan. He's scrolling again.

Evie: *Great.*

> **Amelia:** *Can't wait to hear all!.*

Amelia: *Meeting Victoria for happy hour tomorrow. Join us.*

Evie: *Sorry can't. Got a date.*

I backspace, erase "date", and replace with --

Evie: *Sorry can't. Got a personal thing.*

Amelia: *Say hi to your mom. Check in later.*

Evie: *Have fun.*

DYLAN WAS THE FIRST CLIENT I HAD SEX WITH AND I DID it because I liked him. Wholly. Unequivocally. Purely. We fly to Nashville, arrive early afternoon, and he rents a motel room close to the game's location. We catch a nap, wake up, and fool around. I cheer on his stripper moves. Not only is he enjoying his new 'talent', he's now striving to be the best male stripper ever. Gotta love a competitive guy.

"Woo hoo! Smoking hot! Take it all off!" I shove dollar bills down his underwear, then reward him for real by dropping to my knees in front of him. I slide his briefs down his legs with one hand, grasp his hard cock with the other and take it in my mouth, circling my tongue around the head as he moans. I lick the length of him.

"Evie."

"What?"

"Take off your top."

I pull off my T-shirt and toss it.

He looks at me, licking his lips and my nipples pebble. "Gorgeous."

I take him in my mouth, clasp his muscular ass, drawing him in further and he bumps the back of my throat, over and over.

"Evie. Oh, God." He shudders, groaning, his hands tangled in my long hair, my eyes watering as I take him in, not letting go while he comes in spasms.

We shower together, ostensibly to prep for the gig, but one thing leads to another. He kisses me fiercely, one hand playing with my hair, the other massaging my breasts, teasing my nipples, his erection pushing against my abdomen. My sex is throbbing, my breath coming quicker. "Inside me, Dylan."

He steps a foot out of the shower and grabs a square from his wallet on the bathroom counter. He rips the package open with his teeth and rolls on protection. "Turn." Back in the tub he stands behind me, his hard cock pushed up against the crease in my ass, one hand between my legs playing with my clit. "Lean forward, baby. Hands on the wall."

I do as he asks the warm shower water hitting my back. He slaps my ass a few times and my breath ratches up.

"God, you've got a great ass, Berlinger."

"Awesome compliment coming from the hot stripper with the beautiful dick." I arch my back and grind against him. "This is your best lap dance yet."

He laughs.

I'm on fire for this man. "Inside me, please."

He nudges my legs apart with his muscular one and rubs his hard length against me until he slides in and I gasp from his fullness. He fucks me slowly at first. My eyes flutter closed and I get use to his size, his hardness.

"Baby," he says. "You feel so good." He pushes harder and with each thrust he's deeper inside me, claiming me, making me his. "More?"

I nod, biting my lip.

He grasps the top of my hips and drills me from behind, my ass slapping up against his stomach. It feels so good under the warm water, him inside me, and I push back against him, moaning. His hand reaches around front and finds the hard nub between my legs, strumming fingers over my sex until I'm panting, crying out his name, over and over. "I'm coming, Dylan. I'm coming."

"Good, baby." He thrusts deeper inside me, until he comes, leg muscles contracting, his abs contracting.

We get dressed for real this time and grab a quick bite on our way to the game. A red and yellow flashing neon sign hovers over the large parking lot filled with a smorgasbord of new and old sedans, motorcycles, pickup trucks. It's early afternoon after the lunch rush at Big Tony's a little BBQ joint on the side of the road. Dylan and I share a picnic table and enjoy plates of pulled pork and ribs.

"Yummy," I say. "I could eat this for days."

"I could eat you for days," he says. "I can't believe you're here with me. Part of me thinks I'm hallucinating. Every time I blink I fear you'll disappear."

"I'm not going anywhere. Are you feeling more relaxed? Ready to win the house tonight?" He's got a smear of BBQ sauce on his chin and I wipe it away with two fingers. Still amazed I am here with this beautiful man. Blue eyes, high cheekbones, that tousle of chestnut hair. Feelings percolate in me. Not lust for a change. Something familiar, something I haven't felt in a long time.

"No," he says. "I think we should have sex again. Then I'll be ready." He waggles his eyebrows.

I bite back a smile, pushing whatever this feeling is away. "We can't be late."

"These things never start on time. Look," he says and points to the other side of the parking lot. "That picnic table's way way in the back of the property. Hidden behind a huge pine tree. It's totally private. You could bend forward the way you did in the shower, I'd lift your skirt, pull your panties -- "

"No. A picnic table next to the parking lot is not private."

"We haven't done a quickie yet. I'd feel horrible if I deprived you."

"Sex after the game." I traveled with him to Nashville because I like him. I also traveled here because I desperately want him to get his mojo back.

We arrive at Vanderveen Manor, a large, lush, landscaped, black iron gated estate on the outskirts of town. The greenery's thicker in the South and a heady hint of jasmine wafts through the air. It's early Sunday evening when we're buzzed into the place and instructed to follow the red brick path to the back of the property. The manor's centerfold glossy, with a big money vibe similar to the Schillinger Estate in St. Charles.

"You got this," I say to Dylan as he knocks on the door.

"From your lips to God's ears." He squeezes my hand.

The entrance opens and a polished young woman greets and ushers us inside an immaculate living room with cherry colored hardwood floors. The room smells sweet, like men used to smoke pipes in here and the aroma seeped into the wood. Built in bookshelves line the walls stocked with antique books. A poker table's set up in the far corner, players gathering.

The Nashville help staff is just as polite as the folks in St. Charles and Chicago, but even more polished. The dealer could be a model for men's cologne, slicked back hair, dark eyes. The hostess and waitresses could pass as beauty pageant contestants.

Everything's pristine and pretty when out of nowhere my skin crawls. Like taking a short cut down a city alley when an unexpected wind kicks up, hurling soot and garbage in my direction, trashing me, making me feel dirty.

"Look what the cat dragged in," Glenn, the Fast Food King walks out of the bathroom, eye fucking me as he zips up. "I heard rumors you'd be hitting the Grind City game, McAlister."

"Glenn." Dylan startles. "Didn't realize you'd be here."

"Last minute thing. Awfully nice of you to bring the girl," he says, tongue flicking over thin lips.

"The girl has a name," Dylan says, spine straightening, shoulders squaring. "Evelyn."

"Nice to see you again, Evelyn," Glenn says. "What say I play you for her, McAlister."

Dylan's face flushes red and he practically growls. "Stop being an ass."

I shiver and wrap my arms tight around my waist.

"Come on, church boy. She'd sweeten the pot better than a stack of chips."

"Stop or I'll punch you." His hand balls in a fist.

I step between them. "Dylan."

"I'm a gambler," Glenn says. "Can't blame a guy for trying. Right cookie?" He winks at me and walks away.

"Entitled asshole prick. I'm sorry. You okay?" Dylan asks rubbing my arm.

"Don't let this idiot get to you." I nod as my phone pings. "Get it done. Play well. And for God's sakes, win."

"Lord knows I'll try." He kisses me, turns and makes his way toward the table located at the far corner of the room.

Glenn shoots me another look. Beady eyes disappearing into fat red cheeks topped by thinning oily hair. I don't think Dylan sees it – probably a good thing.

A waitress approaches. "Can I get you something?"

A shower?

"An orange juice, thanks." I slip outside onto a bricked in patio where I'm hoping to get decent reception because Wi-Fi is generally blocked during these events. I check my phone.

Amelia: Where are you?

Evie: Nashville.

Amelia: I thought your mom was in Milwaukee.

Evie: She is.

Amelia: What's going on in Nashville?

Evie: A thing. Talk later.

I check more texts.

Madame M: Contact me.

Evie: Feeling a little under the weather. I'll check in soon.

Madame M: Chicken soup and Vitamin C.

Evie: Good idea. TY.

I sigh and scroll.

Ruby: You around this weekend? My BF and I are coming in town for a concert. Can we crash at your place?

Evie: Which BF?

Ruby: My only BF. Joe.

Evie: Meth head Joe?

Ruby: He doesn't do meth anymore. Just weed.

I roll my eyes.

Evie: *No.*

Evie: *You cannot crash with me.*

Ruby: *Nice of you to be so helpful, sister.*

Evie: *I'm not a nice person. Sue me.*

I make my way back inside, collect my orange juice and move toward the back of the room. Where I stay for the next eighteen hours, hoping and praying this is the game that Dylan turns around. 'He's a good man, God,' I silently pray. 'Send him grace.'

But God's not on speed dial tonight because Dylan's mojo crumbles late in the tournament. He plays loose; checking and calling where Glenn's tight and aggressive, betting and raising on good hands. It's almost as if Dylan's math is off and he's going all in on mediocre hands.

I crunch numbers in my head and I estimate he's dropped over fifty thousand. I feel his confidence blow up like a bomb around me, shards of shrapnel hurtling through the air when once again, Glenn emerges the big winner.

I grab Dylan, his complexion ashen, and get him the hell out of Vanderveen Manor before he loses his shit and punches someone, probably Glenn. We hit Tony's BBQ on the way back to our motel. It feels like we were just here but it was yesterday.

Looking beaten, Dylan pushes food around his plate. "Maybe I need to leave the game. Go back to Texas. Back to the family business – Lighthouse Church. Sing in the choir. Get hit on by every Christian divorcee in the Dallas Fort Worth area. Ugh. Kill me now."

"You're underselling yourself, old man," I take a bite of my BBQ chicken. "You've got classic good looks and with your new stripper moves you're multi-theistic hot. All the non-Christians will be hitting on you too. You'll be the most popular guy in town. But now's not the best time to be making that kind of decision." I point to his plate. "Eat."

"Jeez, you're harsh." He picks up a rib, chewing on it.

"I need you healthy," I say. "Who else is going to give me mind-bending orgasms tonight?"

A pimply teenager holding a fork topped with BBQ at the next table over stares at me wide-eyed, his mouth gaping.

Dylan jabs the rib in his direction. "Not. You. Buddy."

We've been up for over twenty four hours. Back at our room we shower and collapse in bed. I fall into a hard sleep until he wakes me, kissing my breast. "Evie." He circles his tongue around my nipple, the scruff of his beard sending tiny beats of pleasure through me and my pussy clenches.

I sigh, stir, and blink my eyes open. "You okay?" Early morning sunshine pokes through a split in window curtains.

"Right now, I am," he says. He takes my nipple in his mouth, alternating sucking and nibbling. One hand slides down my abdomen. "Spread your knees, baby."

I do as he asks.

"You're so sweet." He kisses me, his lips firm, his tongue exploring my mouth. He grazes fingers down the inside of my thigh, playing with my folds. I'm getting wetter by the second and it's all I can do not to clench my thighs tight against him. "I want you inside me, Dylan."

"Patience," he says, straddling me, his cock already thick and hard, jutting out from his pelvis. He reaches for a small square package on the bedside table, rips it open with his teeth, and rolls on protection.

I reach for him, circling his erection with my hand, stroking its length lightly at first, then firm, harder. He's rock hard. Good God, this man is delicious. "Now?" I ask my body warm, wet, and pulsing with need for him.

"Rub me against you. Play with me like you would with one of your toys. I want to see what you look like." His blue eyes light up with desire. "Watch your pretty face when you come. You're so hot when you come."

I rub his stiff cock against my sex and moan. I'm already turned on, but rubbing his dick back and forth across my sex makes me even wetter, and I'm panting. I push his cock harder, faster against my sex, needing him inside my pussy, needing him to fill me. "Now?"

"Come for me, Evie." He pinches a nipple between his thumb and forefinger, playing, toying with me, taking me to the edge. "You're so sexy, baby. I could watch you forever."

I play with his hard cock across my bundle of nerves, crazy sensations building. I arch and buck and my thighs clench hard against him. "I'm coming!" My orgasm ripples in spasms of pleasure, shooting from clit through my pelvis out to the rest of my body. When the waves settle I take in a deep breath. "Inside me. Now."

He sinks inside me, pushing slowly at first, settling in. He groans. "You feel so good, baby."

"You too." I wrap my legs around him.

"I'm scared I'm losing it." He thrusts inside me. "What if I'm losing it?"

"We'll figure it out. I promise. Right now, just fuck me." I don't care about Dylan McAlister's money. I've never cared about his money. His fortune is slipping away and I still fuck him. I'm not sure when I won't want to fuck him.

He thrusts his cock inside me. He rides me harder, then harder still, burying himself deep, then deeper within me as if I am his last piece of sanity. As if I'm the last bastion between him and the monsters that have come to steal what remains of his courage; the thieves that have come to claim his soul. I lose track of time. The world falls away, and I orgasm. "Oh, God."

He comes moments later in shakes and shudders. "Fuck, Evie. Fuck!" He collapses on top of me, spent, our hearts pounding, our bodies slick with sweat. We catch our breath and I lie in his arms, tracing circles on his firm chest. I'm satiated. I'm happy. I'm a hot mess. My emotions are slinging around like hash browns frying on a grill. Are they mine. His? Right now I don't care. "I had no idea sex could be this good."

"So good, Lucky Charm." He tucks a lock of disheveled hair behind my ear. "But it's past time you go home."

EMPATHIC

EMPATHIC

———————

I BLINK BACK TEARS. "YOU DON'T WANT ME AROUND?"

"Of course I want you around. Hey, don't cry. I'm sorry." He wipes a tear away.

I run the heel of my hand across my cheeks. "I'm a hot mess." Familiar feelings claw at me, shred my heart.

"Hot but not a mess. Look, I'm so comfortable with you, feel like I've known you forever, and that's a problem." He sighs. "Because I'm always going to want you around."

"That's good," I say, sniffling. "That's excellent. When's the next game?"

"Doesn't matter. You're going back to Chicago," he says and kisses my forehead.

"When's the next game?" I ask, more determined.

"Tomorrow. Memphis."

"I'm still on vacation, old man. I'm traveling with you."

"Nope," he says, pushing himself out of bed, walking over

to his clothes lying on the back of the chair. "I've gotten you in enough trouble."

"Who's going to die if I take the rest of the week off?"

"You. Madame Marchand will have your head on a platter." He throws clothes into his carryon suitcase. "She sounds like she tortures kittens for fun during her off hours."

"You talked with her on the phone?" I ask getting out of bed, making my way to him.

"Yes," he says. "After I passed the background check."

"Huh." I didn't know she'd actually talked with him. Why does this feel disturbing? "Behind her hard as nails exterior Madame's a total softie," I circle my arms around his waist, kissing the back of his shoulder. Standing on tip toes to kiss the colorful bite marks on his neck that I gave him when his dick was buried deep inside me. "She's a total marshmallow."

"Bullshit," Dylan says, covering my hand with his large one. His hand fits perfectly on top of mine.

I feel so safe. I feel so – oh fuck am I falling in love with this man? Is *that* what's wrong with me? I haven't fallen in love since I was thirteen years old and that was with Wyatt Wolfe and look how terrific that turned out? We ran over him in Mom's car and broke him.

Jesus Christ, what am I doing? If I go further -- will I hurt Dylan McAlister just like I hurt Wyatt Wolfe? He's right. I need to leave. I need to get the hell away from him. I need to go home now.

"Okay. I'm not going to argue with you," Dylan says. "That's a waste of time. I'm taking you up on your offer."

"You are?" Dread dukes it out with excitement.

"Yes," he says. "Get dressed. We need to eat. We're leaving for the airport in three hours."

"Okay," I say.

'What are you doing?' Queasy wrings his hands. *'This is supposed to be about making money. Not losing your soul.'*

"Three hours?" I ask and think hard, scouring my brain for a way I can make this right.

"Yes," he says and continues to pack.

'Redemption's knocking,' Hope says. *'An opportunity to get it right. Really help someone heal this time.'*

"Dylan, I've got an idea."

"Sure thing, baby. Tell me anything – right after breakfast."

WE JOG DOWN A PATH IN A PRETTY PARK. THE MORNING air's warm, not yet stifling. Dew burns off lush green grass. Dylan's not turning his game around. He says I calm him, but I'm not the human equivalent of Xanax.

There's something else -- not just the game -- that's throwing a fat monkey wrench into his brain, his heart. Something else is cutting him off from his mojo. I'm removed, on the outside looking in. It might be easier for me to identify whatever this thing is and help him change it.

We run in step next to each other, both breaking a sweat. I gather my courage, prepare a big old long speech in my head that sounds rational and smart and cool and just when I have the words perfect, all lined up like little soldiers on parade I forget them and spit out, "Dylan, I like you."

"I like you too."

"What if there is a way for you to turn this losing streak around that you haven't thought of yet? A solution that's not even on your radar?"

"I *don't* count cards," he says, shooting me a disappointed look. He sprints ahead, practically leaving me in the dust.

Anger pops, lighting a fire under my feet. "Hey!" I race quicker, catch up with him, and smack his shoulder.

He slows down. "What?"

"I don't count cards, either, asshole. Don't assume a new suggestion is illegal or amoral."

"You're right." He slows. "I'm sorry. Tell me more."

I take a deep breath. "I'm empathic."

He frowns. "The last thing I want is your sympathy."

"Not sympathy, old man. Empathy. Sounds similar but it's completely different."

"How so?" He stops running, wipes the sweat off his brow with the hem of his T-shirt, and eyes me. He's wearing one of those sleeveless tanks, the muscles cut and defined in his arms and I have to pinch myself to stay on subject.

"I can feel in my body what's going on inside of yours. Literally feel it. That's called *empathy*."

"Okay," he says and grazes a finger down my neck, my shoulder, his blue eyes dropping to my sweaty cleavage. "What am I feeling now?"

Goosebumps prickle on the backs of my arms, my nipples hardening. "Besides you wanting to go back to the motel?"

"Yeah. There's that."

"Sadness and regret."

His eyes widen. "That's a good guess."

"It wasn't a guess. I felt it." I clench my fist tight at my side. Don't care how hot he is – I need him to take me seriously.

"What are my sadness and regret about?"

"The game."

"That's obvious," he says and removes his hand. Disbelief rears up within me. I'm used to being dismissed. Used to being the small voice that people ignore, but for some reason I thought Dylan would be different.

'He's not a mind reader,' Hope says. *'Speak up.'*

I give my head a shake. "Hear me out."

"Fair enough. Tell me more."

I squeeze my eyes shut and search for the memories of his

sadness and regret and I find them. "Glenn was betting bigger with each round. On the third to the last round of the game he didn't. He changed his behavior."

The thick muscle in his jaw ticks. "More."

"You wondered if he was hedging. If his hand was really all that good -- wouldn't he be upping his bet?"

"Go on," he says.

I take his hand, interlace my fingers between his, liking how his palms are a little calloused. I concentrate. "You didn't know if you should check, raise, or call. That's when the sadness hit you. Hit you hard, in your gut," I touch his abdomen. "Like a thief stole the watch your grandfather gave you, then wore it out in public, and bragged it was theirs. I don't know what you were thinking, but that's what you were feeling and that's when you second guessed yourself. Your confidence -- poof – vanished. You wobbled around in that round like a drunk pirate with a peg leg and you folded. And the Fast Food King, who had a weaker hand than you, won the game."

"Fuck me," Dylan says, shaking his head. "You're right. Fuck me. This empathic thing – it's happened more than once?"

"Yes. I pushed it away for a long time but there's a connection happening between you and me. I don't know why but the empathy's back with a fury."

He paces, all ripped muscles and corded emotions. "Did this happen during the Chicago game?"

"Yes."

"St. Charles game?"

"Yes."

"Damn," he says. "How do you control this empathy thing?"

"Exercise, meditation, prayer. You know, things that ground a person. But with you -- I don't control it all that well. In fairness -- I don't really try. When I'm tuned in to you I sense all the fantastic things you're feeling -- "

"And the awful things too." He slams his forehead with the heel of his hand. "Evie, I'm sorry."

"Don't be. You're not doing anything wrong. I can't help wondering if we can play with this? Figure out how to make this empathic connection between you and me work for you. Maybe turn your game around."

"I'm dutifully impressed, Lucky Charm, but I don't get how your empathy can change anything. You feel the past -- you don't predict the future."

"I feel the *present* and I'll lay odds there's something from your past that's screwing you up. An old wound's running you, a messed-up belief's playing out over and over -- like the lyrics to a stupid song that your brain can't turn off. Something dark and dirty and buried is running the show."

"Something old is playing me?" He asks.

"Yes."

"Like what?"

"I don't know?" I shrug. "Unresolved guilt. An old fear."

"Maybe I need to go back to therapy."

"Therapy's great."

"But if you feel these things *when* they're happening --"

"I do."

"What if we can track this old belief down, Evie?" He stops pacing, stands still in front of me. I can practically see the wheels spinning in his brain as he tries to figure it out. "What if we can figure it out?"

"If we figure it out? You face it head on, confront it, and then you conquer it."

"Get my game back," he says.

"Get your life back."

His blue eyes light up. He pulls me to him, lifts me up in the air and swings me around. "Yes!" He kisses me and I'm reminded why I'm playing hooky. Because when Dylan McAlister kisses me my lips tingle, my cheeks flush, my body bathes in stardust after a meteor shower blows through. When Dylan McAlister kisses me time stands still.

What I'm going to do without him when this crazy ride is over?

MEMPHIS

I FINALLY TELL HIM A LITTLE ABOUT MOM ON THE PLANE. About her mental condition. That she's had it a for a long time and it's tough, but she's making headway because of this new treatment. How Ruby and I are trying to support her.

"Not easy, Evie," he says.

I nod. "I know. But she's doing better. Turning a corner."

"Not easy for you either."

"Thanks. Enough about my exciting life – let's talk about you!"

"Let's not," he says. "Tell me more about you. School. Friends. What you want to be when you grow up."

"I have a Master's in Education. I have friends at the Agency, pals on my softball team. What I want to be when I grow up? I'm not sure."

"All that education and you don't know yet? Pick the first thing that pops into your head."

"I want to be, hmm — I want to be someone who puts her own needs first every once in a while."

"That's not what I thought you'd say."

I've never been to Memphis and I'm kind of excited about it until we arrive. Turns out Memphis is simply another airport, another ride sharing service, another motel. I shower, dress, and apply makeup in front of the bathroom mirror. I can't wait for Dylan to kick ass tonight.

We talk about meditating and I show him how to do it. Getting quiet, going still, can actually change the structure of the brain and thicken areas that deal with learning and memory. It can still the chatter, reduce anxiety, and reboot the brain. It's like taking a chill pill without the pill.

I'm crossing my fingers that Dylan will tune into his feelings and together we'll figure it out. He'll get his mojo back and turn his game around. Then we can see each other, meet up on paid engagements. I can still pay for Mom's medical treatments, help Ruby out with school, and keep a roof over my head. He and I are a team. If he gets his shit together we can do this.

I fashion my hair into a messy bun, apply a coat of lipstick and check the mirror. I'll pass. "Ready." I walk into the room.

Dylan's half naked on the floor doing pushups.

"Hello?" I say. "What are you doing?"

"You said that you controlled your empathic reactions with exercise," he says, sweat glistening on his bare shoulders, that muscle ticking in his jaw.

"Yes. Sometimes."

"If I get the blood flowing maybe I can get more in control for the game," he says, straining his breath.

"That's not how it works." I sigh. "It's about letting go. Finding the calm when you're hurtling through the storm."

"Thank you, Obi Wan Kenobi," he says, and knocks out one armed push-ups, grunting on the exhalations.

"Fuck you, Rocky," I say when my phone pings. "Shower and get dressed. I'll wait for you outside."

I PACE ON THE GRASS CIRCLING A FENCED IN PLAY AREA. A few kids dig in the sand, the girls making castles with buckets and water, love and care. The boys race around like their hair is on fire. I check my texts.

Madame M: *Are you feeling better?*

Evie: *Getting there TY.*

Evie: *Chicken soup and Vit C.*

Madame M: *Glad you took my recommendations.*

Evie: *Of course.*

Madame M: *I have a new client for you.*

Madame M: *You're not contagious anymore -- right?*

My throat dries up and I hack. Um...

Evie: *Still coughing...*

Madame: *I'll send him to someone else. Heal up.*

Evie: *TY.*

Madame: *How much longer do you think?*

Evie: *Soon.*

I sigh and scroll.

Amelia: *Victoria and I are hitting a club tonight.*

Amelia: *Join us.*

Evie: *Sorry. Can't.*

Amelia: *Mom?*

Evie: *No.*

Amelia: *A date?*

A door slams and I startle. Dylan exits our motel room. He's wearing a white shirt, open a few buttons and charcoal dress trousers. He's a panty melter for sure and I bite my lip.

Evie: *Nope. I've fighting off a cold.*

Amelia: *You need anything?*

He moves toward me like a guy appearing out of a mirage in a desert in a cheesy movie. Inside my ribcage my heart rattles about and my knees go a little weak.

"Happy?" He asks.

"You're super hot when you're pumped, Rocky."

I text back while I'm still able to feel my fingers.

Evie: *Thanks for the offer but I'm good.*

Amelia: *Change your mind and we can drop it off on the way out.*

Evie: *TY but no TY. Xo.*

Amelia: *Xo.*

"I'm ready for the game, Lucky Charm," Dylan says, our ride share pulling up into the parking lot and he opens the door for me.

"Good," I take his arm and step inside. "You'll get it done tonight."

"I'm feeling it, baby. We might not even need your empathic powers, tonight," He says. "I predict the McAlister mojo is back."

But twenty hours later Dylan's hopes and dreams are ambushed by darkness tearing through him like a hollow point bullet. He loses again and swims in sadness and regret. We collapse into bed, no sex this time. He stares up at the ceiling, and I soothe his bare arm, shoulder to elbow and circle back again. "Sleep. Tomorrow's another day."

"You're young. Your life lies ahead, waiting for you to enjoy it. Time's running out for me."

"It's just a bad turn," I say. "A crappy detour."

"What if it's not? What if this is just the new normal? I'm the king of reinvention but even kings can hit a limit on heartache. Even kings abdicate." He rolls away from me.

I fall into a fitful sleep dreaming of boys lying broken in the snow, birds circling a country field, cawing as they wing their way toward the horizon.

A large one swoops down, sinks its sharp talons into my shoulders, and lifts me in the air. I pinwheel my arms trying to get out from under its black wings but no matter how much I struggle, the damn bird is taking me with him, winging its way through gaps in the clouds.

The ground lies thousands of feet below. Our car that we ran over the Wolfe brothers with is a speck, and I scream.

The bird screeches and releases me. I drop like a stone, the earth coming up below me fast. Too fast, and I slam my eyes shut bracing for the impact.

I wake up in a sweat, the morning sun filtering into the room and Dylan already seated in a chair at the little desk, hunched over his phone. "What are you doing?" I ask.

"I booked a game in Dallas for tonight."

I run a hand through my hair. "You're not taking any time off?"

"Dallas is home turf. Friendly. Buy in isn't bad. You don't have to come if you don't want to. I've got to be at the airport in three hours. I'll book a flight for you back to Chicago." He looks at me, sadness drawing lines in his face. "I'll miss you but I can't let you do this with me forever. It's not right. It's not fair."

"What day is it?"

"Friday," he says, and walks into the bathroom and turns on the shower.

The sun poking through the curtains warms the room but I shiver. It's a cold August day in Memphis, the kind of mean girl cold that doesn't care that it's not supposed to trespass into a warm, luscious southern summer.

Despair and grief are sneaky, malicious thieves, stealing a man's soul in bits and pieces. I fear they have latched onto Dylan the way that black bird latched onto me.

Maybe I should go home, let Dylan's darkness win the round. Mom's voice plays in my head, echoing from the day we ran into the Wolfe brothers: 'Evie, you can't heal everybody. You can't fix everything.'

I've learned over the years that she's right. But I've also learned there are some things I *can* fix. I was scared senseless the day of the accident and yet I crawled out of that damn car and stumbled past one broken boy on my way to the other. I stared down at Wyatt Wolfe lying twisted on the hard snow, not knowing if he was alive or dead. And I wondered—could I save Wyatt if I touched him?

I couldn't feel my hands or my feet. My breath was trapped in my throat, completely useless, so instead I gathered my courage. I knelt down next to him, placed my hand on the soft white divot of skin that lay between his neck and his chest, and I willed my life back into him.

I willed it so hard the warmth abandoned my body and practically bled into his. Paramedics hustled Wyatt into an ambulance and screeched away. I was pushed onto the sidelines and watched first responders hustle Easton Wolfe past me on a rattling gurney.

Mom went to prison for six months charged with reckless driving. Ruby and I went into foster care. My whole world turned upside down and yet I still wondered about the Wolfe brothers. I heard through whispers and school gossip that both boys survived. Easton suffered a badly broken arm, leg, and busted ribs. But Wyatt nearly died.

His organs ripped, bones smashed, his brain injured, he almost bled to death. A friend told me the Wolfe family moved to California to be close to a children's hospital. They pieced Wyatt back together surgery by surgery. Fragment by fragment. And he lived.

Perhaps it was coincidence, maybe fortune, even all the praying, but I wonder if I did something, no matter how small, that gave Wyatt just enough healing to stay alive. That boy did not deserve to die on that cold day just for crossing a damn road. And if I did help Wyatt heal -- I sure as hell am not ready to give up on Dylan McAlister.

An idea percolates in my brain. I follow Dylan into the bathroom, strip off my T-shirt and panties. I step in the shower at the same time he is stepping out, dripping wet, muscles tight, abs ripped. "No shower sex?"

"Not today," he says.

I run soap over my body and rinse off in record time, and step out of the shower. Dylan drags a towel over his hair, across his beautiful body, and wraps it around his waist. "Anyone ever tell you that you're a hot piece of stripper ass, McAlister?" I towel off, throw my clothes back on. I sit on the countertop.

"Sadly, you're the only one," he says, and grabs a tube from his toiletry bag. He squeezes a dollop of cream into his hands and rubs them briskly together.

"Let me do that." I place a hand on his.

He quirks a chestnut eyebrow. "Okay."

"Tell me." I scoop the cream from his palm and smooth it on the scruff of his beard. "What do you feel like when you suspect you're going to win the hand? When you're almost sure the other guy is bluffing?" I draw the cream down along his jaw onto that soft area under his chin.

"Relieved." The artery in his neck throbs under my touch.

"Before relief." I pick up his razor and run it under the faucet.

"Do you know what you're doing with that?" He quirks an eyebrow.

"Not really." I lean in closer. "Trust me?"

"You're one of the few people I do trust."

"Good." I concentrate and draw the razor up across the stubble on his cheeks, shaving in straight lines. A few careful swipes later and I haven't cut him or killed him. Progress.

"Maybe you'll be a barber when you grow up," he says.

"Nope. When you look across the table at your opponent, squaring off at the last person who stands between you and victory and something clicks inside you and you just know— you've got 'em." I run the blade under the water. "You know that moment?"

"Yes," he says, his eyes clouding over. "It's been a while, but I do."

"Tell me." I shake the water off the blade. "What's *that* feeling?"

"Calm," he says. "I feel calm."

"Chin up, please," I say.

He does.

I angle the blade on the upper part of his throat and continue shaving him. "When's the last time you felt calm?"

He knits his sexy eyebrows together. "Months ago."

"Where did calm go?"

"I don't know. It vanished." The big muscle in his jaw ticks. I nick him and he flinches.

"Crap. Sorry!" I wet a washcloth, blot the blood, then fold the cloth and blot off what remains of the soap on his face.

"We've gotta get to the airport, baby."

"We've got time." I seize his hand and place it on my throat. "Humor me. Close your eyes."

He arches his eyebrows but he closes his eyes.

"Tell me what you feel." Warmth courses through my body. My hands tingle.

"I smell the soap on your skin. You're making me hard, Evie. We don't have time for this right now."

"We have plenty of time." I'm dying to put my hands on him, not just to undress him or fuck him. I want to heal him. "Tell me what you *feel*, Dylan. Not what you're thinking."

"Fine." He sighs. "Your skin is soft."

"What else?"

He slides his fingers across my neck. "This vein pulses when you get wound up. It's sexy. I want to fuck you."

I catch my breath under his fingers. "Veins don't pulse. Arteries pulse."

"I watch veins pulse in the necks of people I play card games with." He opens his blue eyes and stares into mine. "It's a subtle tell."

"What else?" I ask.

He moves his hand and tugs strands of my hair. "The way your neck curves into your shoulder." He works his fingers lower, brushing them across my shoulder. "Your collarbone. It's elegant." He lowers his hand to my chest and the V between my legs grows wet. "The way your heart beats faster, harder, when I grow closer to your heart."

He slips his fingers inside my T-shirt and fondles my breast, tugging a nipple. His erection pushes against my leg – warm, throbbing, growing harder by the moment. "Dylan," I say. "Do you still want to fuck me?"

"Yes."

"Lose the towel."

He drops it with a flick of his wrist.

I take his hand and lead him from the bath to the bed. "Lie down," I say and strip off my clothes, tossing them. "On your back."

He does as I ask, his breath coming quicker, his dick growing thick in record time. He reaches for me but I pull back and shake my head. "Tell me details. What changed when you moved from my throat, when you moved your hand toward my chest."

"Your heartbeat increased. Your skin grew warmer. Your lips grew fuller. Biteable." His cock is swollen and hard, bobbing up toward his abdomen.

I caress the top of his hard dick, using his precum as lube. I circle his erection and slide my fist down his dick, crown to base then back up and repeat. "More."

"Evie," he groans. "This isn't fair."

"Life's not fair and yet we find ways to deal with that. Tell me more. Things you haven't told me before. Tell me details."

"Details? Things I haven't told you before? I've told you a lot."

"Something happening in the here and now. Something you feel."

"You have a scar. Right here," he says, reaching his hand an inch into my hairline. "I never noticed it before."

My heart bumps around awkwardly in my chest right before it plummets into my stomach.

'That's your scar from the accident.' Queasy says, wringing his hands. *'Think about all the panic attacks you had. Think about the anxiety you suffered. Don't go there.'*

My scar from the accident with the Wolfe boys is a centimeter within my hairline. I stroke his dick harder, his breath coming faster. My breath comes faster because I'm starting to panic. "Tell me about the scar. How do you think I got it?"

"Knowing you? Doing something fearless." He caresses it with his fingers. "Hiking the woods in the cold winter snow when you were a kid. You tripped and fell into a barbed wire fence. Or, something flew through the air and smashed into your head."

My sister Ruby's tablet flew through the air in the back-seat of Mom's shitty SUV and sliced into my forehead when we hit the Wolfe boys.

I freeze. I am blindsided. Smashed. Just like when those boys flew off our car. I can hear the tires screeching. I can hear the thuds in my head. I wince and glance down at my hands. They're trembling.

"Baby," Dylan says, pushing himself up, staring at me. "What's going on? Are you all right? Evie!"

"What?"

"Are you all right?" He seizes my hands. "Is it your empathic thing?"

"Not my empathic thing," I say, holding onto his hands like they are a lifeline, the irony not lost on me because I'm supposed to be *his* lifeline. I shake my head. "It's something else."

"Can I do something? Do you need me to do something?"

"Yes." I'm so close to helping him and yet I can't do it right now. I just can't go there. "You, Dylan. I need you inside me. Now."

And just like that we switch roles. Protector becomes protected. Wounded becomes healer. He folds me into his arms. He kisses me. He makes love to me slowly. Sweetly. When I orgasm I cry his name.

❧ 14 ❧

DALLAS

DALLAS

WE STEP OFF THE PLANE AT DALLAS FORT WORTH AIRPORT and follow the signs to Baggage Claim.

"You've been to Texas before?" Dylan asks.

"Never had the pleasure," I say.

"A virgin," he says.

"Hardly after what we did this morning."

He smiles and draws his hand down my neck, down my back, heat blossoms on my face. "Welcome to the Lone Star State."

"Sadly, the Lone Star State's seen far better than me. I feel like something the dog rolled in." I pause in front of the Ladies Room. "Give me a moment."

"Take two." He leans back against the wall, and checks his phone.

I use the facilities, stand in front of the mirror, run a hand through my hair that feels heavy and stifling hot on the back of my neck even though the air conditioning is blasting.

I've been gone a week. I'm lying to my friends and my employer. I'm not making any money. We agreed to one last game and then he puts me on a plane back to Chicago. I'll be home tomorrow night. I don't know if I should be celebrating or if I should buy a beer and cry into it.

I'm acutely aware I signed up for this gig of my own accord. I've got some savings stashed away in an account that will cover a few month of bills. But the biggest bill, the one that needs to be paid the first, is Mom's invoice from the Institute. *Tick-tock.* The clock counts down and I'm dangling from the pendulum swinging back and forth between my desire to spend time with Dylan and my need to make enough to keep Mom and Ruby and me above water.

I drag a brush through my hair, twist my locks into a loose bun, and secure it with a pretty clip. I snag a lip gloss from my purse, apply a fresh coat, and check my reflection in the bathroom mirror. Not horrible. I wet a paper towel with cool water and press it against my face, my neck, my chest. I thought Chicago was hot in the summer. Texas heat kicks sand in Chicago heat's face.

Thank God this is just another game and I don't have to impress anyone. I'm here for Dylan. The game's tonight and part of tomorrow. No matter what happens I go home tomorrow night with a clear conscience and a heavy heart. Mom needs healing, Ruby needs babysitting, and my needs do not come first.

I swipe my phone off airplane mode and *ping-ping-ping* am inundated with texts.

Amelia: *Where are you?*

I text back with the truth for a change.

Evie: Dallas.

Amelia: WTF are you doing in Dallas?

Evie: Explain later.

Amelia: I'm worried about you.

Evie: Don't. I've got this.

Evie: I mean -- I think I've got this.

Amelia: You need to tell me what's going on.

Evie: Sure.

Evie: I'll explain everything when I get home. I'm on a tear.

Amelia: A tear?

Evie: Figuring out a puzzle.

Amelia: OK?

Amelia: You can always run stuff by me, you know. I'm happy to help.

Amelia: I'll water your plants.

Amelia: Make sure your Fan isn't walking around naked in your apartment while you're OOT.

Amelia: Playing with your underwear.

I shiver.

Evie: TY for the lovely visual.

Evie: No worries I'll be back tomorrow night late.

Amelia: K. Let me know if anything changes.

Amelia: I'm a little worried about you.

Evie: Will do.

Amelia: Promise.

Evie: Promise.

I check more texts.

Madame M: As much as I like you, Evelyn -- you are replaceable.

Madame M: Just tell me if you don't want to work at Ma Maison.

I sigh.

Evie: LOVE working for Ma Maison.

Evie: Finishing up a personal issue. Sorry. Back soon. Promise.

Madame M: Don't disappoint me.

I scroll.

Ruby: In a pinch. Send $ please. I'll pay it back.

Ruby: Seriously -- need your help.

Crap! What's going on now?

Evie: How much?

Evie: What's going on?

Ruby: Some crazy guy.

Evie: Crazy BF guy?

Evie: Crazy meth head Joe?

Ruby: I won't put up with the kind of stuff like Mom did.

Ruby: I've got to get out.

I frown.

Evie: OK.

Evie: You can't do what Mom did — right?

Ruby: No! This is a once in a lifetime problem. Swear.

I roll my eyes.

Evie: Except this is the third time.

Ruby: Talk later. 'K?

Ruby: Paypal me a thousand.

Ruby: TY!

I log in at Paypal, check my credit, and hit 'Send.' I scroll to the next text.

Mom: Ruby's trying to scam money off me.

Mom: She'll ask you next. Tell her 'No.'

Mom: I have ESP about this shit. Something's hinky. Say 'No.'

Crap.

Mom: I miss you.

Mom: When are you coming to visit me?

Mom: I miss the old days.

Evie: Miss you too, Mom.

Evie: We'll talk in next couple. 'K?

Mom: Love you, daughter.

Evie: Love you back.

And in less than a minute my shoulders have knitted to my ears. I mute my phone, stuff it in my purse, and exit the bathroom. I'll be damned if I'm going to let family drama cut into whatever time I have left with Dylan. My sexy player's leaning against the wall, looking Texas boy next door handsome in jeans and cowboy boots, his casual shirt open a few buttons. My pulse picks up. "Hey, hot cowboy," I say walking toward him.

"Everything okay?" he asks as we make our way through crowded airport corridors.

"Another day, another drama."

"Anything important?"

I shake my head. "Family stuff."

"Know that one well." He's not meeting my eye. The springs are already pre-loading within him, coiling tight.

"You're doing it again," I say.

"Over-thinking?" he asks.

I nod.

"The Dallas game is my opportunity to win back my money. Redeem my pride. Be my Lucky Charm tonight?"

"Yes," I say, trying to keep my heart in check because I can't play this part forever. Being with him forever, for real, just isn't on the table. "I'll be your Lucky Charm tonight. But you've got to chill out. Get grounded. Do the things we talked about."

"Meditate before I hit the game. Center. Get grounded. I'll do it." He pulls me tight to him and kisses me. "I'll do whatever you say, Evie. I'm crazy for you."

My resolve to leave weakens. This man. This delicious man. "Ditto."

But the clock winds down and fear, my old friend, bubbles up. I'm hitting this game to support him and then I'm going home. No more random motel rooms. No more games. No more hot sex with my hot player. I lived without him before. I'll build a damn wall and do it again.

We wait in Baggage Claim for the carousel to dump off our luggage, his possessive, muscular arm draped over my shoulders. I text back and forth with Mom about what she thinks is going on with Ruby – when I sense someone's eyes boring into me. A taller, ruddier, harsher version of Dylan, ambles toward us checking me out.

"Dylan," he says.

My player swivels, and startles. "Patrick? How did you —"

"You told the human loud speaker." Patrick hesitates then walks the rest of the way toward us, stopping short. They regard each other awkwardly. No shaking of hands, no hugging.

"Of course, I told mom," Dylan says. "Patrick -- meet Evie Berlinger. Patrick's my older brother."

"Your only brother," he says, reaching his hand out to me. "Any friend of Dylan's is a friend of mine, Evie."

"Evelyn," I say as we shake.

"Glad to see Dylan's got a girlfriend," Patrick says.

"Me too." Dylan keeps his arm on lock down around my shoulders. "I told Mom to keep my visit quiet. Quick trip and all. Not a ton of time for family stuff."

"You need to re-think that," Patrick says. "Shit's going down."

Dylan frowns. "Mom didn't mention anything."

"She doesn't want to worry you. She wears her poker face with you because you're her baby."

"What now?" My bag tumbles down the baggage chute and Dylan reaches for it, hoisting it onto the tile floor with a thud. "More bad test results?"

"You could say that," Patrick says.

"I thought Mom's thing was under control," Dylan says. "Handled."

"The doctors told her that. But they don't know everything."

Dylan grabs his suitcase from the carousel and sets it on the tiled floor. "We good?"

"One more," I say.

"How bad is it, Patrick? This is a short trip, but I'll make time--"

"Her breast cancer's back," Patrick says.

"Crap." The color drains from Dylan's face. He sways and I grab onto him, my fingers blanching on his arm. I've gotten into the habit of keeping this man standing and that's not changing today.

Patrick hoists my bag off the carousel and places it on the floor.

"Thanks," I say.

"No problem."

"What now?" Dylan shakes his head in disbelief.

"Surgery. After that they run the lab results and figure out what comes next."

"When?" Dylan asks his face stricken.

"Monday," Patrick says.

"Another lumpectomy?"

"Double mastectomy. They're not messing around this time."

My beautiful player's resolve crumbles in front of me like stale cake left out on a plate for too long. "I'll cancel the game."

"Good," Patrick says. "That's for the best. She wants to be with family this weekend. There's the church event, and she'll go, put on her game face, but she's not telling a lot of people."

My stomach plummets and I make a snap decision. "I'm already here at the airport. I'll book a flight back to Chicago."

"No," Dylan says, a hand pinching that small space between his brows.

Patrick nods at me as if we are suddenly in an unspoken partnership. Collusion. "I'm getting the car. I'll be out front in ten minutes." He grasps Dylan's suitcase, rolling it behind him. "Whatever you decide -- nice meeting you, Evelyn." He leaves through the exit doors at the same time the heat from summer in Texas bullies its way inside the cool, air-conditioned baggage claim.

"Shit," Dylan says, running a hand through his hair.

I stare up at my beautiful player. "You need to be with your mom. You need to hang out with family. The last thing you need is me here."

"That's not true." He shakes his head. "I need you here, Evie," he says, whisking my suitcase away with one hand, placing his other on my arm. He hustles me away from the carousel, away from the thinning crowd of passengers to a side wall.

"I'll be in the way."

"Is this your empathy talking?" He drapes both arms over my shoulders, leans me back against the wall, boxing me in.

"No. It's my practicality." I twist a lock of hair around my fingers, pulling it taut, trying to think this thing through.

"Your practicality doesn't get to tell me what or who I need. I need you."

"This is so intimate. It's your family. They're not going to want a newcomer in their midst during a tough time and I don't blame them."

"You calm me. You center me. Stay the weekend," he says prying open my fingers open, my hair falling. "Just a few more days. Stay the weekend and then I'll get you on a plane back to Chicago before Madame Marchand sends out her storm troopers and has me arrested."

"Why do you say that?"

"She figured out what your 'personal problem' was. Why you're 'calling in sick'," he makes finger quotes in the air. "She's been texting me since we landed in Dallas."

"Shit. I'm sorry. She's so smart."

"She's not going to can you for one more weekend. Besides, my mom will love you. I want you to meet her. Actually, I need you to meet her."

"Think about what you're saying."

"I know what I'm saying. Everyone will rally around Mom. Patrick's wife will be there for him. Even though most of them won't know about her surgery – the congregation will be there for Dad. Who's going to be there for me? Mom normally does that, but I can't really ask her to do that right now."

My heart travels full circle and aches for him.

"Who's going to be there for me, Evie?"

"Everyone, Dylan." I blink back tears, unsure if they're mine or his. "Who wouldn't want to be there for you?"

"You mean -- who will be there for me because of the come to Jesus money? There's an awful lot of power and prestige partnering up with a famous preacher's prodigal son."

Crap, he's right. Who *really* will be there for Dylan because he's lovely and amazing versus who will want to be with him because of God's dazzling dollars?

"I told you the pretty story, not the shitty story."

"What's the shitty story?" I ask.

"I'm the black sheep of the family," he says. "I didn't fall in Dad's footsteps. Didn't take on the family business. I took the love of the game we played around a kitchen table to the next level and when my marriage tanked, I left town."

Out of nowhere anger sparks like a brush fire in my chest. It starts small, burns faster, hotter, quickly out of control. It's Dylan's rage. It's spitting lava, a volcano threatening to erupt. Its tentacles root deep down in this man but its branches are stuck in his throat in the form of words that need to be spoken. Words that must be spoken or screamed out loud.

"Home was stifling me. Home was killing me. But I tried," he says, breaking away from me, pacing back and forth like a fighter gearing up for the big match in the ring. "I tried, I gave it my all, but then the shit hit the fan and I blew out of town, left the church. And now I find that there are only two places -- make that three -- that I call home anymore."

"What's that?" I ask.

"A poker game. Hanging with Mom. And being with you. Home is three things and right now, two are dying."

The cold wind blows through Dylan's life and I shiver. Can I help him? Can I save him? "You don't know that. Not about your mom. Not about the game."

"What about you, Evie?" He trains those blue eyes on me.

"I came here for you, Dylan," I say. "I'm just here for you."

"Then stay the weekend."

"Yes." I don't even draw a breath. "Absolutely yes."

✦ 15 ✦

GOD'S MONEY

GOD'S MONEY

I SIT IN THE BACK SEAT OF PATRICK'S ENORMOUS, RED, shiny pick-up truck as we blow past the Lighthouse Cathedral on the way to the family's spread. The cathedral is Je-frick-ing-enormous, bright, and shiny under cobalt blue Texas skies surrounded by black topped parking lots that take up more real estate than the ones surrounding football stadiums. If I were God, I'd dress up in my finest suit, slick back my hair, and shave twice before I walked into this place – it's intimidating.

I text Amelia.

Evie: *Plans changed. I'm staying through Sunday. Medical emergency.*

Amelia: *You okay?*

Evie: Yes. Not me.

                                       Amelia: Good.

Evie: If you wouldn't mind, could you check my place?

                    Amelia: No problem. I'll take Victoria with me in case creepy stalker Fan is there.

Evie: Don't say that.

Evie: Take a guy.

Evie: A big guy. You've got a set of keys, right?

                         Amelia: I think you gave them to me a while back.

Evie: There's an extra mailbox key hanging on a hook next to the front door. It's blue.

Evie: Check the box okay.

Evie: I get this weird feeling that something's not right.

                           Amelia: I'm sure everything's fine.

Evie: Let me know.

                           Amelia: Soon as I swing by.

THE MCALISTER HOME'S A FEW MILES DOWN THE ROAD from the church. We stop at a gated community guardhouse for the few seconds it takes a guard to salute Patrick and wave us through. We motor past gated estates with expansive lawns, not that many trees, each lot situated on twenty or so acres circling around Lake Grapevine.

The guys exchange measured pleasantries but the vibes traveling through the air aren't all that friendly. Patrick pulls into the driveway of a ranch style estate, punches in a code on a security box and waits as the gates open, driving inside. A large house is the hub with an attached five car garage, and four cabins scattered on the periphery.

"It looks the same," Dylan says, opening the passenger, stepping out and holding his hand out to me, helping me step down from the truck.

"Not much has changed," Patrick says.

"Fresh coat of paint. The house is yellow now, not white," Dylan says.

"Mom wanted something bright and cheerful after her last bout with cancer. You haven't been back since then?"

"Of course, I've been back since then," Dylan says. "I arrived at night. When you weren't here."

"Right," Patrick says. He lifts our suitcases from the truck bed onto the pavement and they split up the bags wheeling them up the driveway.

I accompany them into the main house expecting marble floors, gilded mirrors, and giant statues of Jesus. Instead there are honey colored hardwood floors, framed photos on the walls of laughing, smiling kids of all colors.

A thin sixty-something year old woman with sunshine yellow Doris Day hair moves into the kitchen's entrance, sees Dylan, and stops dead in her tracks. She squeals in excitement like a teenage girl, her hands flying to her face. "My baby's home!"

"Mom," Dylan says, dropping the bags, walking the few yards toward her, pulling into a careful hug.

"I'm not china." she says and smacks his arm. "Give me a real hug."

His arms circle her waist more securely. She stands on tiptoes, planting a kiss on his cheek, tearing up.

It's love I see around me. Love and warmth. An older man who could be a shorter, silver haired version of Dylan walks down the stairs toward me: his dad. There's no judgment in his eyes, simply curiosity. "Welcome," he says, extending a hand. "I'm Pastor -- "

"Dad," Dylan says. "Meet my girlfriend, Evie Berlinger."

"Honored to meet you, sir," I say as he grips my hand so hard I fear it might fall off. "Dylan's said so many nice things about you."

"Apparently, you're a miracle worker because he talks to you," he says. "How'd you get him to do that? I've been trying to get him to talk to me for thirty-eight years."

"Maybe he doesn't talk to you, Bill," Dylan's mom says, "because you're always lecturing him. Hi, Evie. I'm Rosemary, Dylan's mom."

"Mom! Give me a half second to make the introductions, please."

"Lovely to meet you, Mrs. McAlister," I say.

"Call me Rosemary. Come with me," she motions. "We'll let the boys catch up on boring guy stuff. Besides it's cocktail hour somewhere and I need a drink. I bet you could use one too after being stuffed in that airplane for -- where were you flying from?"

"Memphis."

She grabs my hand and leads me into the kitchen.

Bill frowns. "Are cocktails prudent Rosemary? You know what the doctors said --"

"Screw the doctors," she says as I follow behind her. "I'm having fun before the cancer games start up again."

"IT'S GORGEOUS HERE," I SAY. "IS THIS WHERE DYLAN grew up?"

Rosemary and I are sitting next to each other at an intricately carved Spanish dining room table in the kitchen. The French doors are open onto a terracotta tiled back veranda. Flowered vines twirl around columns bolstering the portico. Potted herbs: basil, sage, oregano smell delicious.

Rosemary snaps open an old-fashioned silk fan and waves it in front of her face. "This house? Oh, no, honey. This is the house that God's money bought."

A Latina maid dressed in jeans and a T-shirt sets stainless steel bowls on the patio. Three dogs abandon the guys lounging around the swimming pool and race toward the food, gobbling it down like they haven't eaten in days. The green lawn is deep and ends abruptly where it drops off into Lake Grapevine. A boathouse is tucked in a far corner of the property. Crickets croak as the sun sets in a hallelujah chorus of reds, oranges, yellows, and purples.

"We lived in an 1100 square-foot yellow wood-framed home in a poor part of Dallas for the first seven years of Dylan's life," she says. "Life wasn't always green lawns, margaritas, and French manicures."

She's so down to earth it's impossible not to like her. "What was that like?" I ask.

"Long hours for Bill in seminary. Even longer hours ministering at our first church. There was nothing fancy about that parish, the parishioners, or us for that matter. I cut coupons and we ate chicken casseroles. I have recipes for twenty different kinds stuffed in a box somewhere."

"I loved the one with the taco chips on top." Dylan peers in at us from the portico, and tips back a beer. "How's it going?"

"Fine, Dylan. No need to hover. I'll keep Evie safe."

"I'm not hovering." He makes his way to the fridge. "Did Maria make her famous guac?"

"Is it Friday?" his mom asks. "Third rack down. Bring us some and the home made chips while you're at it."

Dylan sets a tray of food on our table. "Holler if you need anything," he says and heads back out to the pool carrying his own stash.

"You like him, don't you?" Rosemary asks.

"Guilty."

"What do you like about him?"

"His honesty. The fact that he works so hard at everything he does. His sense of humor. His kindness. He's so real, so down to earth."

"Hallelujah." She lifts her glass in the air and I take that as a prompt to lift mine. "A toast."

"A toast?"

"Here's to someone finally liking Dylan for who he really is."

We toast and toss back our drinks.

"Dylan needs someone to like him just for him." Rosemary sighs and pushes herself up from the table. It's then I see the tiredness wearing on her. She takes a bit longer to walk to the oven and open it, the smell of comfort food wafting through the kitchen.

"Can I help?"

"Casseroles are almost done, honey. I'm making one for tonight and three for the potluck tomorrow. I'm not going to do the vegetables until tomorrow 'cause they'll just get soggy if I make them too early."

Amelia's words echo in my brain, 'Tell his mother you love anything she cooks.'

"I bet your cooking is great," I say.

"My cooking sucks. Tell me about your upbringing. Where'd you grow up?"

"Wisconsin. Illinois. Iowa for a short stint. We moved a lot."

"Military brat?"

"Nope. Mom, my sister Ruby and I bounced around a bit. The houses were small. The apartments dingy. Not very many chicken casseroles."

"Sounds interesting." She removes the baking dishes from the oven with fat potholders and places them on racks on the large stove. "Was there love?"

"Yes. I just never knew how it would present itself."

"Did your parents have a drug problem?"

"Mental health."

Rosemary dips a tablespoon into the casserole, scoops out two generous helpings and *clack-clacks* them onto plates. "That's tough, honey," she says. "Look, I know coming here is a change in Dylan's plans. Patrick intercepted you at the airport and laid some guilt trip on him. I wish I could tell you I wasn't happy to see him, but honestly, I am."

"He talks about you a lot."

"I wish he visited more but he's still uncomfortable and I don't blame him. Do you know what's going on with him, Evie? He doesn't share all that much with me. If I poke the bear he'll go into his cave and hibernate. Then I don't talk to him for a month."

"He's definitely going through something. I don't want to break his confidence, but if you ask him directly, I'm sure he'll tell you.

"Do you think he'll figure it out?"

A rush of sadness and raw need hit me like I've been punched in the stomach. Rosemary McAlister needs to make sure everything's going to be all right.

"I think so. I'm doing my best to help anyway I can. I'd never bet against Dylan McAlister figuring things out."

"Good. Keep helping him, Evie. He needs no bullshit people in his life. Did he tell you about his ex? Dixie?"

"A little."

"What a fucking disaster she was. A gold digger with dollar signs popping out of her blue contact-tinted eyes."

I cough, nearly choking on my chip.

"Oops, did I say the F word? My husband hates when I swear. But he's not here, is he?" She sets two small plates of casserole on the table and sits back down. "I don't know how much longer I get to be here. I don't know how much longer I'll be around to make things right."

"Mrs. McAlister ..." My phone pings repeatedly.

"Dotting my I's and crossing my T's, honey. You take that," she says. "Maria! Freshen up the cottage for Dylan and his girlfriend."

I walk onto the patio, pluck my phone from my purse, and read my texts.

Madame: *Call me. Now.*

I dial her number and she picks up.

"I don't even have the words to tell you how angry I am," she says.

I walk away from the house onto the lawn. "I'm sorry."

"You're literally taking money out of Ma Maison's pocket," she says. "Give me one reason why I shouldn't fire you."

Damn. "I'll never do this again. I promise. This is a one time thing."

"Oh, please, Evelyn," she says. "I wasn't born yesterday. Once a thief always a thief."

"I'm so sorry. How can I make it up to you? What can I do to make this better? Just tell me and I will do it."

"Prove you still want this job. Prove you still want to work for Ma Maison."

"I'll be home in a few days. Book a client, keep my fee. I'll do a freebie. I won't take a dime. Will that make you happy?"

"It's not about my happiness, Evelyn. It's about boundaries. It's about knowing your place. Clients come to Ma Maison because of our reputation. We vet clients, assign them to the escort we think would be the best match. We help you, but we do not work for you. You work for Ma Maison. And if you stop abiding by our rules, you are free to find other employment."

"Fine." I grit my teeth. "I'll do it. Book it. Tell me where and when."

"It's already booked. The client's in Texas. Dallas actually. Considering you're in Dallas I thought this was meant to be."

"When?"

"Tomorrow night. A wedding. A new client wants a date for a wedding."

How am I going to get away from Dylan? "He can't go stag?"

"Does it concern you why he wants to drop five thousand on a date that lasts six hours?"

"Where and when?"

"The Sycamore Pines Country Club. He passed background checks. You'll meet him at the club. 6 p.m. It's a society event. Wear something upscale. Conservative cocktail attire. I'm thinking you packed that for your road trip with Dylan McAlister, who I'd love to throttle by the way."

"Leave Dylan out of this."

"That's difficult, Evelyn."

"It was my decision to travel with him."

"It was a bad decision."

"It was the best decision of my life. I'd do it again in a heartbeat."

She hangs up.

How in the hell am I going to explain to Dylan that I'm leaving? I'll just tell him I need a few hours away. That I need a few hours to talk privately with Mom. Facetime with her.

A text comes in from Amelia.

Amelia: All's cool with your place.

Amelia: I'm watering the plant in your kitchen.

Evie: Great.

Evie: Hey, can you do me a favor? Text me tomorrow around 5:30.

Evie: Need an excuse to get out of something.

Amelia: Sure thing.

Amelia: By the way you got a letter.

Evie: My name typed. No return address?

Amelia: Yes.

Evie: Open it.

Amelia. K.

Amelia: Another letter from Fan.

My stomach flip-flops.

Evie: Send pictures please.

Amelia: K.

I look at the guys sitting around the pool. Dylan's in the shallow end tossing tennis balls, the dogs paddling to fetch them. His Dad's leaning back in his chair sipping from a long-neck beer and talking about how church needs to stay off the political bandwagon and stick with Jesus's original message about ministering to people. Patrick's sitting next to Pastor McAlister hanging on his every word.

The photos arrive thirty seconds later.

Dear Evelyn,

I hope you got my first letter. Not everyone checks their mailbox anymore.

I've thought about this for a while now. I've run it past a few people. Smart, educated people. They say it's healthy to get things out in the open. Properly communicated feelings do not percolate or fester. They do not become a problem. Even though I've decided to share with you how I feel, I have so many feelings that I don't know where to begin. So, I'll start with the obvious.

Affection.

You're easy to like, Evelyn. I love your smile. I've always loved your smile. Remember when your softball team won that game against the Southside Tigers a month ago? There was a photo on Instagram of your team celebrating. In one photo your head was tilted to the side and I spied a few freckles across the bridge of your nose, spreading onto the apples of your cheeks.

That picture's so sweet.

You weren't wearing any makeup. You looked so innocent. You could be a thirteen-year-old girl.

That's all for now, really. Hope everything's okay by you.

By the way, I haven't seen you in over a week. Don't worry, I'll keep an eye on your place. I don't want anyone messing with my favorite person.

Best,
　　Your Fan

A shiver runs up my spine. I text Amelia.

Evie: *You took someone with you to my place – right?*

　　　　　　　　　　　　　　Amelia: *No.*

Evie: *R U still there?*

　　　　　　　　　　　　　　Amelia: *Yes.*

Evie: *Get out.*

Evie: *Get out now.*

16

MAGICAL THINKING

MAGICAL THINKING

THE COTTAGE IS PRIVATE, AT THE END OF THE PROPERTY just a few yards from the lake, which is tranquil at night. Dylan's sitting quiet in the corner, his eyes closed. He's finally meditating and I'm not going to interrupt and tell him about creepy Fan. I read the letter three times and each pass it feels a little less weird. It's probably nothing.

His eyes blink open and for a change he looks relaxed. "How do you feel?" I ask.

"Good. Calm, centered. I can think more clearly."

"Excellent," I say.

"I have a few questions."

"Hit me."

"Do I have to empty my mind completely when I meditate? Or can I imagine kissing you, then sinking my cock into your sweet, wet pussy?"

I bite back a smile. "The goal is to release all thoughts. Concentrate on one word that brings you back to peace."

"What if my word is 'Evie's sweet wet pussy?'"

"That's four words. Besides, that's not the best way to empty your dirty mind of dirty thoughts."

"I've got a way. Come here," he says, pulls me to him, pulls me on top of him and kisses me thoroughly, teeth scraping my lower lip, tongue exploring my mouth. He tangles his hands through my hair, pulls back a little and tugs on one long lock. "Mom likes you."

"I like your Mom," I say.

"I like you in a different way than Mom," he says, his erection growing in record time, pressing insistently against my pelvis and the V between my legs throbs. He pulls my top over my head and tosses it onto the braided rug on the white wooden floor.

"I hope so," I say, and tug the zipper down his jeans, his erection springing free. We make love like furtive teenagers, quietly, passionately, trying not to wake the folks in the main house a few hundred yards away. I come in soft moans and he follows shortly thereafter. We lie spent and sweaty, limbs entangled on the bed in his parents' bungalow.

"Turns out coming home wasn't all that bad after all," he says. "Turns out coming home is pretty sweet with you here. You might be a miracle worker, Evie."

———

THE SATURDAY SUMMER POTLUCK AT LIGHTHOUSE Cathedral has been on the calendar for months.

Dylan plunks our beers down on a picnic table in the middle of the tree-lined park between Lighthouse Cathedral and a modern building with 'Prayer Hall' painted in giant metallic gold letters on the side. "You sit here. With Mom," he says. "I'll get us plates from the buffet table. Anything special you want, Evie?"

"You pick," I say.

"Mom, you want anything?" he asks.

"Danica already took my order," she says.

Ten minutes pass. Rosemary's surrounded by friends and parishioners hanging on her every word. I doubt any of them knows her surgery's coming up in a few days, and she's not the kind of person to play the sympathy card.

A short, pretty brunette wearing jeans, platform sandals, and a cotton floral print peasant shirt walks up to our table and drops off a plate of food. "Can I get you ladies refills on drinks?" she asks.

"We're good, Danica," Rosemary says, and holds out her hand.

Danica squeezes it tight.

"Thank you. Have you met Evelyn?"

"No," she says and extends a French manicured hand, diamond tennis bracelet sliding over her chunky gold watch. "Danica McAlister. Pleasure to meet you, Evelyn. If I knew Dylan was going to leave you here so long with the prayer ladies I would have prepared a plate for you too."

I get a sweet vibe from her. "Call me Evie."

"Evie it is. How long are you in town for?"

"Not very long."

"Danica!" Patrick calls from a dozen yards away on the opposite end of the park and beckons. He's surrounded by doughy middle-aged men who look like they were just carted in off the golf course.

She rolls her eyes. "The ball and chain beckons. Chat soon?"

"Yes."

She walks in Patrick's direction.

I crane my neck and see Dylan a dozen yards away holding two jumbo-sized paper plates heaped with food, talking with three guys his age. He meets my eyes and nods.

"I'm Becky Littlefield." A coiffed thirty-something woman with dragon red lips and fingernails plunks down opposite me at the table. "Pleased to meet you." She extends her hand and we shake.

"Evelyn," I say, and try not to cringe. Her acrylic nails press so hard into my palm I fear they're leaving indentations.

"Becky Littlefield of the North Dallas Littlefields," she says. "Not to be confused with the Houston Littlefields."

"Right." I pull my hand back, wondering if it needs triage.

"I took back my maiden name after I got divorced. It's so nice to see Dylan again. It's been too long. How'd you two meet?" She sips from her fruit-adorned red plastic cup.

"A set-up."

"A matchmaking service? I've been thinking about doing that too. Is that how Dylan finally got past the whole Dixie debacle?"

"I'll let Dylan tell that story." I sip from my beer.

"I don't know if he shared with you or not." She stares at Dylan and when he glances in our direction and waves, she says, "But the four of us hung out together during college summer breaks."

"The four of you?"

"Dixie, Dylan, Patrick and me."

"Oh." She hung out with Dylan's ex-wife? Awkward.

"We boated on Lake Grapevine. The McAlister brothers talked us girls into skinny dipping with them more than a few times. They're so handsome. A little wild for pastor's boys."

I glance at Dylan. He smiles at me and winks as if we have a secret. I guess we do. I doubt he's told anyone about how we really met.

"I got separated right around the time Patrick got

married," Becky says. She stares at Patrick who's standing next to Danica, her bejeweled hand resting on his arm. "Bummed I missed my window, but Danica's seems sweet, and she's from a good family, you know."

"I didn't."

"The Dixie thing. Don't believe every story you hear about how that went down." She picks at the potato salad on her plate. "In my humble opinion, I think everybody was a little to blame. Where are you from again? Obviously, not from around here."

"Chicago," I say and tip back a cold beer, staring pointedly at Dylan, wishing he would get his ass back here.

"Dixie had her eyes set on the McAlister boys since freshman year in college. She wanted Patrick but he wouldn't pay her the time of day. He wanted someone with a better pedigree."

"Pedigree?"

"Respectable parents. Breeding. Background. Dixie's parents were trailer trash. Patrick always planned on taking over the family business and he wanted a girl who came from a good family."

"Patrick's a pastor?"

"No, sugar."

"Isn't the family business..." I gaze up at the Je-normous cross on the lawn, "Lighthouse Cathedral?"

"Oh, Patrick's not interested in the preaching part," Becky says. "He's got an MBA. He wants to manage the money. He wanted to marry a girl who came from a good family because he knows how judgmental church people can be."

"Got it," I say, glancing around the crowd of at least a hundred people ranging from squidgy babies in bouncers to octogenarians in wheelchairs. The babies look the least judgmental.

"Are you and Dylan an item?"

"Yes, Evie and I are an item, Becky." As if on cue he hustles up and unloads the plates heaped with casserole and salads, fried chicken and biscuits. He takes a seat next to me. "Sorry! I got stuck in the deadly Texas triangle of former high school football friends one hasn't seen in forever."

"Nice to see you, Dylan," Becky says. "Can't blame a friend for asking. I didn't hear you were dating anyone special after, well, you know, your unfortunate breakup. I never forgave Dixie for that, just so you know who's side I'm on."

Well clearly she's on Dylan's side. As well as his front, back, center, and any other square inch of him that she can eye fuck right now while she leans across the table, touching her throat and batting her eyelashes.

"Evie and I also go way back," Dylan says, leaning in and kissing my cheek. "Right, honey?"

"Right."

"Evie says you all were set up."

"Yes. A mutual acquaintance. I spotted her and thought, 'That girl's special. She's got a look in her eyes.'" He squeezes my arm and grins.

"The look was a smudge of eyeliner and mascara," I say.

"And super cute on you. Technically, we didn't start dating until recently."

"I had a feeling it was recent," Becky says, a relieved look washing over her face. She scoops up her designer bag from the picnic table. "Gotta say hi to Patrick. Other folks. Great meeting you, Amy."

"Evie," I say.

"See you around Dylan." She walks away, then pauses. "I told you I got divorced, right?"

"Yes," he says.

I lean into him and whisper, "The hot stripper vibe is already working its magic back in your home town."

"I'm spanking you when we're back at the cottage," he says and we both cover giggles.

Saturday afternoon the McAlister family takes the boat out on Lake Grapevine. Patrick, Danica, and Dylan take turns water skiing. Rosemary hands me a wrapped sandwich from a cooler. Dylan climbs up the boat's steps, and grins as he deliberately shakes his wet head, spraying water in my direction.

"Stop!" I shake my finger at him.

"You ever water ski, Evie?" Reverend McAlister asks from behind the steering wheel.

"No."

"You'd love it," Danica says, tipping back a beer.

"I'll teach you how to water ski," Dylan says.

"I'll pass. I'm not the best swimmer in the world."

"Come on," Dylan says. "Live life!"

"She doesn't have to ski if she doesn't want to," Rosemary says, squeezing sun screen out of a tube onto her palm. "Stop being so pushy."

"We should get back in time for the reception tonight," Bill McAlister says and turns the boat around.

"I'm not going," Dylan says. "I have a game."

"I thought you canceled that," Patrick says.

"I told him not to," Rosemary says. "Stop being so bossy. I'm not going either."

"Do I have to go?" Danica asks.

"Yes," Patrick says.

"Do you have to meet with these people tonight, Bill?" Rosemary asks. "Why can't you do that tomorrow after services?"

"This has been on the schedule for months, Rosemary," he says. "The Bethany Synod elders flew in from Oklahoma. We need to hammer out the details for the convention next year."

"I don't know if I have 'next year'," she says. "I'd rather spend the rest of the day on the water with my family."

A hush falls, just the sound of the engine and the boat cutting through the water.

"You said you didn't want to talk about that this weekend," Bill says.

"I changed my mind." She juts her chin out defiantly. "If I don't say things now, when in the hell am I going to say them?"

Patrick and Danica gaze pointedly out across the water rushing by the motor boat's wake. Dylan eyes me, his board shorts wet, his legs already turning pink because they haven't seen sunshine in God knows how long.

"It's the elephant in the room," Rosemary says. "I'm having surgery in a few days. If we can't talk about our feelings now, when are we going to talk about them? Why don't we just get it all out the next couple of days? Let the shit fly. Let the love fly."

"Hear, hear," Danica says, grabbing another beer.

"Not a great idea, Mom." Patrick runs a hand through his hair.

"I love you, Mom," Dylan says. "I'm sorry I stayed away for so long."

"I love you too, Dylan," she says. "I forgive you."

"Jesus Christ," Patrick says. "Can we just go home?"

"That's the point, Patrick," Rosemary says. "That's what we're finally doing."

DANICA WALKS WITH ME FROM THE DOCK TO THE MAIN house. "I confess I've only met Dylan a few times," she says. "But this is the happiest I've ever seen him. I think you're good for him."

"Thank you."

"Welcome. Look, I know what happened between him and Patrick. A world of hurt feelings. But Patrick wasn't the only shithead responsible for that mess."

"Dylan?" I ask.

She shakes her head. "He handled it the best he could. Dixie was a shithead. She was mad at Dylan for not wanting to be a bigger part of Lighthouse, not taking a more substantial role. She walked out on him and slept with Patrick, who was drunk. Afterwards, he felt like an asshole but Dixie had already bragged to Dylan and the damage was done."

"Yikes," I say. "That explains some things."

"Patrick apologized to Dylan but that fell on deaf ears. What a mess. Possibly the biggest shithead in this whole mess was Lighthouse Cathedral. So many expectations. The bar is set so high that failure becomes more the norm than success." She pauses before walking in the main house. "You coming inside?"

I look at my watch. I have to meet the Ma Maison client at Sycamore Springs Country Club in a few hours and there's something I need to finish with Dylan before I go. Just dotting my i's and crossing my t's. "Nope. I'm wiped from the day."

"Time out on the boat and the sunshine can do that to you."

"I think it was the Lighthouse picnic."

She frowns. "That too. Don't let these Lighthouse holier-than-thou assholes get to you, Evelyn. Trust me, someone's going to try. They did with me."

DYLAN LIES NAKED IN BED. HIS SKIN IS FLUSHED EITHER from too much sun out on the boat or because I'm straddling him, caressing his face, his shoulders, his chest, his stomach – basically everything on his glorious body except for his dick. His cock's rock hard from me brushing my wet pussy across his stomach. Yes, I'm turned on, but more importantly I'm determined to get to the bottom of his messed up core wound, and find the bitter belief that's shutting him down.

"Baby," he says, his breathing coming faster. "You're killing me."

"Me too. Remember a few days ago when you found the scar on my head when we were fooling around?"

"Yes."

"I think we were onto something. We were close to finding the thing that's zapping your mojo. You've got a game tonight. Want to try again? You know — before the game?"

"What do *you* want to do," he asks, eyes wide.

I know he wants me to let this go because right now he just wants to fuck me. That would be the easy thing. I've never really done this before, this sex and empathy and healing thing blended together. I might just make a big fat mess of this and then hopefully we'll both have a good laugh at my expense and I can live with that. What I can't live with is knowing I got this close and I gave up. That's not who I am.

"Mold your hand onto my skin. Mold your hand into the scar." I take his hand and place it on the scar on my head, an inch into my hairline. "Every scar has a story."

"Why are we doing this, again Evie? Are you sure we can't just have sex?"

"No. Trust me, Dylan. Close your eyes. Feel this scar, tell me its story, and then we can have sex."

He closes his eyes. "Scars happen after you've been sliced open. Injured. Suffered."

"Tell me more."

"Scars happen when the body tries to repair tissue because pain has torn into the body. The worst scars usually happen with the toughest injuries."

"Yes. What does my scar feel like?"

He crinkles his forehead. "It feels like it's pushing me out. Pushing my hand away. Something bad happened to you Evie."

"It did."

'Are you sure you want to do this?' Queasy asks, flip-flopping dramatically in my stomach.

'Keep going,' Hope says, throwing an encouraging fist punch, and I get a hit of adrenaline.

"Let's not talk about me right now." I still my hand on his chest. I close my eyes and silently count *three, two, one.* I move into the empathic layer within me. The outside world drifts away and I feel.

I simply feel.

Heaviness fills my chest. I wade into the ocean of Dylan's sorrow, the waters rising. The weight of the world wears on my shoulders and I am eighty-four years old, not twenty-four. His core wound is within me. It's furtive, panting, eyes darting, sneaky, staying one step ahead of me. But it's been stealing from him for a while now, and like any thief who hasn't been caught in a while, it's growing bloated from its undeserved, vampiric success.

I circle it, my hand skimming across Dylan's body as the predator twists inside him. It disappears behind a black veil of fear. Dare I go there? Dare I pull back the curtain? Who am I to confront Dylan's shitty belief? I'm no hero. I boast no supernatural abilities to lift myself up. I'm just a rental date who met him a few weeks ago wearing a borrowed dress.

But I'm also the girl who willed life back into Wyatt Wolfe. I'm the girl who puts others' needs first – my mom's, my sister's. I'm the girl who has to try. I need to identify these sensations. The heaviness, the drowning, feel familiar. And then it dawns on me that I've already been given the answer.

Guilt.

"I love you, Mom," Dylan said to his mother on the boat. "I'm sorry I stayed away for so long."

"I love you too, Dylan," she said. "I forgive you."

Dylan found out Dixie cheated with his brother and it wrecked him and he left. He bailed. He stayed away. He's felt guilty ever since. It's killing his mojo. But the funny thing is, that guilt's not going to make his mom better.

Losing his game, screwing up the life he built is not going to make his mom better. On the other hand, owning these feelings is a big first step toward healing Dylan, healing his relationship with his mother, and getting on with all the love that they share.

I open my eyes and stare into his. "You feel guilty," I say.

"About what?"

"When did you leave home?"

"When I found out about Dixie. Five years ago."

"You left to keep your sanity when your marriage fell apart. You left in anger."

"Yes."

"Now your mom's sick and you're blaming yourself. Magical thinking," I say. "We think we can control everything. We can't."

"But she *is* sick and I *did* leave."

My hand on his stomach starts sweating as that fucked up belief tries to wriggle away from me. I grit my teeth and hold onto that belief. I'm not letting this sucker go. "If your career crashes and burns, it justifies you returning to Texas and

Lighthouse Cathedral. In a strange way, it's doing you a favor, a service. It's making the decision for you."

"That can't be." He props himself up on his elbows, looking a little pissed.

"This life no longer suits you." I don't move my hand and yet I pull that angry predator out of Dylan inch by squirrely inch. "I get a feeling this life has never suited you. You know how on the boat today you mom forgave you for not coming home?"

"Yes."

"How did that make you feel?" I pull the guilt into my hand and I capture it. I can almost see it squirming in my palm all, slick and whiny and entitled. I close my fingers into a fist. What a fucking asshole his guilt is. He doesn't need this wound anymore. He needs to work on healing and get on with it.

"Sad."

"She forgave you," I say.

"I shouldn't have left her."

"Tell me that you could have stayed." I lean forward, run my other hand across his face, a finger across his full lips. I kiss him. This man – this delicious man. "Tell me you could stay after what happened with Dixie."

"You don't know the worst of it."

"I do, Dylan." I slide my hand over his hard dick and he moans. I straddle his thighs, circle his cock with my hand, and lightly run my fist up and down it. "Lighthouse might have a huge congregation, but at the end of the day it's a relatively small, close-knit community. People talk."

"Becky?"

I nod. "And others."

"Do you think I'm an asshole?"

"No. I think you are deserving. I think you are kind. I think you are a bright star on a dark winter night."

"Really?" His eyes are dark with lust and something else – I'm not sure what.

"Look, Dylan." I stop stroking his cock and move my core over his. I hold my closed fist in the air and open it.

"What?"

"Remember when you asked me to wish you good luck at the game in Chicago when we met?"

"I do."

"This is your guilt. Here. In my hand. It's no longer in you. We're letting it go. Releasing it to the wild where it can stalk about, grumble that no one understands it anymore. This guilt is no longer yours. Let's wish it good luck and kiss it goodbye."

"Really?"

"Really." I say a silent prayer.

'Dear God, take Dylan McAlister's guilt. He's carried it long enough. It's time for him to heal. Thank you. In the name of the Father, the Son, and the Holy Spirit.'

"What will I do without it?" he asks as I center my core over his beautiful cock and lower myself onto his hardness. He moans.

I lean forward and fuck him. "Positive things, Dylan. We can work on mantras. 'I am enough.' 'I am forgiven.' 'I am calm.' 'I am strength.' 'I am respect.' Say the words, Dylan. Say them as you fuck me."

He says them. "I am strength. I am calm." He turns me over. He's on top of me now, staring down into my eyes with a fierceness. "I am forgiven. I am enough," he says and thrusts into me harder.

"You are." I wrap my legs around his waist as he penetrates me deep and deeper. He says the words over and over as he fucks me and on the fourteenth or fortieth time, I know he believes them. There's something different in his touch, in the tone of his voice. It's clearer. "Evie. Evie!" He climaxes, groaning, chest slick with sweat.

He owns his pain instead of his pain owning him. I know in my bones, that bent, battered, Dylan has broken through.

My beautiful, broken man is finally healing.

17

PRODIGAL SON

PRODIGAL SON

I PICK THROUGH THE CLOTHES IN MY SUITCASE AND FIND A country club kind of dress that works for the wedding date with this Ma Maison client but would also fit in with Dylan's poker game.

I put on makeup in front of a mirror hanging over a hewn wooden desk in the living room and watch him out of the corner of my eye as he gets dressed, pulling on his pants, shrugging on a light cotton shirt. I don't think I'll ever get used to how handsome he is. My phone pings with an incoming text. Amelia messaged me right at the time we agreed on.

__Amelia:__ I'm fake texting you at the time you told me. Good luck.

I read her text, sigh theatrically, and frown. "Dang."
"Something wrong?" Dylan asks.

"My mom needs me." My nose is growing.

"She okay?"

"I think so." I walk up to him and button his shirt, making my way up his hard abdomen and sculpted chest. Deceit is not something I'm comfortable with. It's a shitty feeling and I promise to avoid it from here on out. "I've got a situation. I can meet you at the game later, but first I need to spend some quality time with Mom." God, I sound like a phony asshole.

"I thought your mom was in Wisconsin."

"She is. But she's wound up and I need to calm her down. Have a heart-to-heart. Facetime for a few hours. I'm going to go to a mall, grab something to eat. Go somewhere I can have private time."

"Malls aren't all that private."

"Malls are malls are malls. Generic. Mom doesn't know I'm on the road. She might have more anxiety if she knew I wasn't in Chicago."

"Okay, Lucky Charm," he says, and kisses me on the lips. "Do you want me to drop you somewhere?"

"Nah, I'll order a ride."

"I'll text you the address for the game. We can meet up later."

"Fair warning," I say. "Mom can talk for hours."

"No rush." He opens the door of the cottage and walks out, but pauses. "Baby?"

"Yes?"

"You're amazing. You heal me. Thank you."

I watch him leave and I blink back tears.

AND SO, AT THE END OF THE DAY, IT'S NOT A MISSION OF endurance as much as one of cutting the cord. The cord of guilt. Dylan doesn't belong in Texas anymore. Maybe at some point when he was a child, being molded by his parents, he belonged here. To a life of service. Duty to an institution. But Dylan's life veered left while his family's lives marched forward. Their separate paths didn't make them less of a family. It just made them diverse.

Dylan McAlister needs to play the game and he needs to do that well. He needs to travel from state to state. City to city. Stay up all night. Sleep all day when he needs or wants. Just because he's different from his family doesn't mean he's worth less. Dylan's worthy of love just like everyone else.

My driver messages that he'll be arriving in five minutes. As I head to the front door I see Dylan sitting in the kitchen with his mom. She's wearing a cotton shift with "Winter is coming and I can't wait!" on it. A globe lamp is glowing overhead, a moth beating against the kitchen screen.

"You always were my favorite, you know," his mom says, and shuffles a deck of cards on the table.

"No, I wasn't," he says. "Patrick was."

"Patrick likes to say he was. But you've always been my favorite, Dylan."

"Mom."

"I'm so glad you came home, honey." She pats the back of his hand. "But if you stay, I'll kick your ass."

"Really?"

"Really. You don't belong here anymore. I know it. You know it."

"What about..."

"Yeah, the cancer," Rosemary says. "Now that the ice is broken, you'll come back more often. We'll see each other more. And we'll figure that part out, moment by moment. Step by step."

"Okay." He sighs and shuffles the deck.

"I like Evie a lot," his mom says. "Do you think you found the right girl?"

Woah.

"Not for you to worry about, Mom." He cuts the stack. "High card wins."

"What are we betting on?" she asks.

"You decide."

"I win, Dylan, you go for broke on Evie. Don't play half-assed for her. Play smart. When the time is right, put all your money on the table. Don't lose her." She grabs his hand, squeezing it.

"I will, Mom. I will once you are squared away."

God, I hope she's squared away soon. *Wait-wait* – does this mean Dylan and I have a future together?

"I win, you don't wait for me." she says. "Dreams have a way of getting away from you if you let them sit by themselves for too long. People do that too."

The tears are coming and I can't screw up my wedding date by showing up with smeared makeup. I walk quietly past the kitchen, open the front door, and see my driver already waiting at the end of the long driveway.

———

THE DRIVER DROPS ME JUST INSIDE THE GATES AT SYCAMORE Springs Country Club. It's a three story L-shaped red brick building surrounded by sweeping manicured green lawns. A brook winds around the grounds, with small, picturesque walking bridges spanning its width.

A Rolls Royce is parked at the club's entrance, where a tuxedoed twenty-something groom is helping the beaming bride out of the back seat. Coiffed women in designer cocktail dresses and suited men make way for the newlyweds. There's a smattering of applause and a few chants of "Kiss the bride!" The cute couple look at each other, laugh, and oblige their fans.

"Evelyn." A meaty hand slides down my bare shoulder and I wince when it lands possessively at my elbow. "So glad you could make it." A shiver runs through me because I know this man's voice. It's Glenn, the Fast Food King. Dylan's poker rival. The portly, sweaty man with the skinny tongue who can't help but lick his lips when he sees a young, attractive woman. Even worse? He's doing it now.

It's all I can do not to make a run for it. I could bolt past the guard at the front gates and squeeze out. Oh man, fuck Madame Marchand for doing this to me. But leaving will just seal my fate. I'll definitely be out of a job. I won't be putting a dent in Ruby's tuition, let alone paying for Mom's medicals in a month from now. I need to bite the bullet and just get this done. "Glenn," I say, and force a smile. "What a nice surprise. How do you know the bride and groom?"

"Dallas Historical Society." He escorts me, one fat hand on the small of my back, inside the richly upholstered lobby. Beet red and gold foiled flecked wallpaper line the lodge; beet red like Glenn's corpulent cheeks. "I'm on the board with the groom's parents," he says. "Imagine my surprise when I contacted Ma Maison and found out you were in town. It almost seems like kismet, Evie."

"Evelyn," I say.

"Evie, Evelyn, Whatever. At five K for the evening at least I didn't call you late for dinner. No wonder McAlister walks around looking like the cat who ate the canary. No puns intended, darling. I'm sure the favor is reciprocal."

I throw up a little in my mouth as we make our way down the hall to the ballroom. The building's air conditioned and yet his palm pressed into the small of my back is slick and sweaty, just like his face. Tiny waves of nausea slop around inside me. I remind myself I don't have to let this guy kiss me, let alone sleep with me.

"What's my old pal, Dylan McAlister up to lately?" He squeezes my shoulder and slides his hand down my arm, his thick gold pinkie ring scraping my skin. He twines fat fingers between mine and I remind myself that for the five thousand dollars he's paying Ma Maison for tonight's date, he's allowed to hold my hand.

"Don't know, Glenn. You tell me." He hired me to be his wedding date. He's probably expecting more, but he's not entitled to more, and I will guarantee you he's not getting it. How bad can this be? How long can a wedding last? How long can I be nauseated and not throw up?

He stops at a small round table in the hallway and peers at the folded cards until he spots the one with his name on it. "Glenn Reynolds & Guest, Table 15. Oh, honey, they must have forgotten to put your name on it."

Just when I think it can't get worse it does.

"Amy?"

Aw crap, I remember the last women to call me "Amy." I turn and see Becky Littlefield, blood red fingernails matching her lips and her cocktail dress. Gold earrings, gold watch, gold bracelets. She matches perfectly with this country club's décor.

"Hi Becky," I say cheerfully, well aware Glenn is still clutching my hand.

"Where's Dylan?" she asks, blinking deer-caught-in-the-headlight eyes.

"Funny, I was just asking Evie the same question," Glenn says. He slides the table marker into his pants pocket and extends his hand. "Glenn Reynolds. Nice to meet you."

Becky yanks her hand back, her face turning in on itself like she just stepped into something foul the cat hacked up. "Glenn Reynolds from Dallas North High School?"

He grins. "I think we did go to D North together, darling. But from the looks of tonight, we've come a long way since then."

THE RECEPTION'S IN THE BALLROOM AND HISTORICAL Society connections or no, I'm thanking God we're seated at a table on the outskirts because Becky's on the opposite side of the room. Glenn doesn't drink when he plays poker but he's been pounding back the single malt scotch from the cocktail part of the evening to the speeches, which is where we are now.

"Have a little something to drink, sweetheart," he says, slurring into my ear, running his hand up and down my arm. "You're so uptight. You never seemed that uptight at the games. Did Church Boy McAlister do anything special to warm you up? I guarantee you I can do better than that loser." He wiggles his tongue in my ear and I lean away from him and glance at my watch.

Another hour drags by and I've successfully made it through the dancing and the bouquet and garter toss without heaving up the salmon salad or even going to the bathroom. I just know Becky will follow me in there and demand some kind of explanation.

"Sweetheart," Glenn says in a sing-song voice. "I didn't pay Maze-on five thousand for just any old wedding date, you know. I want the Dylan McAlister special. I want you to pull my zipper down, take my cock in your mouth. Make me a happy man, Evelyn. Daddy Glenn is such a good tipper."

Ugh. I push back from the table, "Excuse me," I say, smoothing my skirt and grabbing my clutch. "I'll be right back." I get all the way to the edge of the ballroom before Becky's up out of her chair, her round eyes focusing on me, looking like the suburban version of the girl in that spy movie who was dipped in gold. Jesus, how am I going to get through the rest of this evening?

I pick up my pace and exit the ballroom just in time to run right into someone else I don't want to be seeing tonight, or ever for that matter.

Patrick McAlister glares at me and I can practically see the steam puffing out of his nostrils. "You." He's not dressed for a wedding. He's wearing a polo shirt, khakis, and runners. He's got a bit of sunburn on his face or he's just wound up.

"What are you doing here?" I ask, my heart clattering off my ribs before it drops like a stone to my stomach. I don't really need to ask because I already know.

"You and I need to have a little talk." He takes me by the arm and hustles me down the hallway.

WE STAND OUTSIDE THE CLUB'S FRONT DOORS. "OF COURSE, Becky Littlefield called me. She of all people knows what's at stake," he says.

"You can think whatever you want, Patrick. I hate to be a bitch about this, but you and Becky aren't my concern. Dylan is."

"Wow, because you getting pawed in public by creepy Glenn Reynolds just screams how much you like my brother."

"He was not pawing me."

He holds out his phone and pulls up the photos. There's Glenn with his arm draped over my shoulders. There's Glenn, rubbing his hand up and down my arm. There's me watching the bride and groom's first dance while Glenn downs another Scotch and stares pointedly at my boobs, his snake tongue slipping between his thin lips.

"You think the prodigal son can return with his prostitute girlfriend and all will be wonderful?"

"Not a prostitute," I say. "Escort."

"Huge difference, Evelyn. You think the church is going to be down with that? We're such good Christians that we welcome the poor, the tired, the unwashed among us? I. Don't. Think. So."

"I don't care what Lighthouse thinks. I care about Dylan."

"Then you need to rethink what you're doing. Dylan's finally back home. He's here to see Mom. That's the story that will play out when people find out about Mom's cancer surgery. The last thing in the world any of us needs right now is the story about Dylan's girlfriend ho-ing around with some other guy, especially ho-ing around professionally for money."

"You're an asshole." I blink back tears.

"I'm entitled to be an asshole, Evelyn." He pulls out his phone. "This is my world. It's my life, not yours. These aren't your people. Not your flock. This isn't your safe haven. You need to let Dylan get his life back together. Because the only thing that you are in his life right now is a big. Fucking. Liability. I'll be CFO of Lighthouse in a few years. I'll be shepherding its image. I can't allow Dylan to fuck things up like the Dixie thing almost fucked it up."

"*You* slept with Dixie."

"She threw herself at me. It was a thing. It wasn't supposed to get out. Dylan had to pull a hissy fit, leave her, and abandon the whole fucking church. The gossip nearly burned the roof off this parish. I'll be inheriting the Lighthouse legacy, the empire. Not Dylan. That's in writing, signed, notarized, and resting in multiple safe deposit boxes at Dad's lawyer's offices."

A man pulls up in Patrick's cherry red truck, slips the engine in idle, and walks to the passenger side, pretending he's not paying attention.

"Dylan doesn't want what you want," I say, my voice hushed.

"Dylan wants money or he wouldn't continue to play the game. Do you have any idea how much money is in Lighthouse Cathedral? Do you have any idea how much —" He stops and smacks his head with the heel of his hand. "What am I even asking? Of *course* you do. I will not have this church brought down by some two-bit whore who spreads her legs for a living. Jesus might have forgiven the sinners but I'm not as nice as Jesus, Evelyn. Compassion isn't a spoke, let alone a wheel in my wheelhouse right now. Your suitcase is in the truck. Get in."

He walks to the driver's side as the guy opens the passenger door for me.

"I can't just leave Glenn here without telling him..."

"Glenn Reynolds from high school? Loser." Patrick pulls out his wallet and tosses it to the guy. "Cut him a check for whatever he paid for her." He points to the passenger seat. "Get in, Evelyn. Or you'll fuck up the next five years of Dylan's life. Can you live with that? It hasn't been all that easy for me."

18

WALLS, WATCHTOWERS, & MOATS

WALLS, WATCHTOWERS, & MOATS

AND JUST LIKE THAT I'M BACK IN CHICAGO. I'M DEPRESSED.
I'm a mess. And this time I'm one hundred percent sure all
these feelings belong to me. Victoria picks me up and drags
me to Amelia's place for pizza and a movie.

"The cops I talked to said you should keep all the letters
for safe keeping," Amelia says sprawled on the couch aiming
the remote at the flatscreen TV on the wall. "Lock your
doors and windows. Keep the blinds closed at night. You can
contact them if anything concerns you. They said cyber
stalking is pretty common these days and usually nothing
comes of it."

"It's not just cyber stalking," Victoria says. "He mailed
letters to her physical address."

"I told the cops that but they said these days it usually
starts online," Amelia says. "And oh, check the shadows
around your entrance. Be aware of your surroundings."

"Terrific," I say, lying on a love seat. I blow my nose, tossing the used tissue into a wastebasket. "Maybe it's Madame Germaine. She's a horrible person."

"Madam's a shitty person," Amelia says "Setting you up with that asshole when she knew you were with another guy was unforgivable. But I doubt she's your 'Fan.'"

Victoria passes me a beer. "A cold, shitty, horrible person. I don't think she's your fan, either."

"Maybe Madame didn't know that Glenn and Dylan had history?" I ask. "Maybe it was just an innocent mistake on her part."

"Please," Victoria says. "She vetted him. She knew he was a high stakes gambler. She'd have to be a dumbass not to know they played in the same circles. Wedding date my ass."

"I'm sorry, Evie," Amelia says tipping back a beer.

"Madame pulled something horrible on me, too," Victoria says.

"What?" I ask.

"I'd been at Ma Maison for about five months, and met this guy I really liked. I was thinking about quitting."

"I remember that," Amelia says flipping through movie channels.

"What happened?" I asked.

"A 'little bird' told Scott's wife he was seeing someone. Out of nowhere he takes a job in Denver, up and moved the next week. I called. Texted. He ghosted me. Broke my heart into a million pieces."

"That sucks," I say Just a few weeks ago I hated this girl and now I like her. Life can turn on a dime.

"Sucks hard," Victoria says, grabbing a tissue from the box and blowing her nose. "Different movie please. I cannot watch *Titanic* tonight."

"If I see Jack die one more time I'll put a fork in someone's eye," I say.

"Fine," Amelia grumbles.

"Did you ever get a hold of Scott?" I ask.

"Two months later," Victoria says. "He talked cryptically like he was being secretly recorded. He said someone using the Agency's email had contacted his wife and sent photos of dates that we'd been on."

"Ugh. Did you ever figure out who?" I ask.

"No proof," Victoria says. "Who do you think did it?"

"Madame Marchand?"

"That sounds like a reach," Amelia says. "Probably a friend of Scott's wife. How about a romantic comedy?"

I frown. "How about I punch you."

"So bossy." She keeps clicking.

Victoria shakes her head. "I should have known better. I was raised better. 'Don't give the milk away for free,' my grandmother said a million times. 'Never date a married man.' I figured that last one didn't count because we're not actually dating at Ma Maison."

"We're *not* actually dating," Amelia says. "We're just doing a job. Keeping a roof over our heads. We don't plan on more than a paycheck and a decent tip if we're lucky."

"I certainly never planned on falling in like," I say.

"Victoria, is that when you started putting up walls?" Amelia asks.

"Walls, watchtowers, and moats."

"What happened to the guy who took you to Paris?" I ask.

"He's good," she says and tosses her drink down. "He's so good he knocked up his wife whom he was planning on leaving. That's on hold for the next five years or forever."

"I'm sorry," I say.

"Guys suck," Amelia says. "How about Terminator 2?"

"The Arnold Schwarzenegger movie?" Victoria asks.

"Yup," Amelia says.

"The one where Linda Hamilton gets insanely buff and kicks ass?" I ask.

"Yup," Amelia says.

"Perfect," Victoria says.

SUMMER TURNS TO INDIAN SUMMER, A HINT OF AUTUMN chill creeps into the night air. I need to exercise, calm my anxiety, blow off steam. I wheel my bike outside. My mailbox is stuffed with fliers, and my stomach flip-flops. I stick the key in the box, pull out a million paper coupons and find another envelope, my name neatly typed.

'Uh-oh,' Queasy says. *'Better open it.'*

Hi Evelyn,

I waited a bit to drop you a line because I don't want to overwhelm you. It seems the world is split between those who want 'too much' attention and those who don't. You seem like the latter.

You're such a nice girl, kind to everyone you come in contact with, and it goes without saying that you're beautiful. I've been hesitant to bring this up before now, but I checked out that photo again. You know the one I like – the picture your friend took of her Bachelorette party at Navy Pier? You were third from the left wearing the "Team Jennifer Bride" T-shirt." My good God, Evelyn, you put models to shame. You don't need makeup. You don't need fancy clothes. Your beauty, your goodness, shine through, like a lamp lit in the darkness.

And then there's a photo of you with one arm

around your mother. Your mom looks so lost and fragile. But the way you're staring at her, your good intent shines through. You take care of her. You're there for her. Not many people share your commitment or your devotion to family, let alone others less fortunate than you. That photo moved my heart and I look at it every time I need a boost to get me through a stressful day.

You and I are cut from the same cloth, Evelyn. We are both kind, caring people. People that go out of our way to help others, sometimes even putting the needs of others before our own. Please understand, it's not my intention to freak you out, or scare you. Rest assured, I'm not some aggressive stalker. Don't worry that every person you see at a coffee shop or in the grocery store wearing a ball cap pulled low over their head is me.

That person is not me.

I stay in the background. I promise I won't show up on your doorstep. I'm not delusional. I don't presume that you even want me in your life. In fact, feel free to throw this letter away. I am certain you have a fair share of admirers, suitors, whatever.

Thanks for letting me share, Evelyn.

My best,
Your Fan

"Creepsters." I shove the letter in my bike pouch and check my surroundings. It's broad daylight but I still eye the bushes next to the stairs that lead to my walk up; the hedge that lines the squat building next door. I hop on my bike and make my way to the trail adjacent to Lake Shore Drive.

I pedal for miles like a madwoman, blowing past sailboats in the harbor. The author of these letters has to be some socially awkward guy. A harmless weirdo. I'm going to shove this letter in the drawer with the others and ignore this bullshit. Maybe I'll buy a can of pepper spray. Make that two: one for my purse, one for my nightstand. Yeah, that's going on my to-do list.

I slow down as I pass sailboats dotting the harbor, sleek condos, the constellation of wealth gathered like members of a private club hovering around a mahogany bar at Lake Michigan's edge. It's the same route I took a few months ago, but wow, has my vantage point changed.

I've been to these private clubs, sat at the bars. I've visited the sleek condos and been touched by wealth in ways both good and bad. Rosemary McAlister welcomed me into her home and treated me like family. Patrick oozed entitlement and threatened me. Glenn's desperate need for one upmanship made my skin crawl. Scratch the surface of the elegance and you might unearth some dirty bits, find some filthy secrets.

Time passes. A week, then two. No more letters from my fan. Also no word from Dylan. No emails. No texts. No handwritten letters. I Google him, but juicy new gossip doesn't float around the Internet when a big player falls off the grid. It's like he's vanished without a trace. Maybe he was just a dream.

September marches in and I'm back to teaching Kindergarten during the day, taking Ma Maison dates at night and on weekends. Mom calls from the Institute. She's non-manic excited because she's taking a pottery class and is going to be part of a fall arts and crafts festival. Her doctor floats the possibility of her becoming an outpatient in the next couple of months. I think this translates into 'I'll be paying medical expenses and footing the bill for an apartment somewhere within easy ride share distance from the Institute.'

I thought my empathic hits would die down after Dylan and I ended, but they're clocking in more frequently. The rusty gates inside me that creaked open have apparently stayed open. Clients' feelings are popping up inside me more frequently, throwing elbows and shoulders like hockey players fighting for control of the puck. I'm exhausted trying to push them away and so I finally stop resisting. Now, when they jockey about I follow Hope's protocol: identify the sensation, determine if it's mine. If it's not, I follow up by asking the client a few questions.

Most of the guys are thrilled to talk about what's bugging them. They seem relieved to spill their burden. Carrying an old wound is exhausting. Covering it up is even more work. I'm not a priest, definitely not a therapist, but for some reason a girl in my line of work is a safe haven for confidences shared, secrets revealed.

In a weird twist, my tips increase. They're up fifty percent. I'm still not having full blown sex with these men and I'm making more money. Will I spread my legs for a client in the future? That barrier was already crossed with Dylan and I'm open to consensual sex with the right person. Now that I know I actually *can* come with a man, I'm also open to dating someone in real life. The guy from the gym asked me out again, but I wasn't interested before, and now, after Dylan, even less so.

I throw my energy into my day job. I'm helping five-year-olds finger paint pictures of pumpkins and goblins when I get a text from Madame.

Madame: *When can you come into the office?*

Evie: *Tomorrow?*

Madame: *Confirming tomorrow noon.*

I don't bother getting dressed up or applying full makeup. Surely Madame knows what I look like without the prep work. I stand across from her in jeans and a long-sleeved T-shirt, my hair tied back in a ponytail.

"Based on a referral, a new client contacted Ma Maison and wishes to engage your services."

"Oh?" Most clients keep what happens between us private. Guys are territorial creatures; don't like to share. I hope this referral isn't someone hoping for a threesome because that's not on my dance card yet.

"He seems like a nice enough man. Never been a Ma Maison client before," she says. "But this engagement is a little different than what you normally do."

Oh, crap, it *is* a request for a threesome. "My boundaries haven't changed."

Her lips purse so hard I fear they'll snap off her face. I redirect her attention. "Tell me what's different about this guy, Madame. What's different about this date?"

"It's not specifically what he wants." She slides her turquoise cat-eye glasses back on her face. "It's the time he's requesting."

"A morning engagement? I'm not into mornings but I'll make an exception."

"Not morning," she says. "He wants to book you for a week."

"A week?" I cough, and cover my mouth. "Like every night for seven days?" That'll make for some sucky early mornings shepherding five-year-olds.

"No. Twenty-four hours a day for a week."

I plunk down hard in the nearest chair, and pinch my arm, trying to contemplate what this means. It means money. A lot of money. "Holy crap."

"Holy crap indeed," Madame says. "By the way, Ma Maison just raised your rates."

"I'm assuming some of that gets passed along to me?"

"Yes. The client lives in St. Petersburg, Florida, co-owns a minor league baseball team, and a string of car dealerships. According to him, you came highly recommended. The person who referred you said you helped him heal. Said you were a miracle worker."

"I am?" My heart twists because I've heard that phrase before. Those words fell out of someone's delectable mouth. "*Who* referred him?"

"Confidential. I can't reveal that," she says, *clack-clacking* papers on her desk into neat, perfectly aligned stacks. "The person told him that what you did helped him live again. What you did helped him heal."

I know who that guy is. It's the guy I can't stop thinking about. Blue eyes, a smattering of freckles across high sun-kissed cheekbones. Dylan Fucking McAlister.

"Is there something you need to tell me, Evelyn?" Madame asks, staring at me like I'm a bug crawling across the floor. "Something important you need to share?"

"Nope," I say, technically *not* lying through my teeth because Madame Marchand will be the *last* person I share anything, let alone this, with.

"I trust you'll tell me if *healing* turns into a 'thing'? Specifics make for a better, more detailed client experience at Ma Maison. Specifics bring in more money. Specifics can launch a breakout career."

"I'll keep that in mind," I say. "When is the new client coming in town?"

"He's not. His credentials passed with flying colors. You're going to him."

"Aha. St. Pete?"

"Yes. And anywhere in the continental U.S. he wants to travel for the week he employs you."

"Okay," I say, overwhelmed and confused on how the hell I'm going to prep for this date, what I should pack, let alone how I'll manage to take off work from school.

"You're getting a seven hundred dollar stipend for the date's duration." Madame practically reads my mind, reaching in her desk drawer, sliding a debit card across the desk in my direction. "This should cover beauty and grooming necessities. Emergencies."

Hope swift kicks me. *No one's going to give you anything unless you ask for it.*

I clear my throat. "What about wardrobe?"

"What about it?" Madame shuffles paperwork around on her desk, making everything immaculate as always.

I just got a new client, a fat gig, and was bumped up a pay grade. You can bet your life Madame's going to want me to be as high end and perfect as those stupid stacks of crisply aligned papers on her fancy desk.

"I need better clothes," I say, my voice low at first, growing stronger as I grow my courage. "Ma Maison gives Victoria and Amelia a wardrobe stipend. You want your top tier girls to look money. You want Ma Maison to be the most exclusive agency in Chicago, right?"

She sizes me up with a look that for once isn't dismissive. "Three thousand for this engagement and this engagement only. We'll re-evaluate for the future."

'Yes!' Hope high fives me.

"Yes," I say under my breath, clenching a fist at my side.

"What?" Madame asks.

"Thank you."

19

ST. PETERSBURG

ST. PETERSBURG

———

I TRAVEL TO ST. PETERSBURG WHERE ANDREW Courtland's driver picks me up at the airport and chauffeurs me to his vintage 1940s Spanish-style mansion on Snell Island. The place is a rambling, two-story stucco with red tiles. Orange and blush bougainvillea trail over the arched doorways. There's a tennis court in the back yard, tucked behind a swimming pool. The house has gorgeous views of the waterfront, and a shiny motorboat is parked at the dock. The scent of salt wafts through the air.

Andrew seems like a decent guy. He's forty and good-looking in that retired ball player kind of way. A year ago he sold the majority share of his ball club to a corporation. Until recently he was amicably divorced and shared custody of his teenage daughter, Hailey. But lately he's been dropping the ball: canceling visitations at the last minute, screwing up father-daughter plans. He's been pissing off his ex-wife, alien-ating Hailey, and now there's friction.

The first night I arrived, he confessed over dinner that he used to be a cocky piece of work when he was the majority share owner. He sold because he wanted the influx of cash to spruce up the stadium and attract young athletes with better potential to cross to the big leagues. Ten months later, his job as team manager is no longer a given. He's not the golden child in the new owners' minds. They hired a hot shot out of Cleveland to be his boss and Andrew's not all that happy about it.

He's having trouble sleeping. He's drinking more than usual and having anxiety attacks, which hasn't happened since he was a teenager. And for the first time he's being an asshole to his players.

"Evie," he says one night at the end of a game that stretches into overtime as we're sitting behind the dugout alongside the players. "What was I thinking selling the majority share? I gave up too much control. Maybe I'm no longer qualified to manage the team. Maybe I should hire someone to do the grunt work while I sit in the clubhouse instead of the dugout, drink too much beer, and entertain corporate big shots. Is anyone really going to miss me?"

I look around the field and take in all he has done. The renovated stadium. The athletes scouted from all over the world. A devoted mid-sized fan base cheering from the bleachers. My stomach sinks, uncertainty crawling about in my gut. It's so beautiful here and yet somehow it's not perfect.

And I realize these feelings aren't mine: they're Andrew's. There is no room in him for anything less than perfection. I gaze up at his ruggedly handsome face and it dawns on me the answer isn't going to be found on the field. It's going to be found within Andrew Courtland. Over-achiever. Perfectionist. Second-guesser.

Suddenly I'm dying to know if I can crack open the wound that broke him, the same way I cracked open Dylan's. I sleep with him that night. The first time we have sex is nice. When I close my eyes I can almost imagine Dylan.

Andrew's a considerate lover, well aware that a girl has needs. The second time we have sex is about helping him relax, getting him to let down his guard. But the third time I do what I did with Dylan. I tell him when and how he can touch me.

I call the shots during these healing sessions. There's no kissing or touching without my consent. I ask the questions and he answers. I compare his responses to the feelings that rise up in me. His sadness weighs on my shoulders. His heaviness carves my heart. And I feel his bitter belief within me. Spot the dirty thread at the bottom of his lovely, second-guessing soul. No matter what he does, no matter how hard he works at anything he does, Andrew doesn't believe he is good enough.

"You can kiss me, Andrew. Now."

He does.

"Touch my breasts, Andrew."

He fondles my tits like he's a teenager and they're the first breasts he's ever felt. "That feels good. See how my nipple pebbles under your touch? You're so hot. I have a question for you. Tell me how why you're not good enough."

"I shouldn't have sold the company. I must have fallen short or corporate wouldn't have hired the ringer from Cleveland. Let me fuck you, Evelyn."

"Not yet." I run a hand through his short blonde hair. With my other hand I trace my fingers down his abdomen and brush back and forth just inches away from his erection.

He moans. "Why not?"

"Because we've got a ways to go." I place my hand over his heart because this feels like the source of the poison. I need to touch him here. I visualize tugging on that toxic thread, coaxing it out from where it's hiding deep inside him. I pull it to me inch by inch. "Tell me more about falling short. Where else have you fallen short in life?"

"Do we have to talk about this, Evie?"

"Yes."

Days pass. He takes me out on his boat. We go to a party at the yacht club. We hit more ballgames and I meet the players. We end up back in bed and I question him. Each twinge of pain he's carrying rolls through me. He's desperate to do all the right things.

I place my hand on his heart and feel the bitter belief, the wound within him. The thread turns into a cord. I think it's all going to come out so easily. Like excising an encapsulated tumor. But the tumor isn't encapsulated. Its roots are terrified with angry tendrils that fire up when they realize their existence is threatened. Andrew's fear isn't going to leave easily. It fights back.

"Why are we playing this game, Evie?" Andrew asks. "I didn't fly you down to Florida to play a stupid game."

"If you wanted regular sex you could have a hired a local girl to suck your cock for a fraction of what Ma Maison charged you," I say, and run a finger over his lips. "Listen to me. Do this my way, please."

"Fine," he grumbles.

Andrew doesn't want to let go of the old, doesn't want to release what has worked for him up until recently. But my resolve is firm. We play a game of tug of war and I refuse to let go when that wound slides through my hands. I don't let go when it burns and tries to suck itself back into the abyss and disappear. I hold tight until we get down to the nitty-gritty. Until we circle closer and closer to the messed up belief that is his undoing. "Do you want to keep working for these people?" I ask. "Is managing this team that important to you?"

"I don't know," he says. "Part of me wants to quit this job. Part of me wanted to quit it before I even sold the company."

Interesting. "What do you want to do instead?" I run my hands up and down his body, lightly running my palm over his hard dick.

"You're killing me, Evie."

"What do you want to do instead?"

"I want to spend time with family," he says and moans. My parents are getting older. My daughter's growing up so fast."

"What's stopping you?"

"I've been doing this for fifteen years. I'm a hard worker. I'm not a quitter."

"You always will be a hard worker, whatever you do."

"Not true. When things get tough I quit. I quit visiting my grandmother when she went into a home. I quit my marriage. What if at the end of the day I'm just a guy who quits when the going gets tough?"

Bingo. Paydirt.

He's scared of being a quitter. He's scared that if he's a quitter, he's a shitty, worthless person. "Your guilt about your grandmother is different than this job. Whatever's going on with your ex-wife is different than this job. You're letting it all spill into the same stew. It's bubbling up within you. It's shutting you down. It's acting out in anger and anxiety."

"Damn," he says. "You might be right."

"Don't look at leaving this job as quitting. Reframe it as graduating. Moving from high school to college. Do that right now with me, Andrew. Do whatever you want with me."

He kisses me, touches me, sinks his cock inside me and a few minutes later he comes. The bitter belief is revealed for what it truly is: a hoax. And once the hoax is called out and confronted, like any bully it loses its power.

He drops me at the airport the next morning and we hug. "I can't believe I'm letting you leave a day early," he says. "But Hailey wants to hang out. I'm going to take her to the mall. Shopping. Then we'll go to a movie. Dinner wherever she wants. Probably pizza."

I smile at him. He's sweet. "You should hang out with Hailey the whole weekend."

"I already talked to my ex about that."

"What will you do when Hailey leaves?"

"Work on my resignation letter. Thank you, Evie."

"You're welcome."

"This might sound weird. Feel free to say 'no.' You really helped me. Do you mind if I refer a friend to you?"

"No. As long as he's as honest and hard working as you." I stand on my tiptoes and kiss him on the cheek. "Thank you for being sweet. Gotta go."

"Go," he says.

The flight home is uneventful. Madame summons me to her office the next day. "You did a great job, Evelyn," she says. "Mr. Courtland is pleased."

"Good." I practically topple off my chair because I'm not used to her praising me. "You called me into the office to tell me that?"

"Amongst other things. One. We're raising your rate. I thought you should know."

"Great." Did someone secretly replace Madame with a person who cares?

"Second, we have a new client for you."

"Excellent. FYI, I'm back to working weekends and nights. I've taken enough time off work."

"About that. Ma Maison pulled your financials." She clicks her tablet, swivels it toward me, and voila, there's my credit report. The score is low, the debt is high, and I break out in a sweat.

"You can't, that's not right, I, I..."

"Hear me out, Evelyn. I have a proposition for you. Ma Maison can help you wipe out all this debt quickly," she says. "How quickly is up to you. Will teaching kindergarten do that?"

"I love teaching. I will not quit being a teacher." I stand up. "You can't make me quit my day job."

"What if Ma Maison is your day job? Teaching kids can be something you do in Sunday school, or volunteer for an after school program at the library. You could have the best of both worlds."

"But I went to college. I have a Master's in Education."

"Yes, I can tell that by looking at your student loans. Andrew Courtland called me after he dropped you off at the airport. He couldn't have been happier. He's referring a friend."

"I know. He told me."

"The man already called. He's in St. Louis. He owns five breweries and a racetrack. We're in the process of vetting him."

"Okay."

"I've heard gossip about what happened with you and Dylan McAlister. You helped him get his mojo back. You have a gift, Evelyn. You're able to help powerful, broken men heal. It's a unique combination of skills that restores their confidence."

"I don't know..."

"I do," she says. "This is your breakout. It's big money, not only for Ma Maison but for you. If we market this correctly, your debt disappears, you'll never worry about taking care of your mom or sister. Take a few days and think about it."

I didn't see this one coming. "I'll think about it," I say.

"But don't hold your breath." I text Amelia on my way home on the el.

Evie: *Need to talk.*

Amelia: *We're getting ready for a Halloween party. Come with us.*

Evie: *Didn't think I'd be home in time for Halloween. Don't have a costume.*

Amelia: *I've got something from last year. Just come over.*

We hit a Halloween party at a club west of the Loop. The place is popping. The DJ spins Michael Jackson's 'Thriller.' Victoria and Amelia are dressed as super heroes. They're smoking hot in their spandex and bustiers. Guys are practically salivating as we elbow our way through the crowd. I, on the other hand, am a Tootsie Roll. "I look like an idiot."

"You look adorable," Victoria says as we move past the dance floor toward the back of the place.

A vampire guy squeezes past me and flashes his fangs. "I'd take a bite out of you."

"Be gone with you, Boris," I say.

We edge up to the bar. Amelia flags down the bartender, thrusting her recently enhanced Wonder Woman cleavage in his direction. "Three Black Magic Cocktails, please."

"Coming right up, Diana," he says.

"What do you think?" I ask. "It sounds kind of crazy, right?

"It sounds smart," Victoria says. "Get everything in writing. A contract. I've got an attorney you can run it by."

"But... " She was supposed to agree with me. She was supposed to say this was a ridiculous, terrible, crazy idea. "I'd miss teaching. What if quitting St. Matthew's Elementary and working at Ma Maison is a horrible mistake?"

"Then you go back to teaching," Amelia says, lifting the cocktails off the bar and passing one to each of us. "I put in my resignation last week. I'll be working full time at Ma Maison too. I second Victoria's lawyer referral."

I spend all weekend thinking about going to work at Ma Maison full time. Quitting the day job sounds so weird. I meditate on it a few times. I hit the gym and ask God for clarity before I start working out. You'd be surprised how many answers come to me after I clear my mind. In the middle of running my third mile on the treadmill I realize it's okay to shift gears. It's okay to let go of the familiar path.

I quit my job as a teacher on Monday and feel some of the same 'quitter' feelings that had ping-ponged inside Andrew Courtland. I won't tell Ruby or Mom I quit until it comes up in conversation. Besides, I don't know what to say I've replaced my job with.

"Corporate consulting," Victoria says a few nights later when we hit a movie. "I told my family I took a job as a consultant for Fortune 500 companies. That explains my wardrobe and why I'm always busy in the evenings."

"A part of me is freaking out that I might be able to earn enough money to sleep at night," I say. "Enough money to reach for the check when we go out for a beer and burgers. It all feels oddly uncomfortable."

"You might get used to it," Victoria says. "You ever go to therapy?"

"A long time ago." I think of all the therapists I saw after the car crash but I don't really want to talk about that.

"You'd love my shrink," Victoria says, and messages me his contact information. "He's non-judgmental, insightful, a safe harbor in a storm."

I would love a safe harbor. I start therapy with Victoria's

therapist just in time for more Ma Maison referrals to come in. And with my new empathic 'specialty' comes money. Big money. Crazy money. Debt-erasing money.

At times the work is glamorous. I wear beautiful clothes. I stay in gorgeous homes. I converse with high powered, interesting people. Other times it's crawl out of my skin uncomfortable. I wade through these men's destructive feelings. I wear their pain. I cry their tears. I tremble with their fear.

But I keep digging through their messed up beliefs and core wounds, doing my best to find the breakthrough they need. At the end of the day I don't heal these men. They heal themselves. They just need a push in the right direction.

Every few weeks Madame raises my rate as well as my clothing stipend. The work's emotionally exhausting. And finally, three months later just when I think I'll never hear from him again, Dylan McAlister contacts Ma Maison. He's got a gig in Vegas and wants me to fly out, and join him for the weekend. I practically fall onto my knees and cast a prayer up to the heavens, thanking God for finally taking my call.

"Madame?" I ask. "Did you give Mr. McAlister my new rate or the old one?"

"New rate," she says, toggling between two laptops on her desk.

"Is he okay with that?" I clench one hand at my side, digging my fingernails into my palm, hoping he doesn't cancel, because after everything we've been through now I cost too much.

"He didn't hesitate. He didn't skip a beat."

Holy crap. I'm going to see Dylan McAlister again.

20

LAS VEGAS

LAS VEGAS

I FLY OUT A FEW DAYS LATER AND CATCH A RIDE TO THE Wolfe, the luxury boutique hotel where I'm supposed to meet Dylan. The irony's not lost on me. It's a weird coincidence that I'm reuniting with the guy I helped heal at a hotel carrying the same name as the boys I helped break.

I pause along a cascading water wall at the far end of the lobby and pull a compact from my purse to apply a coat of lipstick, check my reflection, and run a hand through my hair. I'm wearing it down. Dylan loves my hair. He likes to tug on it during sex. He likes how it drapes across his body, tickling him when he's naked and I'm straddling him, holding tight to his shoulders when we have sex.

I'm nervous. I haven't seen him since that horrible, heart-stomping evening. We haven't talked since I left him high and dry at that game in Dallas after I was blindsided by creepy

Fast Food King's bullshit one-upmanship and Patrick's need to be in charge.

I pinch the acupuncture spot on the web of my thumb to ground myself, take a few calming breaths, and gather my courage before I walk through the door of the darkened bar. The bar is crowded with people of all ages. My heart flutters in my chest like a teenager's, my pulse building. But I don't see Dylan.

What if he doesn't show? What if for some twisted reason this is some kind of revenge plot? There are so many people here. I crane my neck but I still don't see him. What if this is a way to get me back for leaving him with no explanation? Where is he? My palms break out in a sweat and I glance around the bar.

'He's not that guy,' Hope says. *'He's not petty. Keep moving. One foot in front the other.'*

I resume walking, past a bottleneck of people clustered at the bar, and that's when I spot him. Dylan's sitting at a small table in the far corner checking his phone, a lock of hair falling over his forehead. A bouquet of flowers rests on the table. Goose bumps sprout on my arms. I don't think I've ever been so excited to see anyone in my entire life.

I toss my hair over my shoulder, count *three, two, one*, and make my way toward him, my heart beating fast, practically carving a hole in my chest. "Hey, old man."

His eyes light up and he springs to his feet. "Evie." He pulls me into a tight embrace. My breasts press against his hard chest, our hearts *thump-thump*. "God, Evie. You're finally here."

"Finally." I cling to him. He smells like hope and dreams. He feels like love lost and love found. I want to disappear into his arms forever, and it's all I can do not to burst out crying.

"I missed you," he says.

"I missed you back." I inhale his scent and draw a hand over his neck. We fit together like long-lost puzzle pieces snapping into place. He wraps one broad, protective hand around my shoulders, the other around my head. He weaves his fingers through my hair and kisses me. He explores my mouth with his tongue, tasting me, claiming me, devouring me.

I'm home, Dylan. Oh, sweetheart, I am home.

HE KISSES ME, TANGLING HIS HAND IN MY HAIR. HE SHUTS the door of his penthouse suite behind me with his foot. "God, I missed you, baby." He feathers kisses on my forehead, face, lips and neck, and pulls at the zipper of my dress.

I unbutton his shirt. My breath comes quicker. He shrugs off his shirt and I run my hands over his muscular chest, and shoulders. I'm getting turned on by every muscular rip and swell. My cocktail dress falls to the floor and I step out of it. He palms my breasts through my lace bra, rubbing a broad thumb over first one nipple, then the other. They pebble under his touch. His breath comes faster. The muscle in his jaw ticks as he unhooks my bra. I inhale. My bra gapes opens and I shrug it off.

He runs fingers down my neck, my chest, tracing circles around my breasts, pinching my nipples between his thumb and forefinger. I moan, electricity spreading in bursts to my arms, my fingers. He unzips his pants and kicks them off, then yanks off his underwear. His hard dick springs free, bobbing up toward his abdomen.

He's bigger than I remember. Dylan McAlister's got a gorgeous cock. Tight balls. Flat stomach. Muscular shoulders. Be still my fucking heart. He pulls my lace panties down my legs and kneels in front of me, his breath warm on my abdomen. "Spread your legs, Evie."

I do.

"So good." He kisses my stomach, running a hand toward my core and I grow wetter. He reaches between my legs and circles a finger around my pussy. "My mantra," he says. "Evie's wet pussy." He strums his thumb across my clit and eases two fingers inside me.

I groan. "Your cock inside me, now, Dylan."

"I'm in charge tonight, baby." He drops his mouth to my sex. He scrapes his teeth over my clit, the scruff of his beard tickling the sensitive skin on the inside of my thigh. He thrusts his fingers in and out and I moan. "Come for me. I want to watch you come." He looks up at me. That muscle in his jaw ticks again. His eyes are heavy with lust, his cheeks flushed. He runs those talented fingers over my clit as my breath comes quicker.

"Yes." I grab his hair, threading my fingers through its thickness. I arch my pelvis, riding his hand that's fucking me and I gaze down into his brilliant blue eyes. My orgasm circles and I'm panting by the time it hits me, strong in my core, tingles shooting down my legs, up my stomach to my breasts, my arms, my heart.

He wraps his arms around me and smiles. "How you doing, Lucky Charm?"

"Yeah," I say catching my breath. "Yeah."

"Bed," he says and points. "On your back."

I lie on the bed on my back. He grabs a condom from his wallet on the floor, rolls it on and then lines his beautiful cock up with my center and enters me. I am filled. I am whole.

He fucks me, thrusting in and out. I want even more of him. "Harder, Dylan." I wrap my legs around his back, moving with him as he pounds into me. I want to feel every inch of this man. I want to burn his memory inside me. Carve him in my bones. I claw the skin down his back. The world flies away somewhere I didn't know existed before I met him. There will always be other clients. But there will only be one Dylan McAlister.

"Evie." He leans in and kisses me, then grabs my hair and pushes it back from my sweaty forehead. He curls my hair around his hand and kisses it, before dragging my hair down his neck, down his chest, down his stomach.

He's so fucking hot.

"You're gorgeous, Evie," he pants. "I'm coming. I'm coming..." He holds onto that lock of hair as he shudders, his head tilting backward, and pushes even harder into me.

He collapses on top of me, spent, and we catch our breath. I run a hand over his sweaty back. The longer I travel down this road, the more I get lost in the fantasy of what life would look like if Dylan and I were playing this game together for real. And I'm okay with that. I'm good with that, actually. Maybe all we really needed all this time was each other.

WE SIT ACROSS FROM EACH OTHER IN A BOOTH AT A NEON lit, crowded, casual trendy restaurant, two beers on the table. He holds my hand and turns it over in his palm. He runs his elegant fingers up and down the inside of my wrist. Sparks dance in the air around us.

"Mom's in remission," he says. "It's a bitch of a fight and yet she's up for it."

"She's a warrior. I'm so glad. I adore your mom."

"How's *your* mom?"

"Slow progress. Kind of hard to tell. I think she's happier. Not as swingy."

A waiter drops off two mile-high burgers surrounded by sweet potato fries.

"What's going on with the church?" I ask.

"Lighthouse is still Lighthouse," he says and shrugs. "Frankly, it's not my concern anymore. I put in my time. I served my eighteen-year penance. I cashed in my chips and I'm out of that game forever."

"Patrick?"

"Bless his heart," Dylan says.

I cover a laugh.

"My brother can fight over every last dime that's squirreled away. Mom confided one night over a bottle of Jack that the will isn't what Patrick thinks it is."

"Mom's drinking Jack?"

"Mom's doing whatever the fuck Mom wants. She's done with people telling her how to live her life."

'L'Chaim!" I hold my glass up in the air and we toast.

"About the will. Patrick's not getting the lion's share that he's been planning on. It's going to an orphanage in Puerto Rico. The rest will be divided between the two of us when that day comes."

"Good on the orphanage. Does Patrick suspect?"

"Don't know. Don't care." He shakes his head. "And I'm not going to be the one to tell him. Ha."

"Tell me about the game."

"The one here? Private. High stakes. Got in with a big money guy I met in L.A. A good man. A little gruff."

"Gruff? Translation – asshole?"

"No. A little rough around the edges."

"Good. Is it good?"

"It's very good, Lucky Charm. He owns this hotel, among other things."

'That's weird.' Queasy flutters in my gut. 'Wolfe. Same last name as those brothers.'

"So, the gruff guy who owns this hotel -- he's like the CEO of a ginormous conglomerate or something?" I ask, chewing on a fry.

"Yes on his being the CEO. No on the conglomerate. It's a family-run company. He owns the majority share. He's some kind of wunderkind. He had a weird accident in high school and it set his brain on fire. He was a multi-millionaire by the time he left Stanford. He brought his brother into the business and they expanded."

Queasy's wound up like a Golden Retriever doing anxious laps around my stomach. And I know it's one of the Wolfe brothers. The guy Dylan's talking about is either Wyatt or Easton Wolfe. "What's his name?" I ask, my palms sweating.

"Easton Wolfe."

I stop chewing. The blood drains from my fingers. "Did you meet his brother?"

"Nope. You okay? Is there something wrong with the food?"

"The food's great. I think I know the guy."

"A lot of people know Easton Wolfe. He's got his finger in a lot of pies. He has companies all over the globe."

"This is different," I say.

"Different? *Oh.* He was a client? Did something happen? Say the word and we can change hotels. We don't need to stay here. You're more important than a comped room."

"*Not* a client." I shake my head. "Just a guy I know from a long time ago. I haven't seen him in years."

"And I doubt you'll see him here, either. I've played a few tournaments at this hotel and I've never run into him. Easton Wolfe is constantly traveling. But it's your call, baby. I'll do whatever you want me to. I want you to feel safe. I want you to feel comfortable."

I hate lying, I'm shitty at it. I might be forced into the occasional white lie in the course of work but I will not lie to myself. Those days have come and gone. The universe has a fucked up sense of humor. I've circled back around to the Wolfe brothers. They just don't know it yet. But I do. Can I live with that?

'Yes,' Hope says. *'You are not a rickety shed. You survive when the storm blows through. This isn't even a squall.'*

And I remind myself I'm not just here to have fun or be comfortable. I'm here for Dylan and I'm here for the job. "I'm okay. We can stay here. It's fine." I will deal with these feelings later.

"Good," Dylan says. "Not that it matters but my room's comped. The food's comped. A few shows are comped."

"Am I comped?"

"No, darling. You're definitely *not* comped." He leans over and kisses me. He tugs my lower lip with his teeth. His breath is warm against my face, and I want his mouth everywhere on my body. My neck. My breasts. My sex. I give my head a shake. I've got to leave the pleasure zone and return to business. Get straight for the game. I reluctantly pull away from him.

"By the way," Dylan says. "Your rate's doubled."

"About that..."

He shakes his head. "I'm good. Don't worry about me."

The waiter stops by. "Can I get you more drinks?"

"No thanks."

"We're good, thanks," Dylan says.

"I can't drink before a game," I say. "Probably shouldn't have had this one. I'll fall asleep and then I'll snore. They'll never ask you back."

"They'll ask me back as long as I'm staked and capable of losing money. I forgot to tell you," he says. "I already played the game. I did pretty good. A hundred thousand up."

"Dylan!" Tingles zip up and down my spine. I'm so excited I practically topple off my seat.

He beams like a kid coming home with A's on his report card. "I'm winning again. Winning fairly consistently. I've been meditating, drilling into that core wound we discovered, reciting affirmations, chanting mantras. My shitty old beliefs might derail me on occasion, but those fuckers will never own me again."

"Yes!" I mouth a quick, 'Thank You' to the heavens. "But, why am I here?"

"To celebrate. Who else would I celebrate with, baby?"

"Get out!"

And that's what we do for two solid days. We go to Cirque du Soleil, our seats ten rows back from the stage on the aisle. Close enough to see everything. Not so close to be overwhelmed. He leans in and asks, "Do you think we can do what they're doing right now on stage?"

"I am not a double jointed fire eater who can swing from a trapeze."

"Come on. At least try the trapeze for me?"

"God, you're demanding," I say, swallowing laughter.

He takes me to a five-star French restaurant where we eat delicately sauced dishes with names I cannot pronounce. We swim for hours in the aquamarine, warm waters of the hotel pool. We get a couples' massage at the spa. Dylan hires a helicopter to take us far enough out into the dessert to see the brilliant night stars. I cling tight to his arm because heights freak me out a little.

We play blackjack at one of the hotel's casinos, when a suited-up security guard taps Dylan on the shoulder. "Mr. McAlister?"

"Yes," Dylan says.

He holds a hand up to his ear and whispers into it.

"Yes, I see," Dylan says. "Tell him I'll contact him shortly."

"Excellent. Have a good night." The guard walks off into the crowd.

"What was that about?" I ask.

"A business opportunity. I'll hit the guy up later."

We take in a concert. Center stage five rows back. "I loved this guy when I was a teenager," I say, jumping up and down along with everyone else in the auditorium. "No one rocked a pair of purple tights, platform shoes, ratted hair, and eye liner like Johnny Stone did."

"Throw your bra on stage and flash him your boobs," Dylan hollers over the din.

I smack him over the head with a glo stick. "You just want to see my tits."

"Yes, please." He waggles his eyebrows.

"Dirty old man."

"Some things never change, baby."

He fucks me in the shower, pulling my hair back, wrapping it around his hand. The water beats down on us and he slaps my ass, his other hand curved around the top of my pelvis as he pounds me from behind. His cock fills me. His warmth envelopes me. He feels so good and I'm moaning.

"You miss me, Evie?"

"So much, Dylan."

"Not as much as I missed you." He reaches a hand around and strums his fingers over my clit until I cry his name and arch and buck against his hand, pleasure coursing through my body. Pleasure comes in rocky waves, crashing everywhere within me. I bite my lip, hit the tipping point, and come in shakes and shudders – little earthquakes.

When I can finally breathe again I grind back against him, taking all of him deep, then deeper inside me. "Come for me, Dylan."

He roams his hands over my breasts, pinching my nipples, his breath coming faster. I push back against him almost as hard as he's taking me. It feels like we're on a roller coaster and I think we've known each other forever. Maybe God created us to be together. Maybe this was God's plan all along.

"Do you want to go shopping?" he asks the next day.

"Don't care, old man."

"I'd like to get you something to go with the necklace."

"You don't need to."

"I want to."

An hour later I stare at all the brilliant baubles in the jewelry cases, the diamond horseshoe pendant he gave me resting comfortably on my breastbone.

"Do you have any earrings that go with her necklace?" Dylan asks the clerk.

"Happy to show her options," he says, unlocking a drawer, pulling out small black velvet boxes and placing them on the glass countertop. "The round cut two carat studs would go perfectly with your necklace. Try them on."

I remove my earrings and put in the studs. "They're gorgeous. Dylan. What do you think?"

He's wandered a few yards away. He's staring into a different case. He's looking at engagement rings. For a second I forget how to breathe and I tug on a lock of my hair, winding it around my fingers. "Dylan, what do you think?"

He walks toward me, a funny look on his face. "About? Oh, the earrings. They look great. Do you like them?"

"I love them."

He kisses me sweetly. "Sold. Ring them up, please."

Two days spin by in a flash. It's laughter and sex. Glamour and sex. Affection and sex. We're back in our 'old married couple's routine, finishing each other's sentences, egging each other on.

We lie next to each other on a king-sized bed in his suite at the WW Vegas boutique hotel and casino. Electric candlelight flickers from sconces across the thin green and gold pinstriped walls cocooning our suite. There's a view of the Strip in one direction and the brilliantly lit aquamarine pool in the other. Vegas is the epitome of glitz but this place is elegant. And yet a part of me misses that that kitschy little motel in Sugar Grove.

I trace Dylan's freckles with my finger, drawing constellations on his high cheekbones. I know we're only got this weekend. The time to let him go draws closer but I'm going to hold tight to him for as long as I can.

I've never really experienced anyone like him. Because of Dylan I learned my biggest weakness could also be my strongest strength. My empathic reactions — my most tragic wound — is transformed into my super power. My life would be perfect if I could have Dylan in it every day go to bed with him every night and wake up every morning spooned up against him.

Will I meet another man I'm attracted to as much as Dylan? Who knows? What I *do* know is that it's finally okay for me to be empathic. No more pushing it away, no more keeping it under wraps. It's mine to own. Using my empathic ability with clients is already a big messy stew of passion and sex and sadness.

But if I can help heal these broken men, help them get their power back, I'm cool with that. I'm signing up for a wild ride, but I joined this ruthless rodeo when I was born into my crazy family.

"We never actually talked about why you left me swinging in Dallas," Dylan says, playing with my hair.

"Yeah, about that," I say, unsure if I should share the details.

"Patrick told me he scared you off."

"He did?" Did Patrick also tell him what went down with creepy Glenn?

"He said he gave you some kind of 'Come to Jesus' lecture about you not being the right girl for me."

I nod. "I'm sorry I left the way I did. Everything got overwhelming really quickly."

"You had to go, Evie. Ripping off the bandage was probably best for both of us. How else were you going to take care of your mom? Hey, there's something I've been meaning to talk to you about."

"What?" I say and tickle that spot under his ribs, the one that always earns a smile. I take a mental picture of the creases around his eyes, he way his long, brown lashes brush against his high cheekbones. I burn his laugh into my memory forever and ever, fucking-amen. I tuck that laugh inside my heart, in a file that reads 'I Will Never Forget' because I will never forget Dylan McAlister's laugh. He's water on a stifling hot summer day. He's love on a cold, hard, mean winter day.

He tucks a lock of hair behind my ear. "It's going to sound weird."

Dylan McAlister's the man who marked me with a diamond necklace. The first man to make love to me in years. The first man to make me come. He's the real deal. I'll give this man my soul. I'll ink his name on my skin. He's already burned in my heart forever. "Tell me what you want."

"Your hair," he says. "I want to cut your hair."

21

DECEITFUL BED

DECEITFUL BED

———

MY BODY FLUSHES HOT, THEN COLD, AND SOMEWHERE IN the middle my throat closes off. My hand flies to my waist-length ponytail, clutching it protectively. "What do you mean you want to cut my hair?"

"I want you to cut your hair," he says, and runs his fingers down the lock trailing over my breast. He grazes my nipple and it pebbles under his touch – *damn my traitorous body* – then he places his hand possessively on my waist.

"Why?" I say, breaking into a sweat, my guts dissolving into a pool of panic. "I thought you loved my hair."

"I do. Look, it's complicated. Trust me on this one, okay? I'll take you to the best salon in Vegas. We'll do it right. You've got a gorgeous face. You'll look terrific with short hair."

"No." My stomach twists and I stumble out of this deceitful bed, putting distance between myself and the man who up until a few seconds ago I trusted more than anyone else in the entire world. "I've been growing my hair since I was thirteen." Since the accident. But he doesn't know that.

Dylan sits up and glares at me, determination wearing on his face, resolve blazing through blue eyes. "You hide behind it."

"What's gotten into you? I do *not* hide." I slip behind the chair next to the desk and shove an upholstered armchair between us. "My hair is me. It's my look. It's who I am."

He climbs out of bed and pulls on his briefs. "It's a liability," he says. "You tip your head when you need quiet. A wall of hair slides in front of your face when you check out." He seizes my hand, easily navigating the blockade I just erected.

I jerk away. "Not true." I look at my suitcase, my purse. Should I stay and figure out what the hell has gotten into him or should I grab my stuff and run? Is this what Mom felt like right before panicked and split? Oh, holy crap, am I turning into Mom? Fuck. *Fuck.*

"You mess with your hair when you're nervous," Dylan says.

"I don't." My knees feel wobbly. The ground I thought was solid is shaking.

"You do. It's a tell to anyone who moves in these circles."

"A *tell? Circles?* You're the only gambler I know, Dylan. The only player I've dated." My pulse races so hard it could be trying out for the Olympics.

"The circle isn't just poker, Evie."

"Don't treat me like a child, Dylan." My knees knock. "Don't you *dare* treat me like a child."

"The circle's *money*. Big fucking money. Only people with money can afford to play games like this. Only people with big money can afford to hire a girl like you."

"Then you shouldn't have sent them my way." I jut out my chin defiantly.

"I referred a few guys to Ma Maison who are like *me*. Good people you could help heal. They're not the problem. Predators are the problem."

"Then don't send me predators."

"Jesus, Evie. You think I would knowingly send you assholes, let alone sociopaths?"

"No."

"Listen to me. Predators *love* big money circles. They're lions to zebras. Cons to marks. It's out of my hands. Word's out and it's a hell of a lot bigger than me." He shakes his head. "You, Evie Berlinger, help powerful, rich men heal. You get them back on their game, help them regain power."

"So?"

"Power's money. I'll bet the bank Ma Maison's inbox is spilling over like a crimson fucking tide at an Alabama game. Filling up with inquiries from billionaires who want to hire you."

"You're exaggerating."

"I'm not." He shakes his head. "I ran into a guy the other day who told me about *you*. *Not* the other way around."

"What are you talking about?" I'm shaking. My hands. My heart. My recently acquired belief in myself. "You're talking like a crazy person."

"Listen to me. I knocked back a few drinks with this guy after a tournament a few weeks ago. I had two to his four. The more he drank, the meaner he talked. He asked if I had heard about the escort out of Chicago who helps a guy get his game back. I almost shit my pants."

"It could totally be someone else." And yet the way my stomach's twisting I know it's not. I know that guy was talking about me.

"Really?" He quirks an eyebrow. "'People say she's the real deal,' this shithole said. 'I think she's some stupid bitch who reads tarot cards.'"

"What'd you tell him?" My heart is *pound-pounding* in my chest so fiercely I fear it might break free and make a run for it. I glance at the door. Maybe I should be doing that right about now too.

"'Never heard of her,' I said. He replied, 'I'm going to get ahold of her agency – Ma Maison I think it's called – and give her a spin. I'll share her with friends, split the cost. She can suck my cock while someone hits her from behind and we'll benefit from the tarot or palm readings or whatever crystal ball she has shoved up her ass. You in?' he asked."

My throat squeezes shut and I hyperventilate. "He's talking bullshit."

Dylan runs a hand through his hair. "Evie, I can't take that risk. This guy is bad. Narcissistic, sociopathic, destroys lives kind of bad. His business that wasn't doing all that well? Burned to the ground in a mysterious electrical fire. The business partner he was feuding with? Vanished one day, never to be heard from again."

"Tell me his name. I promise you I'll never date him."

"It's not that easy. For better or worse the word is out." He wrings his hands. "All I can think is, what if he hires Evie? Will she be safe? Or will someone just like him mess her up?"

"I know how to take care of myself. I've taken care of myself for a long time."

"A predator will watch you flick that long, beautiful hair. Watch you toy with it when you're nervous. Figure out your weaknesses. Determine when and where, how and why you're vulnerable. And then he'll ruin you, Evie. Someone like that guy will fucking destroy you."

"Oh, come on." *Bzz. Bzz.* Fear bores thin, painful holes in my bones. "How many people actually know all of this?" I'm in a sinking ship, ocean waters lapping over me. Ten seconds from now I won't be able to breathe.

"Doesn't matter how many," he says. "It only takes one. A narcissistic predator is as dangerous as cancer."

Tears rise, unbidden, un-wanted tears. "There's stuff you don't know..." A layer splits inside me, and I cling to its walls because I do not want to slide into the abyss. But I lose my foothold at the same time my tears decide they will not be ordered about. They defy me and trickle down my cheeks. "Why are you doing this? Are you mad at me for leaving you in Texas?"

"Yes. No," he says, looking tormented. "It's not about Texas. It's about being in love with you."

And I realize *he is*. Just as bad? I'm in love with him too. Holy crap, what have I done?

"I looked at rings today, and for a second I dreamed. I went there. My heart and mind went to the cute house with the white picket fence, a dog, a cat and a jungle gym in the yard. But I can't get down on one knee and ask you that important question right now, Evie. I can't ask you to travel with me and be my girlfriend. That wouldn't be fair." He balls his hands into fists. "Someday my fortune might change. Then we'll be playing a different game."

He looks so sad. Worse, I feel it within me and my heart cracks, grief mixing with disappointment, the bastard fruit falling off the tree of perpetual sadness, splitting open when it smashes to the ground. "I don't need..."

"Think about it for the future. But right now the thing I need most in the entire world? I need you to be safe."

"Safe?" I wipe away ugly tears.

"*Safe*. I can't give you a diamond ring but I *can* give you a bit of savvy. Some protection. I just want you to cut your hair, Evie. At the end of the day is it really that big a deal? Trust me. Please?"

The snow's falling again. It's here in this hotel room, drifting down from the ceiling, melting in droplets from the electric candle sconces. It's in the air outside our window, sifting onto Sin City in sand and silt and all the dreams that are born here, played, here, killed here. Soon I will be buried.

"The concierge gave me the names of the best stylists in town," Dylan says. "He'll get us in to whomever you pick with one phone call. You'll be in the best hands, baby. What do you say?"

"Yes." I grab his elegant hand and squeeze it. "Yes. Because I'll be in *your* hands. You cut my hair, Dylan. Do it now before I change my mind."

22

A MILLION PIECES

A MILLION PIECES

I SIT ON THE MARBLE COUNTERTOP NEXT TO THE BATHROOM sink wearing silk panties and one of Dylan's long-sleeve dress shirts. He rubs my wet head with a thick, white towel. He lifts the towel, tosses it, and my hair tumbles down my shoulders.

"We should brush it first, I think," he says, fingering it.

"Okay," I say, the pulse in my wrist that I grip with my other hand feeling thin and threadlike.

He gently pulls the brush through my hair in sections. I grew my hair long after we ran into the Wolfe brothers. It was a small thing I could control because I didn't have much control over anything else. He pulls a pair of grooming scissors from his leather men's toiletry bag resting on the countertop and leans into me. "My beautiful, brave Evie. Ready?"

"No."

'Don't you dare let the past control your life,' Hope says. *'Take a chance.'*

Screw indecision. I grit my teeth. "I mean, yes. Do it."

He cuts.

The slice is crisp, precise, surgical, but no one's administered anesthesia and I shudder. A hunk of thick wetness smacks my shoulder, tumbling awkwardly down my breast. Fire grips my chest at the same time numbness settles around my ribs.

It is a cold winter day. I am thirteen years old. Mom is manic again, tossing all kinds of crap into our SUV. I am panicking, but I'm not allowed to panic. I have to hold it together for my sister's sake.

He cuts.

Chunks of hair drop chilly and wet onto my thigh. I shiver and peer down.

I wear mid-calf length galoshes with dangling laces. I focus on the laces. If they can stay attached, I can too.

"Breathe," Dylan says, lifting a section of hair, tugging it toward him, angling the scissors.

He cuts.

Mom throws the car in drive and we pitch forward. Thick clouds bump across the open skies open, like the heavens unzipped them.

Nausea rises in small tsunamis inside me and I gag. "Dylan... I don't know..."

"You're in control," he says, kissing my cheek, the stubble from his chin brushing my face, its gritty scratchiness grounding me. "Just tell me if you want to stop, Lucky Charm. I only took off six inches. We can end this now. Not a big deal. Not a big change."

The heavens spill out a sloppy mess of snow. Fat flakes hit the windshield harder. Colder. Meaner.

I glance down. Broken pieces of hair litter my legs, knees, the floor. Broken like the Wolfe brothers. Broken like Dylan used to be. "Keep going," I say.

He cuts.

A wet hunk of hair slaps my hand and I wince.

The car pitches forward and I fly back into my seat.

He cuts.

A thick piece of hair dives and I flick it away, my fingers trembling. What will my fingers do when I no longer have all this to hide behind?

Ding-ding-ding the approaching train shrieks. The gates close in front of us.

He cuts.

Faster now. Split ends, ragged pieces, flutter around me, cover me, damp, wet. The sounds blur, the *cut-cut-cuts* coming faster. I close my eyes.

I am thirteen years old. The disco ball hanging from the gym's ceiling spins panes of light across the room and I stare up at Wyatt Wolfe's beautiful, pale face. His mean dad and my crazy mom twist our lives into tangled webs, and yet together, Wyatt and I make it bearable. Our future lives beckon, bright and promising, spinning like the light off that ball. Wyatt bends his head, touching his lips to mine. I always thought that one day I would marry him but I'll never marry him because we ran him over and I broke him.

Mom's latest boyfriend, Kyle, is strange. My lips burn like I brushed them against hot sauce – the kind of hot sauce Kyle liked on his chips on football game day. Kyle scares me. Mom is broken.

Easton lies – his limbs twisted and tangled – staring up at me with hatred blazing through his eyes. "Fuck you," he says. Easton is broken.

Wyatt's lips turn blue and he slips away from me. The muffled shriek of the ambulance, red lights blinking in contrast to the white against all the snow take him away. Did we break him for good? Did we break him forever?

"Evie? Evie?" Dylan calls to me.

"What?" My fingers tremble against my thighs.

"Evie. I'm here. Where are you?" Dylan brushes his fingers against my face and neck. He takes my hands in his, pumping blood back into them. He pulls me back to present.

"Here," I say, clinging to him – *boomp-da-boomp* – my heart re-starting. "I'm here, Dylan."

"Good." He brushes his lips against mine. He whisks dead hair off my shoulders and it falls, coming to rest on the cold, porcelain tiles. "It's really good. You look amazing. We'll go to the stylist the concierge recommended tomorrow. He'll finish the job. But it's good, I swear."

"Really?" I want to be here with him – not in the past – not in the past with boys that I haven't talked to in over eleven years since that horrible, shitty day. Boys who were forever scarred when a twist of fate met Karma, met a mental breakdown, met a really bad day. The perfect shitty fucking storm.

Dylan places his arm around me tenderly. "It's gorgeous. You're gorgeous. Do you want to see?" He runs one hand through my new hair.

I don't feel like myself. The new me is lighter. I shiver. "Okay." I lower myself off the counter and stomp my feet on the ground. The solid ground. *Three-two-one,* I count silently, turn, and face the bathroom mirror.

My long hair is gone. It brushes against my neck, not even hitting my shoulders. I'm not sure I recognize me. The new Evie has big eyes and high cheekbones. The new Evie has nothing to hide behind. It's freeing. It's exhilarating. It's terrifying.

"I love you," Dylan says and pulls me tight to him.

I melt against him. I kiss his mouth. I kiss his full lips. "I love you, too."

WE MAKE LOVE ONE LAST TIME. I COME TWICE — ONCE with his mouth on my sex, once with his cock buried deep within me as he stimulates my clit with talented fingers. We climax moments apart from each other and collapse against each other, a tangle of sweaty limbs, passion, trust, secrets shared. Respect.

I bide my time until my beautiful player dozes. I watch him sink into a deeper sleep, waiting until he's out cold in REM. I force myself out of bed and head to the bathroom. I startle when I see my hair in the mirror. Most of it has been tossed in the wastebasket. A few sad hunks remain on the floor.

I run a wet cloth over my body and swipe on blush and mascara. I move quietly to the bedroom and pull on clothes, jot my personal, private number on a pad of paper and leave it on the bureau next to Dylan's phone. I take one last long look at my beautiful player.

How can I leave him? How can I do this? What is wrong with me? I don't know. I just know I can't stay. Something's changed. I bow my head and offer up a silent prayer:

Thank you, God for bringing Dylan McAlister into my life. He's been redeemed. He's earned a second chance. He's no longer broken. Take care of my beautiful man and You and I are good. In the name of the Father, and the Son, and the Holy Spirit. Amen.

I wheel my bag toward the door and see my dead hair lying in clumps on the bathroom floor. My throat tightens. I grab tissues from the countertop dispenser, rescue a few pinches, and tuck them in my purse. I carry my bag into the hallway and close the door with barely a sound.

I walk away from Dylan McAlister my heart *beat-beating* in my chest, doing my best not to cry because I hate crying. If I'm lucky I'll make it out of the hotel before I explode into a million pieces.

MINUTES LATER, I MAKE MY WAY THROUGH THE LOBBY. According to the message on my phone my driver will be outside in seven minutes. I spot the obligatory Vegas wedding party and think about what Dylan said about our future. Do we have one? Is getting married ever, to anyone, even in the cards for me?

I check my phone. My driver's running a few minutes late and I pause to take in the fantasy as Sheryl Crow's "Leaving Las Vegas" plays in the background.

Four bridesmaids, a gaggle of twenty-somethings are wearing glittery jewelry and are dressed in fitted raspberry silk dresses. The bride is about my age and has long, shiny blond hair. She's giggling with her friends. "Going to the chapel and we're going to get married," one of her pals sings off tune.

Behind them are the groomsmen wearing charcoal tuxes, spit-polished black shoes, and white shirts. They're all handsome. One man walks with a pronounced limp.

"Dude, this is your last chance to bail," a ruddy guy says, punching his arm.

"Fuck you, Peter." The bride clocks him with her beaded purse and he feigns pain.

I cover a smile.

"It's too late for me," the man with the limp says. "My beautiful bride's been training at the gym. Save yourself, Peter." The crowd parts.

The groom is a little under six feet, thin, lean and athletic. His floppy black hair brushes against his white collar. He laughs and it strikes a familiar chord in me. I notice his shoulders, his jacket, his feet, and for a second I swear I can see galoshes. I shake my head. Not galoshes. Spit-polished black dress shoes.

"Oh man - I'm getting married today." He turns in my direction, and all the air is sucked out my lungs in a mush-room cloud-sized whoosh.

Tingles blast down my spine and I break into a sweat. I know this man. I loved this man. I was in the car that ran over this man twelve years ago when he was still a boy.

This man is Wyatt Wolfe.

My phone pings. My driver's arrived. He'll wait five minutes but then he's leaving. My hands are shaking too hard to message him back. My feet turn to concrete and I can't move. My low-heeled sandals morph into galoshes. They grow roots, tethering me to this spot, to this man.

The last time I saw him, he was boy bleeding out into the hard, cold snow. My hand lay on the soft skin on the divet right above the bone in the middle of his chest. The last time I saw him I willed my life back into him so hard I went cold.

And after all the years, after all my anxiety. After love earned and love lost, the storm blows through, and yet here I am again — still tethered to Wyatt Wolfe.

Now, he takes the arm of the pretty girl he's about to marry, leans in, and kisses her. "Love you, darling," he says. "We're in this forever."

When I was thirteen I dreamed I would marry Wyatt Wolfe. But I am changed. Different. Shorn. I will never be the girl that marries Wyatt Wolfe.

A firm hand grips my arm, a grip much harder than I'm used to. I turn, expecting Dylan, already trying to figure out the best way to tell him that as much as I want to stay, as much as I love him, I have to go now before anything else bad happens. But the man gripping my arm is not Dylan.

It's Wyatt's older brother. Easton Wolfe.

"What in the hell are you doing here?" he hisses.

"Easton?"

"Who the fuck do you think you are?"

"What do you mean? What are you talking about?" Shock tingles on the backs of my arms.

"Dylan McAlister can stay here. Play tournaments anytime. But he's not allowed to bring you."

"I'm not with Dylan anymore. I'm leaving."

"Good," Easton says. "You're not welcome in my hotel, Evie Berlinger. Any of them. You're not welcome in any club I own."

I don't know what to say. I don't know what to think or feel. I'm not even sure I *can* feel.

"You're not welcome anywhere near anyone with the last name Wolfe," Easton says. "Not now. Not ever."

"Fine. Let me go."

He drops his hand from my arm but he's still seething.

"Leave."

"I'm leaving, Easton. My ride's here."

"And don't you dare mess with my brother today. It's his day. Not the day to remember the girl from the crazy family who left us broken and bloody and forever fucked up on the side of the road."

He moves away from me and I sway. I try to remember how to walk. I put one foot in front of the other and keep going until I stumble out the hotel door.

❧ 23 ❧

LEAVING LAS VEGAS

LEAVING LAS VEGAS

I WAS LATE AND MY DRIVER LEFT WITHOUT ME. I GET INTO the back of a Yellow and Black cab. "Where to?" the chick behind the wheel asks, pulling off into Vegas traffic.

"Anywhere but here. And preferably a place that doesn't have weddings. I don't have a lot of luck in the wedding department."

A half hour later I sit at the retro-styled bar at The Jester's Court – a drag bar close to the airport – and nurse my drink. My hand shakes a little less with each cocktail. A Gaga impersonator lip-synchs on stage and maybe I've completely lost my mind because I think she's pretty good.

"Sweet Jesus, your night has been caterwampus," the husky Jayne Mansfield impersonator says from behind the bar, sliding a cocktail in my direction. "Tell me that part again, honey. The part with all the men."

I grimace and take a slug of my drink. "I just walked out

228

on Dylan, the guy I'm in love with, and I'm standing there in the middle of the lobby and my hair is gone, poof, vanished," I say, running a hand through my layered short hair.

"Poof, vanished." She pats her wig nervously. "Were you growing your hair a long time?"

"Since I was thirteen years old." I reach for the basket of chips, shove one in my mouth and chew it half-heartedly. "This has no taste."

"They never do, honey. You've got to go to the good bars for taste. Not the ones close to the airport."

"Fuck me."

"I wish I could sugar, but it's just not my thing. Please don't be mad. But I do have a sympathetic ear. Tell me more. It's good to get it off your chest."

I take another sip of liquid courage. "I'm standing there watching this wedding about ready to go down and suddenly I realize I'm in the middle of the wedding of the boy I thought I was going to marry someday."

Her hand flies dramatically to her mouth. "The same boy you ran over eleven years earlier?"

I nod.

"Oh honey, that's so messed up," She reaches over and pats my forearm. "Tell me more about the hot, angry brother."

"Easton? He's angry all right." I throw back the rest of my drink and a shot of anger courses through me. I pull a fifty from my wallet, throw it on the bar, and stand up. "I never said he was hot. We good?"

"Yes. Change?" she asks.

"Keep it." I look at my watch and pull the handle of my carry on bag up with a snap.

"Good luck to you, honey," she says and clears my drink off the bar.

"Thanks."

"Sugar!" she calls after me.

"What?"

"You forgot to tell me the rest of the story about the hot, angry brother."

"I never said Easton was hot. Besides, I'm sick and fucking tired of people ordering me around. Sick and tired of people thinking they know what's right for me. Sending me away, cutting my hair, acting like they own me."

"They don't own you," she says pointing a finger at me.

"They. Don't. Own. Me." I jab a finger back, punctuating each word. "I'm the *only* person who owns me."

"That's right, sugar."

"And in regards to Easton Wolfe? As far as I'm concerned, Easton Wolfe can go fuck himself. Hard."

She applauds. "Preach."

I walk out the door because I've got a red-eye to catch and tonight can't get any suckier.

❦ 24 ❦

A COVERING

A COVERING

Two years later

I BLINK MY EYES OPEN. I LIE ON THE CHAISE LOUNGE IN room 4B at Ma Maison. The white envelope resting on my chest contains details about the man who calls to me so strongly the universe picked the playlist with "Leaving Las Vegas", the song that will always be Dylan McAlister's song.

Dylan changed my life. He was my mentor, almost my maker, so-to-speak. We fell in love and yet two years later he still can't commit. "Some day, Evie," he says to me every time we meet up for a game or a long weekend, or a special event. "Some day I am going to slip a ring on that important finger.'"

"Right, Dylan," I say, inhale and puff my cheeks out. "Look. I'm holding my breath."

"You doubt me," he says. "Don't doubt me, Lucky Charm." And he kisses me, and I giggle and and breathe. I

231

breathe him in again because it's so hard to let him go every time I see him.

I'm not going to push him into something he's not ready to do. I'm also not going to sit around and wait for him, either. I visit his mom in Texas every few months but I don't share that with him. My friendship with Rosemary will continue no matter what happens with Dylan and me.

Being an empath at Ma Maison hasn't been a picnic but it's paid a lot of bills and it's made for an interesting ride, that's for sure. And at the end of the day, using my empathic ability to help clients heal is my decision.

It's my decision to embrace the thing that has existed in me forever. The thing that I was born into. The thing that was forged in the fire of crazy moms, mean dads, and bloody accidents. It's a rollercoaster but it's a life of service I will not refuse.

I can't a take vacation right now. Can't go to the lake house in Wisconsin. But I can't help but wonder what kind of damaged man am I supposed to help this time? I pull out the packet of information contained in the envelope.

Ah. Him. The famous actor. Everyone knows him. What screwed him up? What demons lurk in his soul? My string of successes is unbeaten, yet with each posi- tive outcome, *tick-tick-tick* I am closer to taking a fall. That much closer to encountering the man I cannot heal. The bent, broken, damaged man who is too much for me.

I slip the papers back in envelope. Stand up, run a hand through my hair, and leave the room. I pass Jay who's still manning the front desk. I glance up at the clock. It's been forty minutes. It could have been a week. "Madame Germaine busy?"

"Not for you," he says, and gestures to the door. "Never for you."

I make my way into her office, take a seat, and toss the open packet on her desk where it lands with a crisp thwack.

She hangs up the phone, her face scrunching in that way that makes her look like a pickle the handful of times I've turned her down "So?"

"Why can't Scarlet or Lily help this guy?" I ask.

"His people specifically requested you."

The envelope lies on the immaculate desk, the packet white and clean – unlike my profession.

Pristine – unlike my past.

Tempting – how I envision my future.

"He's an actor."

"Movie star," She corrects me.

"Whatever. He's in L.A. I'd bet the house his agent is the one looking to hire me. The actor might not even be on board with this."

"The manager guides the actor's career," Germaine says. "He's been with him for twenty years. The actor will do whatever the manager says."

"What's he looking for?"

"Hope."

"Not the manager. What's the actor looking for? He's the one who's broken."

"Redemption, Evie."

I sigh and tap the envelope on the pristine antique desk. "Aren't they all?"

I'LL HEAD TO L.A. TO DO MY BEST TO TAP INTO THE PSYCHE of a broken movie star and find the twisted, messed up core belief that shut him down. As per usual, I'll give my all. I'll push myself like I always do for my beautiful broken men to help him heal. But first – a girl needs to beautify.

I hit up the usual high end places for hair, nails, waxing. Undoubtedly my new client will give me clothing. Expensive, pretty dresses and jewelry. Chances are he'll want to show me off to his friends and business associates. The guys usually enjoy that at the beginning, before we get down to doing the dark, dirty, gritty work.

But I'm not a child, and I don't expect him to wave a wand and make all my teenage girl clothing wishes come true. Handsome Movie Star isn't spending insane amounts of money to hire Dress Up Barbie. Handsome Movie Star is hiring a Healer.

Nordies is my go to place for cocktail dresses and I nab a few. I hit Shoe Factory for new runners. I'll convince Movie Star to exercise with me and release endorphins from his gorgeous body. He already hits the gym, does yoga, Tai-Bo, whatever his role, his handlers, and his job call for. Exercise and endorphins are a terrific tool in my bag of tricks to break inside men's psyches and make him reveal secrets. I scoop up athletic wear, tights, T-shirts, and running bras at a pop-up store on State Street.

It's 9 p.m. and the store guards lower protective gates, gearing up to close. I'm starving by the time I walk into my favorite falafel joint under the el train tracks on the way home to my condo in Greektown. I bit the bullet last year and rented a place with an option to buy. A few months ago my accountant said it was time, so I bought.

I stand behind the counter at Queen's House of Falafels. The sixty-something proprietor with the immaculate salt and pepper hair looks expectantly at me. "What'll it be, Evie?"

I order what I always get. "Gyros, pita and hummus plate to go, Mr. Katsis. No time to make dinner tonight."

"You look healthy and happy," he says.

"New haircut," I say. "How are things?"

"Me? I'm up, down. Left, right. My oldest, Constantine, is divorcing the wife." He looks sad.

I can feel his melancholy, his fears. *No grandkids for me. Only the restaurant.*

"I'm sorry, Mr. Katsis," I say, searching for things to say that will make him feel better. "I predict more daughters-in-law in your future. Constantine is a handsome man."

"You interested?" He waggles his eyebrows.

"I fear he's out of my league." I frown, wring my hands, and sigh dramatically.

"Ha." He cracks a smile. "How's your mother?"

"She's good, thanks. We're going on vacation one of these days."

"She's coming to visit you here in Chicago?" His eyes light up like a kid catching candy at a parade. "When? For how long?"

"Do you have a crush on my mother, Mr. Katsis?" I smile and hand him a twenty.

"She's so nice every time you bring her in here. Like mother, like daughter. I put some extra chips in the bag for you, Evie." He hands me change. "No extra charge. I know how much you like them. Besides, you're getting a little thin."

"You're a sweet man. Are you trying to make me fat?"

"No, Evelyn. I'm trying to bribe you into bringing your mom back to my restaurant next time she comes to town."

"That can be arranged."

I walk out the door of the hole in the wall joint swallowing a smile, the chimes on the door ringing as I leave.

INSIDE THE ELEVATOR AT MY CONDO BUILDING I PUNCH THE button for the 12th floor. The gears engage, hum, and grind, as the lift rises to my loft condo on the top floor. I pull open the accordion door and transfer my purchases into the hallway.

I pick them back up, three in each hand, and walk down the hallway to my corner unit. I drop one handful and dig through my bag for my keys. I twist the key in the top dead-bolt but it doesn't open with the clunk that I expect because it's not locked. It's already open.

How is it already open? Weird. Oh, holy hell have I been robbed? My hand trembles as I slide the key in the bottom lock where it catches. I turn the key, the tumblers clunking over. I nudge the door open with my knee and peek inside.

The TV is still on the wall, the computer still on the recy-cled barn wood dining table. There are no broken windows visible. I probably forgot to bolt the door on my way out. In my haste to get everything done before I leave tomorrow I forgot to lock the deadbolt.

I ease inside my condo, place the bags on the floor, and toss the dry cleaning over a chair next to the dining room table. Nothing appears an inch out of place but the hairs on the back of my arms are raised and something feels off.

I walk down the hall to the bedrooms. The movie posters are all hanging straight on the walls. The framed photographs of my mom, my sister and me that could pass for a smiling department store family are grouped neatly on their own space.

I poke my head in the guest bathroom. The towels are straight, the toilet lid down. The organic lavender soap in the plunger bottle is still next to the glass bowl. I open the door to the smaller bedroom. The futon is bright and cheery with the cover I bought from a seller on Etsy. The windows are intact. My second computer hasn't budged an inch. And still, I can't shake the weird feeling that something's not right.

I wander down the hall and enter my room. There's a gap

in the center of the curtains and my bed is still made, but that's where the similarity ends.

A six by six inch blue box with a white bow rests in the center of the bed. It wasn't there when I left this morning. It could pass for a box from my favorite jewelry store.

My heart *thumpity-thumps* in my chest as I make my way to the bed. My breath ratchets up a notch. I untie the bow and lift the lid. There's a wafer-thin page ripped from a book. It's fragile and yellowing – could be antique. It's a page from a Bible and one verse is highlighted in yellow:

"But if a woman has long hair, it is a glory to her: for her hair is given her for a covering.' 1st Corinthians 11:15"

What–?

There's a white card with typed letters. It's been a while since I received one of these notes, but it looks awfully familiar.

Dear Evelyn:

It's been two years. I had hoped by now you would have grown your hair back. But there is no covering, there is no modest Evelyn, there is only boastful Evelyn. Proud Evelyn. Evelyn who flaunts everything she has.

And this disturbs me.

I'm not sure what to do about this. I'm weighing

options. I'm just a mess inside and yet you sleep easily. Some days I can't eat and worry gnaws at my bones.

And I wonder — what if Evelyn doesn't have a covering and some kind of sicko realizes that and picks a fight with her? Evelyn used to be awfully nice, but she's changed. She shows off. She's entitled. Now she's putting herself out there. Right there in the crosshairs for just the right predator to come around and take, take, take whatever they want from Evelyn. Whatever they crave.

What do you think they'll take first, Evelyn? Your covering's gone. I'm disappointed in you. So very disappointed. I've been silent a while, but I can be silent no more. I just had to say something. I hope you don't mind.

I only want your best, Evelyn.
    I am, as always,
    Your Devoted Fan

My hand trembles as I set the note and the page aside. It continues to shake as I unfold the white tissue paper.

Clipped hair lies is in the box. Silky, shiny, clipped hair. It could be mine.

I think it just might be mine...

DEAR READER: I HOPE YOU ENJOYED THE PLAYER #1. Evie's journey continues in THE MOVIE STAR #2 . Gorgeous movie star Jake Keller's on track to win an Oscar.

But Jake's shutting down, going off grid, doing nothing to help promote his chances. Evie travels to Hollywood to try and help discover what -- or who -- broke Jake. But dirty little secrets prefer to stay buried...

One click THE MOVIE STAR #2! Or turn the page to view an excerpt .

21st CENTURY COURTESAN is a **sexy, dark, addictive** series filled with love, lust, family loyalty, deceit, revenge, and all the *sweet little things in life worth killing for...* Sign up for my NEWSLETTER to learn about new books and bookish developments.

If you love steamy, angsty, and funny royal romantic comedy that's been described as "... Ms. Congeniality meets Sex and the City..." check out the first book in THE CROWN AFFAIR series The Prince's Playbook #1.

SIGN UP FOR MY NEWSLETTER AND ENJOY BREAKING news about books and special offers.

I'd love for you to join my readers' group at Pamela DuMond's Dirty Darlings.

Xoxo

Pam DuMond

EXCERPT: THE MOVIE STAR

BEFORE

Blood pumps through my arteries, my muscles gear up to throw punches and dodge bullets while my brain tries to figure out if there's really a problem. My body knows when someone wants to hurt me. It's had a lot of practice.

One Saturday afternoon in the 6th grade I hung out at my friend Emily's house. The music was loud. Her sister was hosting a pizza party after a high school football game. A guy with bloodshot eyes stared at me from the far end of the kitchen, his hand caressing the watery drops beading on his soft drink can. Just looking at him made my stomach lurch about like the pizza I'd eaten was bad.

I didn't want to get sick at Emily's house, so I went upstairs and grabbed my coat from her bed. When I turned to leave the guy with the bloodshot eyes was standing in the doorway breathing heavily and staring at me funny. I slammed the door in his face. I jammed the lock and sat on the bed, my heart rattling about in my chest like a ghost haunting a closet.

He knocked and knocked. I squeezed my eyes shut and hugged my arms around my ribs because I knew no one would hear me over the music if I hollered for help.

When the music finally quieted, I popped open the door and peered into the hallway: he was gone. I bolted down the stairs and didn't stop running until I got home. A few months later that guy's face was plastered across our local paper because he had hurt a different girl at a different party.

"It's him, Mom," I said.

"See what I told you about respecting your instincts?" Mom made stir fry, the frozen vegetables simmered in the pan. "I bet that girl didn't do the smart girl thing."

"But what if she did?" I asked. "What if that girl fought back and hollered but no one heard her scream over the music?" My stomach knows when a situation is dangerous.

My bones know when someone dies. I was seven when Grandma Berlinger popped up in my dream shaking her owl-head baking spoon at me, fussing that she was taking a trip. "I'm out of here, munchkin," she said. "I'm putting you in charge of taking care of your Mom."

I woke with a start, the covers still tucked around me and yet there was a coldness in my bones, a heaviness that hadn't been there when I'd nodded off. Sure enough, Mom got the phone call the next morning that Grandma Berlinger had passed away in the middle of the night.

Now it's been seven long, heartbreaking days since we ran into the Wolfe brothers. A week since they bounced off our car, flew through the air like broken birds, and no one will tell me if they're alive or dead.

No one will answer my questions. No one will take me seriously because I'm just that poor girl whose mother had a psychotic split. I'm that 'sorry child' who crawled out of the car toward the brothers bleeding on the cold, hard, white snow. I'm the– 'Shh, don't say that loud enough for Evelyn Berlinger to hear' that her mother is going to jail for this you know' girl.

I bet rumors are circulating about the Wolfe boys back at Beethoven Middle Grade school, but I'm not there to hear them. Mom's been taken away, Ruby and I have been split up and sent to different foster homes. I'm staying in a different town with a perfectly nice woman in a house with other sad kids. But in spite of everything I know in my bones that Wyatt Wolfe is not dead.

If only I had Bones on speed dial. I'd pay my entire monthly allowance to hear him pick up. 'How may we help you?' Bones would ask.

'Just calling to find out if Wyatt Wolfe's still alive?' I'd pinch myself as a reminder to keep breathing, not hold my breath and pass out because I'm so dizzy from the anxiety wriggling under my skin.

'He's not only alive, Evie, but he's doing great,' Bones would say. 'A few of us were broken in the accident but we're all healing up now. Thanks for asking.'

'Oh, good,' I'd say, relief coursing through me like a sugary soda. 'I've been wondering 'cause he and his brother Easton haven't been back to school. And I need to tell them how incredibly sorry I am. I need them to forgive me."

'Give it time.' Bones would say. "Forgiveness can take some time.'

One click MOVIE STAR #2 now.

PRAISE

"I FLOVED this book. It moves quietly along **packing punch after punch..**" Maura

"a roller coaster of emotions and had me hoping that Jake Keller could be helped. " arthistorygirl

"Who wants to come to Hollywood and help a **super-sexy movie star,** who is also a really nice guy, regain his mojo? Oh, and it might involve **glitzy parties, star-filled movie premieres, and lots of hot, juicy sex**. Me me me!!"
Beverly Diehl

One click MOVIE STAR #2 now.

BOOKS BY PAMELA DUMOND

THRILLERS

21st CENTURY COURTESAN

Psychological Thriller series (Steamy)

THE PLAYER #1

THE MOVIE STAR #2

THE BELOVED #3

THE HUSBAND #4

THE DEVOTED FAN #5

MORTAL BELOVED

Historical Fantasy Time Travel series (PG-13)

The Messenger #1

The Assassin #2

The Seeker #3

The Believer: Jack & Clara - STAND ALONE

COZY MYSTERIES

ANNIE GRACELAND COZY MYSTERIES

Stand Alones

Cupcakes, Pies, & Hometown Guys

Cupcakes, Paws, & Bad Santa Claus

Cupcakes, Diaries, & Rotten Inquiries

Cupcakes, Sales, & Cocktails

Cupcakes, Bats, & Scaredy Cats

Cupcakes, Bars, & Rock Stars

Cupcakes, Lies, & Dead Guys

Cupcakes, Spies, & Despicable Guys

The Annie Graceland Mystery Set: Books 1 - 4

The Annie Graceland Mystery Set #2: Books 5 - 7

VON PUMPERNICKLE COZY MYSTERIES

GOLDMITTEN: Cozy Animal Mystery #1

'SWEETER' ROMANCE

ROYALLY WED

Romantic Comedy series (PG-13)

Part-time Princess #1

Royally Wed #2

Part-time Poser #3

Royally Knocked Up #4

Royally Wed Box Set: Books 1 - 4

PLAYING SWEETER

Romantic Comedy Stand Alones (PG-13)

Ms. Match Meets a Millionaire

The Story of You and Me

'HOT' ROMANCE

THE CROWN AFFAIR

Romantic Comedy series (Steamy)

The Prince's Playbook #1

His Majesty's Measure #2

The American Princess #3

The Duchess's Decision #4

The Crown Affair Collection: Books 1 - 4

PLAYING DIRTY

Romantic Comedy Stand Alones (Steamy)

The Client

The Matchmaker

The Bodyguard

A Playing Dirty Duet

BOOKS in the WORKS

Dr. Strangedove: Von Pumpernickel Cozy Animal Mystery

For more details please visit Pamela DuMond Author.

ABOUT THE AUTHOR

Pamela DuMond is the *USA Today* Bestselling author of *Part-time Princess* © 2014 and other modern fairytales. Pam writes her own books. #Iwritemyownbooks

Pam writes witty, swoony rom-coms and cozy mysteries. She balances the giggles with darker reads: historical fantasy and psychological thrillers.

Pam's books have been optioned for Film/TV, licensed by Chapters Interactive Stories as games, and featured in *Glamour UK*.

A Midwestern girl at heart, Pam landed in L.A. where on occasion she sticks her toes in the ocean, consumes audio books, and asks 'What do you want now?' to her two funny cats.

———

Sign up for Pam's Newsletter .

Like Pamela DuMond Author on Facebook.

Join Pam's reader group at Pamela DuMond's Dirty Darlings .

Follow Pamela DuMond on Bookbub for timely deals.

For more information...
www.pameladumond.com

ACKNOWLEDGMENTS

Thanks to to Kelly Hartog for editing. Thanks Marissa Shor and Lori Jackson for the gorgeous graphics. Thanks Amber Hamilton, PA for handling so many bookish tasks! Thanks Colleen and Itsy Bitsy Bloggers, Catherine Anderson of Catty Jane Book Blog, Caitlyn O'Leary, Maggie Marr, Sylvie Fox, Cindy Sample, Carolyn Haines, Christine Ashworth, Samantha Beck, and "Pamela DuMond's Dirty Darlings" for being such awesome cheerleaders.

Thanks to my readers and supporters Jeanie Whitmire Jackson, Carrie Hartney, D.C., Cheryl Cavitt Carlson, Joan Brady, Christine Ashworth, Beverly Diehl, Maria Seager, Joe Wilson, Kristin Warren, Monica Mason, Nic Conway, Melissa Black Ford, and Rita Kempley, to name a few.

Thank you romance bloggers — you are the best. And a huge thanks to all you readers. You rock!

Xo,

Pamela DuMond